Pride Publishing books by Alyssa Rabil

Single Books
Splinters of the Heart

I0689697

SPLINTERS OF THE HEART

ALYSSA RABIL

Splinters of the Heart
ISBN # 978-1-83943-962-9
©Copyright Alyssa Rabil 2021
Cover Art by Louisa Maggio ©Copyright March 2021
Interior text design by Claire Siemaszkiewicz
Pride Publishing

SPLINTERS OF
THE HEART

Chapter One

Gay for Pay

Aaron sat on the edge of the bed with his hands in his lap. The man behind the camera clicked something and a red light blinked to life.

"Shy?" asked the man.

"Cold," answered Aaron.

"Shy plays better for the camera," said the man. "But I can also work with stubborn denial." There was that smirk again. "Introduce yourself."

"Aaron. Do you need my last name?"

The man rolled his eyes. "No. And you've ruined the take." He took a breath. "Introduce yourself."

"Aaron."

"Good boy. I'm Farley. Your Dom will be in shortly. You will call him 'Sir' or 'Master'."

"Okay." Aaron shifted on the bed. He wanted to move his hands—make a point and prove he wasn't afraid—but that would probably just earn more snide comments from Farley. He didn't like being the only one naked. Then again, he wasn't sure how much better it would be once the other naked guy joined them.

Will he be naked? Aaron wondered. *Please be naked. Or don't. Maybe he won't show up.*

It wasn't too late to run. He hadn't signed a contract or anything. The money was still in a bag in the corner of the room. He could bail at any time.

"Why are you here?" asked Farley. He nodded to the camera.

Aaron wasn't sure where to look. He settled on Farley, who rolled his eyes. "I need the money," he answered.

"Is this your first time doing porn?"

"Yeah." Aaron glanced at the camera. "I mean — I've been filmed before, but — "

"Shut up." Farley held a marker up to the lens. "I'll cut that out later. Don't elaborate."

Aaron sighed. He could leave, drive home as fast as possible, take a long hot shower and forget this ever happened.

"Are you gay?"

"No," answered Aaron.

"Then what brought you here?" asked Farley.

"Money," answered Aaron.

Farley held another marker up to the lens. "Is it even remotely possible for you to look less like an angry mountain gorilla and more like a virginal twink?" he asked. "I understand your IQ may only extend to that of a mountain gorilla, but surely you can follow basic instructions."

Aaron glared. "What's a twink?"

"Christ," said Farley. "Fine. Never mind." He paused again. "Why do you need the money?"

"Uh — " began Aaron. "It's — that's personal."

"Girlfriend?" asked Farley.

"No," answered Aaron.

"Just say it's for your girlfriend."

"It's for my girlfriend."

Farley rolled his eyes. "Ever sucked a cock before, Aaron?"

"No."

"Ever thought about sucking a cock before?"

Aaron glanced between Farley and the camera. "Yes."

"Tell me about that."

"It—it was a long time ago."

"Care to elaborate?"

"I got curious back in high school," answered Aaron. "It wasn't a big deal."

"Man of few words," said Farley. "That's fine. You won't need to do much talking today. Ever thought about having a cock in your ass?"

"I guess."

"Any idea what you're in for?"

"I googled some stuff." Aaron had spent the entire week leading up to today scouring the internet for advice. He'd taken seven showers in the past three days and hadn't eaten for two days. He'd told himself he was just being thorough—that it wasn't because he'd lost his appetite or because he'd felt dirty after hanging up the phone to confirm the meeting. He'd told himself it was just sex. Men liked sex. Sex wasn't a big deal.

Farley pulled a sheet of paper from the desk behind him. "Do you know what makes my business such a special production company?"

"Your warm and fuzzy personality?"

Farley grinned as he looked down. "Authenticity," he said. "Everything is consensual, of course. Men like you come in for whatever reason—overcompensating for their nerves with masculine bravado—but they don't leave until all parties have been thoroughly satisfied."

"Yeah, you need a money shot," said Aaron. "You said that in the email." He'd found these guys online. The ad had been vague, but had promised a shitload of money for two hours' worth of work. Aaron had emailed them, called them, then showed up in person. Farley had even flashed him the money before Aaron took his clothes off. It wasn't a high-class setup by any means, but it was about what he'd expected from a vague 'call for adult actors'. He probably should have told someone where he was in case things went south — but then someone would know he was here doing this.

"No fake orgasms," continued Farley. "Our audience likes to know what you're feeling is real."

"Okay," said Aaron.

"Your safe word for this Dom is 'grace'. Use it wisely. If things are not going well, I'll switch out for someone I think will be more successful."

Aaron nodded. He felt a little nauseated and closed his eyes for a moment.

"You read my mind," said Farley. He crossed the room and tossed Aaron a piece of fabric. "Tie that tight over your eyes, and no peeking."

Aaron bit his lip, but did as he was told. "Like this?" Suddenly something soft hit him in the face. "What the hell?" he shouted. He fumbled with what felt suspiciously like a pillow and threw it away from him.

"Just making sure you can't see."

"Dammit," muttered Aaron. He heard the door open. He heard Farley return to his position by the camera and heard another set of footsteps approach the bed.

It's not too late. Fuck this and go home. No one has to know I was here. I can find the money somewhere else.

"Hello, Aaron," said a deep voice. A firm, calloused hand ran through his hair. "Do you have any idea what you're doing?" asked the man — Master.

"No," breathed Aaron.

Farley coughed.

"No, Sir," corrected Aaron. He could feel his body shaking, but he told himself he was just playing along. Farley had told him to be a virginal twig or twing or something. He was acting. He wasn't scared.

Master thumbed over Aaron's lips. "Open your mouth," he said. Aaron obeyed.

Master nudged his leg between Aaron's knees, forcing his legs open. "Hands behind your back," he said.

Again, he obeyed.

Run. It's not worth it. Sell a kidney. Sell sperm to a rich lady. Learn to juggle and join a circus.

Something warm and wet touched Aaron's lips and he jumped. Master ran his fingers through Aaron's hair again, and pulled him back. A kiss. The Dom was kissing him. He trailed a line of kisses to Aaron's ear.

"Are you all right?" whispered the Dom.

Aaron leaned his face away from Farley and the camera. "Yeah," he answered. "Sorry."

Nerves."

"Let me know when you feel uncomfortable," he whispered. He nibbled at Aaron's neck.

"Safe word is 'grace', right?" asked Aaron.

"Right." Master kissed Aaron again and breathed against his lips. "I promise, I won't hurt you." He stood up, fingers once again entangled in Aaron's hair. "Open wide," he said.

Aaron did as he was told, and this time he was about ninety percent sure the thing he tasted was a dick. A quick thrust from the Dom confirmed his suspicions. Master was slow at first, keeping his movements steady and shallow. One hand had a vise-like grip on Aaron's hair while the other caressed his cheek.

Considering the many awful ways this decision could come back to destroy him, Aaron was surprisingly relaxed.

Suck him off. Then you get off. Then you go home. It's not that bad. Just an hour and a half more to go.

Suddenly, Farley snapped something. "Cut," he said.

Master pulled away from Aaron. "What could possibly be the problem? You've been rolling for under a minute."

"His sad little deflated cock is the problem," said Farley. "No one wants to see that."

"Give him some time," said the Dom. "He's nervous."

"Sorry," said Aaron, sensing his paycheck might be on the line. "I can get hard." He gripped his dick in his hand and gave it his best shot.

They're watching me. Get hard. Get off. Get paid. Get out. Get the money to Daniel.

Aaron felt nauseous again. If his little brother had any idea where this money was coming from, he'd probably never speak to Aaron again.

If Dad knew —

If Robert Beaumont knew, he'd make sure Aaron never saw Daniel again. "This is pathetic," said Farley.

"Let me try," said the Dom. "Aaron, lie on your back."

"What are you going to do?" asked Farley.

"This is a lot to take in," said Master. "We need to ease him into it."

"I don't want to waste your time," said Aaron. "I can do this."

"And yet here you are, wasting my time," said Farley. He sighed. "Silas, give us a moment, won't you?"

"No. We can figure — Who are you calling?" asked Master.

Farley must have picked up the phone. He shushed the Dom. "Send in Regina. She has the edging equipment. Tell her we need Ralph."

"This isn't an edging scene," said Master.

"Don't get your panties in a twist," said Farley. "Regina knows what she's doing. Now get out."

Master ran his fingers through Aaron's hair again. It was pleasant, but it didn't stop Aaron from trembling.

"I can do this," mumbled Aaron.

Master untied Aaron's blindfold and knelt down between his knees. He placed a hand on Aaron's thigh and rubbed small circles into the muscles with his thumbs. Master was also naked. He had dark, messy hair. His eyes were icy blue and beautiful. He was beautiful.

"This line of work isn't for everyone," said Master. "There is no shame in leaving if you're uncomfortable."

"No," said Aaron. "I can do it."

"For God's sake," said Farley, "get up. I should have paired him with Ralph in the first place."

"Don't put him with Ralph. He's too rough," said the Dom.

Farley rolled his eyes. "You can't fall for some doe-eyed little virgin."

"I told you we shouldn't work with amateurs," said Master. "It's too risky."

Farley muttered something that sounded like 'savior complex' and put his phone into his pocket. "New rule," he said. "Every time you hold up a scene to have a little heart-to-heart with the actors, I'm taking a nickel from your paycheck."

"That's not fair," said Aaron.

"Ignore him," said the Dom. "He has to be petty to stay alive, the same way a shark must keep swimming."

The door opened. A woman entered carrying a large duffle bag. A tall man with a scruffy beard followed her.

"The cavalry has arrived," said Farley. "Silas, leave."

"No, I—"

"You want to cost this young man his money?" asked Farley. "He needs someone more forceful."

"Then why partner him with me in the first place?" asked Master.

"I was being kind," snapped Farley.

Master turned back to Aaron. He looked scared. "You can still say no."

"Leave now, or you're fired," said Farley.

"Go," said Aaron. "I've got this." He tried to force a smile. Master searched his eyes.

"How about this," said Farley. "You can stay and slow down production and make sure we don't hurt this precious boy, and I'll just cut his pay in half and you won't get paid at all for today."

"No," said Aaron quickly. He shoved the Dom away. "Leave. I know what I'm doing."

Master got to his feet and stepped back.

"Go," said Aaron. No contract. No witnesses. Of course these guys could cut his pay. He wasn't exactly a member of the amateur porn worker's union.

Master clenched his jaw. He turned, jabbed a finger at the new man in the room and whispered something.

The man ignored him. Master left, slamming the door behind him.

"Lock it," said Farley. He turned to Aaron. "Sorry about all that. You weren't what I expected. Normally a two-hour shoot only takes two hours."

Aaron glanced at the clock on the bedside table. "It's only been forty-five minutes," he said.

"And of those forty-five, I only have three usable minutes, and those are all your bumbling interview."

Shit.

"So how much longer?" asked Aaron.

Farley glanced at his watch. "Two hours. Maybe less. Don't worry. Ralph is very good."

The new man, presumably Ralph, approached Aaron. "Do you want this done fast or do you want to enjoy it?" he asked.

"How fast is fast?" answered Aaron.

"Two hours. Maybe less." The man echoed Farley.

"What if I want to enjoy it?" asked Aaron.

"No guarantee that you will."

Aaron took a deep breath. "Fast," he said.

"Good. I'm your new Dom. Call me 'Sir'. You're allowed to talk, but you must show me respect or you'll be punished. Understand?"

"Yeah," answered Aaron.

Ralph grabbed him by his hair, flipped him onto his stomach and slammed his face into the mattress. He slapped Aaron's ass so hard, he was sure it had left a welt.

"Son of a bitch," shouted Aaron. "Yes, sir. Fuck."

Ralph hit him again, harder.

"God dammit," said Aaron. "What did I—"

Ralph hit him again.

Aaron bit his tongue. After a moment of silence, Ralph pulled Aaron's face out of the mattress. "Do you know what you did wrong?" he asked.

"Yes—sir," said Aaron.

"You are worthless. Understand?"

"Yes, sir."

"You are mine."

"Yes, sir."

Chapter Two

Safe Word

Ralph grabbed the blindfold and tied it over Aaron's eyes.

It was too tight and his dick was still limp and now his ass hurt. He focused on the wad of cash waiting for him in the corner. *Two hours. Two more hours.*

Ralph grabbed Aaron's wrists. "Rope," he said. He bound Aaron's arms behind his back, which was probably for the best. Aaron wasn't sure he could resist the urge to hit this guy in the face, the way the session was going.

He rolled Aaron onto his back. "Farley, make a note to cut this part and delete it. He might scream. Regina, do your stuff."

Someone grabbed his dick and started jerking him off. Aaron assumed it was Regina, but surprise, surprise, it wasn't any easier to get it up with her. He felt her squirt what he hoped was lube onto his dick.

Remember Ashley. She used to do this. She was great — and flexible. Think about Ashley.

Something wrapped around his balls and the base of his cock. Aaron flinched.

"Close enough," said Regina. "I'll tie him off here. You're responsible for the rest. He won't come until you're ready."

"What are y—"

Ralph was on him before he could finish the sentence. He yanked hard on Aaron's hair and pinched one of Aaron's nipples. He twisted so hard Aaron was afraid it would tear.

"Stop," said Aaron.

Ralph twisted harder.

The ties around his dick tightened. He tried to wriggle free, but he was lying on his arms. Aaron kicked against the bed to push himself away.

Ralph released his nipple and shoved him onto his stomach. Aaron felt a knee settle in the middle of his back. His cock was hard now, but it hurt.

"Bar," said Ralph.

"Stop," panted Aaron. "I don't want to do this."

He couldn't tell how many hands were on him now, but they managed to hold him down and separate his legs.

"Grace," shouted Aaron. "Grace—please. I can't."

Ralph slapped his ass again, which was, at this point, more humiliating than it was painful.

"God dammit, stop!"

Ralph hit him again and again. Someone wedged something cold and hard between Aaron's ankles and he felt cuffs snap closed around them. Ralph wouldn't stop hitting him. Someone was laughing.

"Grace," cried Aaron. "Isn't that the safe word?" He felt tears welling up in his eyes—from pain, shame or something else, he wasn't sure.

Ralph stopped hitting him. "Hand me the gag."

"No," said Aaron.

"Then shut up," said Ralph.

"What's the safe word?" asked Aaron. "I really don't think I can do this. Keep the money. Just let me go."

Something slick ran across the crease of Aaron's ass. "What the fuck was that?" he asked.

Farley laughed. "As entertaining as this is, how long before we get something we can use?"

"He'll wear himself out in a minute," answered Ralph.

The slick thing wormed farther between Aaron's cheeks and brushed against his hole. A finger. It had to be a finger. Aaron tried to kick away, but the bar between his legs was now tied to something else and it anchored him to the bed. Ralph's knee weighed heavily against his lower back. His arms were going numb. His heart was beating too fast. He had to remind himself to keep breathing.

"I don't want to do this," said Aaron. "Let me go. Keep the money. I can't do this."

Suddenly Ralph stopped teasing and shoved his finger into him.

Aaron screamed.

Ralph pumped his finger in and out, setting a relentless pace. "Record now," he shouted. He pulled against the tight ring of muscles and inserted a second slick finger. It burned.

Aaron was sure he was bleeding. He bucked against the bed then recoiled when his dick hit the mattress. Aaron could feel Ralph's fingers moving inside him. He felt them prod and scissor and stretch. One finger bent and hit something that made Aaron see stars. He was crying now. Any semblance he had of dignity was gone.

Ralph hit the spot again and again, then added a third finger. Aaron was shaking all over. He was too hot. Every wave of pleasure from those fingers was followed by a wave of nausea. His mouth filled with saliva and salt. He was going to vomit. He was going to get fucked in the ass, tied to a bed, face down in his own vomit, and he was going to come like a whore. The whole thing would be posted online for everyone to see. *Aaron Beaumont got fucked in the ass and loved it. Aaron Beaumont is a bitch. Aaron Beaumont is pathetic.*

Ralph's fingers wriggled in and out. They crawled around inside him and he felt every damn touch. Three, then two, then three, three, three, prostate, stretch, two, prostate, prostate, prostate, prostate.

Aaron turned his head and vomited.

Ralph cackled. Farley kept rolling—or maybe he didn't. Maybe at this point they were just having fun.

"Grace," breathed Aaron. The stench of sweat, puke and sex was strong. He tried to turn away from the mess he'd made but he couldn't escape the smell, couldn't escape their voices.

"Grace," he said again.

"Poor boy," said Ralph. "That's not *my* safe word."

Aaron wasn't sure if he screamed again. He heard laughter. He felt something hit him. He heard something heavy slam against something solid. He heard a loud bang. He heard screaming. Ralph pulled his fingers away.

Aaron's stomach clenched and he dry heaved. He turned his head toward the bang. It had come from the front of the room near the door. He tried to dislodge the blindfold but failed. The room fell silent.

"Get off of him," said a voice.

"You shot the camera," said Farley.

There was another loud bang. The weight on Aaron's back disappeared. "Everybody out," said the voice.

Aaron heard footsteps. Seconds later, someone pulled the blindfold from his face and Aaron found himself staring into familiar icy blue eyes. The Dom was clothed now and had a long coat tossed over one shoulder.

The Dom didn't ask any questions like "are you all right?" or "did they hurt you?" He worked quickly to untie him. Hands first, spreader bar second. He untied the bindings around his dick. Aaron didn't dare look down.

"They'll be back," said the Dom. "We have to hurry."

Aaron nodded, blinking hard against the too-bright lights of the room. He clutched his stomach. "Put your hands on my shoulders," said the Dom. "We'll stand together."

Aaron did as he was told. His knees trembled but didn't give.

The Dom pulled his coat from his shoulder and wrapped it around Aaron. He tucked his gun into the waistband of his black pants then, in one smooth motion, lifted Aaron into his arms.

Even weighed down by Aaron, he was fast. He walked briskly to the door and stopped. He stooped and released Aaron long enough to collect the bag sitting in the corner and the pile of Aaron's clothes. He dumped the collection into Aaron's lap then gripped him firmly and stood.

Voices echoed down the hall behind them. The Dom broke into a run and Aaron clung to him. He kicked the front door open and they burst outside into the cool night air.

"Which vehicle is yours?"

"Black one," answered Aaron. He pointed to a car parked nearby.

"Keys?"

Aaron fumbled through the pile of clothes in his lap and retrieved his keys. The Dom set him down gently and Aaron clutched his belongings to his chest.

He opened the door for Aaron, then hurried to the driver's side and got behind the wheel. Aaron didn't protest.

Farley was already to the front door of the building, flanked by Ralph and God only knew who else.

The engine roared to life, and the Dom threw it into reverse and hit the gas. They sped backward out of the driveway until they hit the main road. The Dom switched the car into drive without stopping.

They made it. Aaron twisted around in his seat and watched the roof of that terrible place fade away behind the trees. He turned around and slumped down into his seat.

He glanced at the man driving his car, adrenaline surging through him. "I don't even know your name," he said.

"Silas," he answered.

Aaron nodded. "Thanks, Silas. I owe you."

Chapter Three

Secure

"Where do you live?" asked Silas.

Aaron pressed the heels of his hands into his eyes. "Just go to your place. I'll drop you off and head back home."

"Do you have someone who can look after you?"

Aaron swallowed hard. Robert should be home, unless he was still at the bar. If there was a God in heaven, he'd still be at the bar and he wouldn't be around for Aaron's walk of shame.

"I'll take that as a no," said Silas.

Aaron must have taken too long to respond.

"My dad," said Aaron. "I live with my dad."

I'm twenty-one and I still live with my dad because I can't get my shit together.

"Is it safe for you there?" asked Silas. "Will he take care of you?"

"Don't worry about it." He shifted in his seat and his ass stung. The ghost of Ralph's hand brushed over him. "Pull over," muttered Aaron.

"What's wrong?"

Aaron clutched his stomach. "Just pull over," he growled. Silas slowed the car and came to a stop in the grass.

Aaron threw open the door and leaned out headfirst. There was nothing left to throw up. He hung out of the car, dry heaving.

Silas touched his shoulder and he jerked hard, almost falling onto the ground.

"Aaron," said Silas softly.

"Don't," gasped Aaron. Ralph's hands were all over him.

'Good boy.'

Aaron stumbled out of the car, one hand still clutching the door. The grass was cool and wet with evening dew. He heard the driver's side door open and close.

Silas knelt down so he was at eye level. "I think you should go to the ER," he said.

The ER. It wasn't an emergency. He hadn't been raped. He was just being a bitch. He needed to nut up. He needed to stop shaking. "I'm fine," muttered Aaron. His stomach lurched again.

"You need a doctor."

"Can't," said Aaron.

Can't let anyone see me like this. And God for-fucking-bid I see someone I know at the hospital.

"Then I respectfully request you let me take you back to my place," said Silas. "I was a doctor in another life. But I understand if you don't trust me."

Aaron finally looked up from the ground.

Silas' eyebrows were pinched in concern. His expression echoed Aaron's pain.

"I will need to know what happened — if they drugged you and how they hurt you — but I don't want to make you uncomfortable."

"He just shoved his fingers in my ass and smacked me around a little," said Aaron. "That's it. Not a big deal." He swayed slightly and tightened his grip on the door. "No big deal. I'm just overreacting. I do that sometimes. Probably to get attention. It's not a big deal."

"Aaron." Silas' voice was still soft, but it had an edge of authority. "This is a very big deal."

"It's not," said Aaron. His vision blurred and he was going to fucking cry again. He didn't deserve to go home. He didn't deserve his father or his brother.

"Are you able to get into the car?" asked Silas. Aaron closed his eyes and nodded. "Do you need assistance?"

Aaron shook his head. The least he could do was stand up on his own. He got to his feet, knees still shaking. Silas shut the door behind him then returned to his place behind the wheel.

"My house?" asked Silas.

"Yeah," muttered Aaron.

Silas drove quickly. When they reached his neighborhood, he circled the block several times. He said it was to make sure no one was waiting for them. After his search, he pulled into the driveway and parked the car.

"Aaron," he said, voice still gentle, "I need you to take the keys and sit behind the wheel with the doors locked. I'm going to check the house and yard and make sure we're alone."

"You shouldn't do that by yourself," said Aaron.

Silas almost looked offended. "I assure you, I'll be fine." He handed Aaron the keys and retrieved his gun. "If you hear anything suspicious or see anyone approaching that isn't me, don't wait—drive as far away as you can as fast as you can and don't look back."

Like hell I will.

"Okay," said Aaron.

Silas nodded, though he didn't seem entirely convinced. He shut the door and waited for Aaron to lock the car before leaving. Silas disappeared quickly into the shadows and Aaron lost sight of him. The next ten minutes dragged on painfully slowly.

When the porch light came on, Aaron let out a breath he hadn't realized he'd been holding. Silas returned and gave Aaron a thumbs-up as he approached the car.

Aaron grabbed his clothes and the bag and got out of the car. Silas offered to carry him again but Aaron refused, his shredded dignity having undergone enough abuse for one day. Silas led him to the living room and told him to wait on the couch while he locked the car in the garage.

He returned a few minutes later. "Your car is secure. The alarm system is armed and all of the doors and windows are locked. The motion sensor light is on in the backyard and I'm leaving the front porch light on so it will be harder to sneak up on the house undetected. You will be safe here."

"Porn star, doctor, security expert?" asked Aaron.

"Ex-military," answered Silas.

"Okay," said Aaron. "Didn't see that coming. Army?"

"Something like that."

That explained a lot. "Military doctor?" asked Aaron.

"Yes." Silas circled to the front of the couch. "May I approach?"

"Sure."

Silas stepped closer, head tilted and eyebrows creased. "I'd like to examine you," he said. "But I don't know if that would make things better or worse for you.

Physical trauma is my area of expertise. I don't have much experience with psychological trauma."

Aaron leaned his head against the couch. He was still wrapped in Silas' coat, still clutching his possessions to his chest. The reality of the past few hours was fading in and out. He was teetering between numbness and mania. He wanted to scream.

"I don't want to puke on your couch," said Aaron.

"I think your system is empty," said Silas. "When was the last time you ate?"

"I'm not sure," said Aaron. "Day before last?"

"Jesus," muttered Silas. "You need to eat—nothing heavy, but your body needs energy. I suggest a shower, or bath depending on how steady you feel, then I would like to examine you, then feed you."

"Go for it," said Aaron.

Silas sighed. "Will you allow me to escort you to the bathroom?"

"Yeah."

'Yes, sir.'

Aaron covered his face with his hands. Thirty showers wouldn't even begin to wash away what had happened. Aaron was dirty. He was going to have to live with that.

He allowed Silas to drag him to his feet and lead him to the bathroom.

"Shower or bath?" asked Silas.

"Shower," answered Aaron. "I don't want to soak in filth."

Silas ran his thumb lightly over Aaron's shoulder. He turned the water on and tested the temperature. "Do you need help bathing?"

Aaron looked down at the tile floor and his head was suddenly too heavy to lift. "No," he mumbled.

"Are you sure? I've helped patients bathe before. I won't hurt you."

Aaron choked back a sob. He should have listened to Silas when he'd said Ralph was too rough. He should have insisted on staying with Silas. He shouldn't have been greedy. He should have just taken the pay cut.

"The safe word didn't work," Aaron said to the floor. "I tried, but—" He bit back another sob. The white noise of the shower made it easier to talk, made his own voice sound smaller and farther away.

"They are monsters," said Silas. "I shouldn't have left you."

"How can you stand to work with people like that?" asked Aaron. He regretted it as soon as he said it. Silas wasn't a monster. He didn't mean it as an accusation.

"I've been with them for two weeks," said Silas. "This is the first time I've witnessed them do something so abhorrent. Though I think shooting at my co-star and director means I've officially tendered my resignation."

Aaron laughed. It felt good to laugh. It pushed the memories farther away. He looked up at Silas.

Silas gave him a sort of sad half-smile. "I must confess I am partially, if not entirely, responsible for what happened to you," he said.

"How the hell do you figure that?"

"Revenge," answered Silas. "They say I take too long and my scenes are not convincing. They punished you to punish me."

"I doubt that," said Aaron. "Farley was already pretty pissed before you walked through the door."

Silas sighed. "I'm so sorry I left you alone with them. I knew better."

"It's not your fault," said Aaron. "I told you to leave."

I brought this on myself. I got hard.

28

Aaron returned his gaze to the floor.

Silas' hand was still on his shoulder. "I will not let them hurt you again."

Aaron nodded, but pulled away.

Silas let him. "Call me if you need help," he said.

"I will."

Silas turned and left the room, pulling the bathroom door shut behind him.

Chapter Four

Soup and a Coat

Aaron scrubbed his entire body until it was raw. His dick was a little bruised and the hot water stung the skin where Ralph had hit him. He leaned against the tile and turned the spray on hotter until the burning felt normal and the steam became too thick for him to breathe. The pain of the heat canceled out the pain from Ralph. He told himself this was why he was hurting. The shower was too hot. It was a pain he could control. Alone, under the water, his mind cleared. When he closed his eyes, it was almost like he was home and nothing had changed — like the last twenty-four hours had never happened.

When he climbed out of the shower, his skin was red and steaming. He dried off and saw Silas had left two piles of clothes for him on the toilet seat. One was his own clothes — what he had worn to the shoot. The other pile was unfamiliar, soft, and smelled freshly washed. He opted for the new clothes. He'd probably burn his own once he got the chance.

He started to dress, but remembered Silas had said something about examining him. For some reason the idea of dressing then undressing again made him sick. He wrapped a towel around his waist and leaned over the sink.

There was a knock at the bathroom door. "I heard the water turn off," said Silas. "Are you still all right?"

For one brief, horrible moment Aaron wanted to kick the door open and beat Silas until he bled. One more question, one more prodding note of concern, one more implication that Aaron was too weak to handle himself. Then just as quickly as it appeared, the rage was gone.

"Aaron?"

"I'm good," said Aaron. "Can we get the exam over with?"

"Do you feel up to it?" asked Silas, still talking through the door.

"No, but it's probably a good idea, right?"

Silas paused. "I'm not sure," he answered. "I've never dealt with a rape victim before. I don't want to cau — "

Aaron grabbed the toothbrush holder from the edge of the sink and threw it against the wall. The container turned out to be ceramic and it shattered. "I wasn't raped!" he shouted.

Silas opened the door, eyes wide.

Aaron stared at him, then stared down at the broken pieces of pottery. He backed away from the door until he bumped up against the wall. He slid down to the floor, his face in his hands.

He heard Silas approach and sit down beside him.

"I apologize," said Silas. "I was never known for my bedside manner."

"It's not you," mumbled Aaron. "I'm just a little fucked up right now."

"You're entitled to be fucked up," he said. "I shouldn't rush you."

"I'll buy you a new toothbrush thing," said Aaron.

"That's really the least of my concerns at the moment," said Silas. "Do you feel like you could eat some soup?"

Aaron huffed. "Honestly, I'd rather you just examine me. I think I'm bleeding and I don't want to bleed on your clothes. And I really don't want to keep sitting on the bathroom floor naked."

"All right," said Silas. "Are you regularly taking any medication?"

"Does liquor count?"

"No — well, technically no — but I'll make a note of that."

"Then no, I'm not on anything."

"How about drugs? Herbal or chemical."

"Nope. Just liquor."

Silas nodded to himself and stood up. He kicked a few ceramic shards to the side and rummaged through the medicine cabinet above the sink. He retrieved several bottles then tilted his head to the door. "Follow me."

Aaron pushed himself up and trailed after Silas back into the living room. There was a bowl of warm water and a washcloth on the table, as well as a meticulously organized and extensive first-aid kit.

Silas noticed Aaron eyeing the supplies as he set the pill bottles on the table. "I wanted to make the process go as quickly as possible," he said. He opened a bottle and shook a pill into his hand. "Have you ever taken Xanax before?"

"No," answered Aaron.

He handed Aaron the pill and a glass of water. "That's one milligram. It will help with anxiety and stress. You might feel sleepy. If your vision begins to blur, or you feel confused or generally ill, tell me immediately."

Aaron hesitated before taking the pill.

"You don't have to take it," said Silas. "I wanted to offer it to help relieve your stress."

Aaron took it. He'd trusted Silas this far. He swallowed the pill then waited, then felt stupid for expecting an immediate reaction. A snapping sound caught his attention.

Silas was putting on a pair of latex gloves. "I thought I'd check your anus first," he said. He suddenly seemed to have trouble maintaining eye contact. "The rest of the exam will be significantly less invasive."

"Let's get it over with," said Aaron. "Should I bend over and grab my ankles?" He tried to laugh, but it stuck in his throat. Apparently his brain thought it was too soon to make jokes.

"If you could lie on your side on the couch with your knees apart, I think that will work best," said Silas. He handed Aaron a pillow and spread a towel over the cushions.

Aaron didn't have a retort for that, so he lay down as Silas instructed, with the pillow between his knees.

"It's important for you to communicate with me while I do this," said Silas. "If I hurt you, tell me. If you are uncomfortable, tell me. If you feel stressed, tell me."

"I've been stressed since five this afternoon," said Aaron.

"I'm going to touch you now," said Silas. "I won't probe you. I will just spread your cheeks apart."

Aaron groaned and sucked in a breath. "Do me a favor," he said. "Don't narrate."

"Understood," said Silas. After that he kept his mouth shut. His fingers were slick, but not sticky like Ralph's. His hands were warm and firm, but still gentle. He did not invade or push. If Aaron flinched, Silas would pause before resuming the exam. The whole ordeal was over in about five minutes.

"You do have some tearing," said Silas. "It will heal on its own, but I would like to apply an ointment to help with pain and prevent infection."

"Okay," said Aaron. He was facing away from Silas and staring at the light blue couch cushions. He had a throw pillow clutched to his chest.

"I also need to apply a cream to your buttocks where Ralph hit you. The skin isn't broken, but it is inflamed. This will help with the pain."

"Okay," said Aaron.

He felt Silas touch his ass, then spread his cheeks again and rub something cool against his entrance. Thirty seconds was all it took.

Silas snapped off his gloves. "You can carefully turn onto your other side now."

Aaron rolled over and Silas was ready with another towel to cover him.

"Next I need to check for bruising and signs of trauma to your penis and testicles," said Silas.

Aaron stared up at the pillow.

"Again, communication is important."

"Got it," said Aaron.

Silas snapped into another pair of gloves and lifted the towel. He gently nudged Aaron's knees apart, similar to the way he had when they'd first met that

34

afternoon—when he'd been 'Master' instead of 'Silas'. Aaron was vaguely aware that his foot was shaking.

"How old are you?" asked Silas.

"Twenty-one," answered Aaron.

"How long have you owned that car?" Silas lifted Aaron's penis.

Aaron tried not to flinch. "Dad gave it to me last year."

"How long have you lived in town?" He gently pressed his fingertips into the surrounding area.

"We've lived here on and off. Every few years we leave, then every few years we come back."

"Do you have any other family nearby?"

"My little brother," answered Aaron.

Silas tugged at Aaron's knees, signaling for him to relax his legs again. "How old is he?"

"Seventeen," answered Aaron. "Heading to college in the fall."

Silas replaced the towel over Aaron's waist and removed his gloves. "What will he study, has he decided?"

"Law," answered Aaron. He glanced down at Silas, who was perched on the edge of the couch.

"It must be nice to have a lawyer in the family," said Silas.

"Yeah," said Aaron. "He's a smart kid, too. No idea where he got his brains. Must have come from Mom's side of the family." He inhaled sharply as soon as 'Mom' left his mouth.

Mercifully, Silas didn't prod. "You must be very proud."

"I am," said Aaron.

"I'll bring you some clothes. Do you think you can eat now?"

Aaron's stomach answered for him with a growl.

Silas smiled and stood. He returned a few moments later with the clothes from the bathroom. "I'm going to heat up some soup. Do you have any allergies?"

"No," answered Aaron.

"Are you a vegan or vegetarian?"

Aaron laughed. "No."

"All right. Get dressed and I'll get you some food."

Aaron wasn't sure why Silas had switched from overprotective mother hen to removed doctor, but he welcomed the change. He suspected it had something to do with him throwing things earlier.

He stood and eased himself into a pair of Silas' boxers. He heard a scraping sound down the hall and felt a little guilty. Silas was probably cleaning up the mess he'd made.

He pulled on a well-worn, stretched-out pair of sweatpants. They fit Aaron, but he could only imagine they barely hung on Silas' hips. He was slender, and shorter than Aaron. The T-shirt was a little snug, but it was also soft. Aaron eyed the coat now hanging in the entryway. He felt a weird urge to hide himself in it.

Just do it. He just smeared cream on your ass like you were an infant. If that didn't cross the WTF line, wearing his coat won't either.

Aaron felt a little groggy as he made his way to the coat, but he didn't second-guess himself.

Maybe it was the Xanax talking. Whatever it was, he liked it. He slipped into the coat and wrapped it tight around his torso, hugging it closer to his body. Like the pants, the coat fit Aaron better than it fit Silas. *It must be a hand-me-down.*

Of course Silas chose that moment to reappear.

"I have beef and vegetable or chick — oh," said Silas. He tilted his head to the side.

Aaron was about to explain, but Silas interrupted.

"Or chicken noodle," he finished. "I admit, I never learned to cook more than eggs and toast, and most of the time they come out burned. I hope canned soup is all right."

"I'm not picky," said Aaron, still awkwardly hugging the coat to his body.

"Do you want to eat on the couch or in the kitchen?" asked Silas. "I advise you sit on the couch, as it's softer."

"Uh — couch then," said Aaron. "Hey, I — I should have asked." He half gestured to the coat. "I just — I don't know. I don't have a good reason."

"You don't need one," said Silas. "As far as I'm concerned, this is your safe space and you can do whatever you want. What's mine is yours." His cheeks suddenly flushed bright pink. "I'm glad I can offer something that brings you comfort."

Aaron felt the overwhelming urge to rush forward and bury his face in Silas' neck, to hold him and let himself be held. Instead, he hugged the coat tighter. "You saved me today," said Aaron quietly. "I hope you understand that."

Silas' eyebrows pinched together and his hands started fidgeting. "I feel like I should embrace you now, but I do not want to make you uncomfortable or disrespect your boundaries."

"Uh," said Aaron, "You can — yeah, you should do that. The embrace thing, I mean."

Silas closed the distance between them in two quick steps and pulled Aaron into his arms. Aaron wrapped his arms around Silas' neck and hid his face. Silas flattened his palm against Aaron's back and ran his hand in a soothing circular motion.

And God dammit, Aaron was crying again. Silas inhaled a shaky breath and Aaron noticed he wasn't the only one disturbed by the day. He nuzzled closer to Silas and Silas responded by holding him tighter. In that moment, Aaron realized Silas must also have a story. Somewhere in his life, something had gone wrong and made him feel broken. Something had happened that made him able to empathize with Aaron right now. At some point, someone had hurt him.

Aaron closed his eyes and scowled. Silas was a saint. Aaron would kill any son of a bitch who made him feel like he was anything less. Without thinking, he pressed his lips against the exposed skin of Silas' shoulder.

Silas took another shaky breath and made a small sound. "You are safe with me, Aaron. I promise you."

"You're safe with me too, Silas," said Aaron. He ran a hand up Silas' neck and laced his fingers through Silas' hair. "I dare those fuckers to try to come after us."

Chapter Five

Secrets

Silas made chicken soup and they ate together on the couch. He turned the TV to something benign.

Aaron watched Silas from the corner of his eye and his imagination crept in, painting a picture of rainy day. Maybe that day the ex-doctor wasn't feeling very well. Aaron thought about cooking for him, making him his mother's chicken and dumplings soup from scratch—minus the secret ingredient. She'd died before she could tell him what it was. He'd created the recipe through memory and years of trial and error.

After years of over-salted broth, chewy dumplings, and mushy vegetables, Aaron felt confident he'd learned from his mistakes and conquered the texture. Danny always said it was good. But he had been a baby when their mom had died. He didn't have anything to compare it to.

Robert usually wouldn't eat it. On the rare occasion that he did, he'd give Aaron a few words of advice. *'She'd brown the vegetables first'* or *'she always complained about the dough being too sticky.'* Aaron had rebuilt his mother's recipes through his own broken memories and whatever his father was willing to share. He told Danny stories and kept her alive in their house for as long as he could. She would have loved Daniel and he would have loved her.

Aaron blinked hard. The idea of crying again today made him feel sick. The idea of puking again made him feel worse.

He glanced across the couch and his imagination continued its painting. Silas would love the soup. He'd love anything Aaron cooked for him. He'd insist he didn't need Aaron to take care of him. Aaron would insist he needed to stay wrapped up. Silas would remind him he was the doctor.

Aaron smiled at the idea of a grumpy, bed-headed, rosy-cheeked Silas arguing with him, but ultimately giving in. Aaron would help him to bed—he'd probably catch whatever Silas had and— Aaron dropped his spoon back into the bowl.

Shit.

His skin tingled and a nasty, cold feeling slithered through him and coiled in his gut. He glanced over at Silas. Yes, he was attractive. Yes, he was kind. Yes, Aaron had enjoyed kissing him earlier. Yes, Silas was the only good thing about today. Silas was the only good thing about a lot of days in recent memory.

"Are you all right?"

Apparently Aaron's internal freak-out was not so internalized. "Yeah," he mumbled. "Just tired." He needed to go home. He couldn't be gay again. Robert would take Daniel away. Robert would tell Daniel all the ways his big brother was bad and shatter the illusion of Aaron.

Silas took the bowl from his hand. "You're trembling." He touched two fingers to the inside of Aaron's wrist. "And your heart rate is higher than normal." He took Aaron's hand into both of his. "I'm here if you want to talk about it."

"I've already talked about it," said Aaron, hoping Silas was only referring to what had happened earlier.

Can't go home. I'm filthy. Robert will smell it on me.

"Are you ready for bed?" asked Silas. "I'm sure you're exhausted."

Aaron's heart skipped a beat. They hadn't discussed sleeping arrangements—or had they? He couldn't remember. Did Silas want him to stay? Where would he sleep? Would Robert know that, too?

"What time is it?" asked Aaron.

"Almost midnight," answered Silas.

If he wasn't invited to sleep here, he'd sleep in the car. He retrieved his phone from the pocket of his borrowed sweatpants. It was the first time he'd checked his phone in hours. No messages. No missed calls.

Silas moved his hand up and rested it on Aaron's shoulder. "You should sleep. I've got some pills for you to take before bed." He gripped Aaron's shoulder and stood.

Aaron stared at his phone. If he went missing, how long would it be before someone went looking for him.

Silas touched his shoulder again and offered a handful of various pills. Aaron took them all at once. He heard Silas sigh behind him.

"I will sleep on the couch," said Silas. "Let me put fresh sheets on the bed, then you can rest." Aaron closed his eyes and sank into the couch.

"I'll sleep out here," he said. "You've done enough."

"Doctor's orders," said Silas. "You need to have room to stretch." He left without giving Aaron a chance to argue.

Aaron stared at the TV, not really taking in what he was watching, until Silas returned. "There is a box of medicine and a bottle of water on the table by the bed. You've got two painkillers, an antibiotic and another Xanax. If you need more, let me know. I'm not keeping medication from you, but I do need to keep track of your dosages." Silas stood in front of him with his head cocked to the side, watching.

Aaron decided to deflect. "How do you have so many pills?"

"My sister runs a pharmacy."

Aaron raised an eyebrow. "So you're not really supposed to have this stuff, are you?"

"Technically, no," huffed Silas.

Aaron had hit a button that triggered something in Silas. He couldn't help himself. For once, he wasn't the one under the microscope. "Are you still a doctor?"

"Yes. I will always be a doctor. But if you're asking if I have a license, then no."

Aaron blinked, then grinned slowly. "You've got secrets," he said.

"I do," answered Silas.

Aaron got up from the couch, Silas' coat still wrapped around him. "Ex-military, unlicensed doctor, pretty damn good with a firearm, family drug hook-up, ex-porn star and gay? Or was that part of the act?"

"Gay," confirmed Silas.

Aaron nodded. "What other secrets you got?"

"I practice mixed martial arts and I have a brown belt."

"What the shit, Silas? Seriously?"

"Yes. I intend to reach black belt next year."

Aaron laughed. "Well, fuck. I asked for secrets and you didn't disappoint."

Silas' lip twitched and he almost smiled. "You should rest, Aaron."

"Is that your way telling me to stop asking stupid questions?"

"No, that's my way of taking care of my patient," answered Silas. He turned and headed to the bedroom, not waiting for Aaron to follow.

Aaron rolled his eyes and trailed after Silas.

His unofficial doctor turned the covers down and showed Aaron where his medicine was.

"If you can't sleep, I have many books. The ones on the top shelf are my favorite, so obviously I recommend you start there." He held up a small box. "This is your medication. Each slot is labeled with the name and description of the pill it contains. You should go ahead and take the antibiotic now." He set the box down and held up a tube of something. "This is for pain relief on your buttocks." He held up a different tube. "This is for anal tearing."

Aaron picked up the container of pills. Sure as shit, each slot was clearly labeled and each pill had a description in case Aaron got them mixed up.

"If you wake up in pain and need help with anything, come get me, call me, shout for me. Whatever you are capable of doing." He pointed to a small note on the table. "That's my cell number. I'll have my phone on and by my side all night."

Aaron sat on the edge of the bed and smoothed his hand over the fresh white sheets. He looked up at the doctor.

Silas rubbed his neck and blushed for the second time that night. "I also have an air mattress," he said. "I wasn't sure how you would feel about being alone tonight. I wanted to offer you the opportunity to — um — to have company."

"It's your room, Silas," said Aaron. "You don't have to ask —"

"Yes, I do." The blush faded quickly and Silas' eyes turned cold. "I told you I wouldn't hurt you. I meant that."

Aaron broke away from the stare and glanced around the room. He jumped suddenly when he saw a red light glowing in the corner and a dark figure standing beside it. He blinked, and it was gone. He turned to Silas, who was suddenly kneeling in front of him.

"The trauma will haunt you for a while," he said. "I wish with all that I am, that I could take that pain away. I'm sorry this is all I can offer."

"Stay with me," said Aaron quickly. He blurted out the words before he thought about what he was asking.

Silas nodded, then stood.

Aaron grabbed his hand. "I meant here." He gestured to the bed. "Unless that would weird you out."

The chill ebbed from Silas' expression. "Not at all." He pulled away from Aaron's grasp and turned to his bookshelf. He pawed through several volumes before returning with a worn-out paperback.

"*Jurassic Park*?" asked Aaron.

"It's a fascinating story of creation," said Silas.

"I'm adding 'mad scientist' to your list of secrets," said Aaron.

Silas' lip twitched again. "I'm going to shower. I thought you might like a distraction while I'm gone. That's usually the book I use to distract myself."

"Thanks, Silas." Aaron turned the book over in his hands. He'd clearly read it several times before. The spine was broken in multiple places where Silas must have repeatedly opened the book to a specific part. Aaron decided to start from the first crease.

Silas left and the shower turned on.

Aaron tried to engross himself in the story. Instead, he found himself searching the pages for quotes and lines, trying to figure out which parts of the book were Silas' favorite and why.

Silas returned sometime later. His hair was wet and he was wearing pajama pants and a T-shirt. He seemed small and tired.

Aaron wanted to hold him. He shouldn't have asked Silas to sleep here. He shouldn't have accepted Silas' offer to stay at the house. He shouldn't have read between the lines of Silas' favorite book in an attempt to decode the man. He shouldn't care, shouldn't want this, shouldn't need the comfort.

"Do you need anything?" asked Silas, nodding to the table.

"No," answered Aaron. He set the book aside and wriggled out of the coat. He hung it on the edge of the headboard and crawled under the covers.

"Lights on or off?" asked Silas.

"Off," answered Aaron.

"The lamp beside you works," said Silas. "If you change your mind and want a light, it will not bother me." He flipped the switch.

Aaron watched the doctor's silhouette approach the bed. He closed his eyes. One night. He would allow himself one night of comfort, then he'd move on.

The bed dipped as Silas moved beside him. He pulled the covers over himself, but Aaron noticed that Silas stayed above the top sheet. It created a barrier between them.

Aaron sighed. "Thanks, Silas."

"It's the least I can do," he said.

Aaron rolled over, expecting to find himself facing Silas' back. Instead he found Silas starting at him.

"Good night, Aaron."

"Night, Silas."

Chapter Six

Jurassic Park

Aaron saw the spider move out of the corner of his eye. He turned to crush it, but missed. It was small, white and fast. It was going to kill him. He couldn't remember the species, but it was something terrible.

If it bit him, he would die. If he let it leave the room, it would scurry down the hall to Robert's room then Daniel's. They were asleep. They'd never know it was coming.

To his horror, Aaron realized the crack beneath his bedroom door was growing wider. He grabbed a blanket from his bed and shoved it under the door. He'd lost track of the spider.

His room was bright. He couldn't find the damn light switch. Something told him that if he could turn off the light, the spider would glow and he'd be able to see it.

Something tickled his arm and he jumped away. The spider scuttled across his body and up his chest. He couldn't brush it off. He started tearing at his clothes. It was looking for a place to hide. It was going to nest somewhere on him and attack Daniel the next time Aaron left the room.

Aaron pounded his fists against his body in a desperate attempt to crush the spider. His arms ached. His chest ached.

Everything ached. His flailing slowed. He slumped against the door. The spider stirred near his ear. He could feel it. He couldn't move. The spider was going to get out. It was going to kill Daniel.

It crawled down his back, leaving a trail of wet, sticky web as it went. Aaron realized he was naked. There was nothing to stop it from biting him.

"Dad," he called. "I can't kill it."

Someone growled something from the other side of the door. Aaron couldn't understand them. "Help!"

The web covered his entire body, glistening and unbreakable. Aaron caught another glimpse of the creature as it crawled across his stomach. He felt each little leg tapping against his skin as it hurried out of sight again...

"Aaron!"

He jolted awake and the room spun violently around him. He gasped for air, clutching his chest. The web was gone. He was clothed. He wasn't in his room. There was no spider — no threat to him or his family.

Someone ran a hand over his back and Aaron's stomach lurched. He clasped a hand over his mouth and ran to the bathroom.

Silas. He was with Silas. His memories came back to him as he hung his head over the toilet bowl and hurled for the second time in twenty-four hours.

He heard someone approaching. He clutched the bowl with one hand and held the other out, palm first. "Don't," he panted. "Give me a second." His torso seized again and he threw up the remaining contents of his stomach. He dropped his hand and stretched one arm across the toilet seat. He let his head slump to the side.

"May I approach?" asked Silas. His voice was soft, probably with the intention of sounding respectful and soothing.

Instead of calming him, Aaron felt hot breath ghost against his ear—heard someone whisper *'good boy'*. Aaron coughed. His chest hurt. He realized he was leaning against the side where Ralph had grabbed his nipple. He shifted slightly, but didn't turn his head. He couldn't look at Silas. He couldn't look at anyone right now.

He heaved again, drooling into the toilet. The smell of stomach acid and sweat made him cringe. He felt fingertips tapping down his spine, moving lower and lower. He heaved again.

Silas was still standing behind him—probably regretting letting him stay. Aaron clung to the toilet with shaky hands. Silas was watching him. Aaron could feel his eyes on his back. Silas knew what he looked like underneath his clothes. He knew Aaron's body. He could only see what Aaron allowed, but that wouldn't stop him from imagining.

Aaron thought of the way Silas had kissed his neck. He gasped for air, his whole body convulsing now. He'd just slept in the same bed with Silas—with his *Dom*. Jesus—there was no telling what Silas had done to him while he was asleep. He'd taken so many pills since he'd arrived.

"Aaron."

Why had he given them his real name? Why had he let them call him that? Why had he let them touch him? For money? Was it worth it? He should have fought back after the safe-word had failed. He should have tried harder. There was a moment, before the bar had been between his legs, when it had been just Ralph's weight holding him down... Aaron should have been able to roll over and run.

"Aaron."

'Yes, sir?'

He hurled again. Nothing came up. He released the toilet and covered his head with his arms. Maybe he could drown himself. How hard would that be? He could just hold his breath until he passed out, then his face would be in the toilet and he'd drown.

Something warm moved beside him and he flinched again.

"Don't worry," said Silas. "I'm not going to touch you. I just want to make sure you're all right." His voice was distant again — clinical. It was less that simpering 'poor baby, are you okay?' and more removed.

Aaron's breathing echoed in the toilet bowl.

"I am concerned you will hyperventilate if you stay in that position," said Silas. "Can you sit up?" Aaron took a shaky breath and uncovered his head. He kept himself propped against the bowl and kept his eyes closed.

"Much better," said Silas. "You are rocking back and forth."

He hadn't been aware he'd been doing that.

"I'm worried that will make you feel more nauseated."

Aaron stopped rocking. Now that he wasn't moving, he could tell how much his hands were shaking. "Sorry," he muttered.

"You have nothing to apologize for," said Silas. "I'd like to take your pulse. May I touch your wrist?"

Aaron didn't answer — he just held out his arm. "I know it's fast," he said. "I can feel it." Silas wasn't like the others. Of course he wasn't — he'd literally kicked down the door and walked in, guns blazing, to rescue Aaron. Silas was *good*.

"I have a suggestion," said Silas.

"I'm listening."

"I think you should sit across from me with your hand over my heart."

Aaron cracked his eyes open and turned to look at Silas. He was in full-on doctor mode. He watched Aaron carefully with his head tilted to the side. "What will that do?" asked Aaron.

"It is a breathing exercise," answered Silas. "It's to help you make your breath match mine. I will also count."

"This sounds like some yoga bullshit," muttered Aaron. Nonetheless, he turned slowly away from the toilet and sat cross-legged in front of Silas on the bathroom floor.

"Place your hand here," said Silas. He tapped a spot high to the left side of his chest.

Aaron inched closer and raised a shaky hand. He hiccupped when he tried to inhale again. He splayed his fingers across Silas' chest.

Silas smiled. "Good. Now, inhale. One, two, three, four, five. Exhale. One, two, three, four, five, six, seven."

Aaron felt Silas' chest expand and fall beneath his fingertips. His hand was glistening with sweat. He realized he still had drool covering one side of his face. He tried to wipe it away with his free hand.

"Inhale. One, two, three, four, five." Silas handed him a nearby towel. Silas was always prepared. Maybe it was the doctor in him. Maybe it was another secret.

Aaron followed Silas' breathing until his hiccups subsided and his arm stopped trembling. Somewhere along the way, his hand had formed into a fist and he was clutching the front of Silas' shirt. He let go and pulled away. "Sorry," he said again.

"The first few nights are the worst," said Silas. "But I promise it will get better."

Aaron ran a hand over his face. He felt sticky again and his breath smelled awful. He couldn't even take care of himself. Silas didn't deserve to be burdened with him.

Silas flushed the toilet beside him and closed the lid. "Would you like to watch a movie?" he asked. "The sofa converts to a bed and I have all of the *Jurassic Park* movies on DVD." He paused. "I should be honest. It's very hard to resist the urge to put you on bed rest and insert an IV into your arm to make sure you stay hydrated."

"I'd much rather binge-watch *Jurassic Park*," said Aaron.

"Could I persuade you to lie propped up on the sofa bed in case you decide to sleep?"

Aaron huffed a laugh. "Yeah."

"Could I also persuade you to see if you could keep down some wheat toast and water?"

Aaron sighed. "Silas, I should go home. It's late. Dad and Daniel are probably asleep. You'll be up all night if I stay."

"I have nothing better to do," said Silas. "If you leave, I'll be up all night worrying about you, and I cannot guarantee that I can stop myself from following you home to stand guard."

"That's insane."

"I'm aware."

Aaron shook his head. "*Jurassic Park* it is."

* * * *

Silas essentially built a nest in the center of the pullout. He fussed over how Aaron should prop, took his pulse again, debated with himself over whether Aaron should take another Xanax. He brought in two pieces of wheat toast and a glass of ice water.

Aaron patted an empty space in the pillow fortress beside him after Silas handed over the meal.

"I'm not sure I should sit with you," said Silas.

Aaron bit his lip and pulled his hand away, because duh, what the hell was he thinking? Forget the sudden urge to cuddle up on a couch with a man. The last time Silas had tried to comfort him, he'd puked. Not to mention the fact that he was dirty and stained in a way that could never be cleaned. And on top of that Silas had been forced to cater to Aaron all damn day. The very least Aaron should be able to do was sit on the couch by himself.

Aaron took a bite of the toast and grimaced. "Is this cardboard smeared with oil?" he asked.

"It's wheat bread with a butter substitute," said Silas. He left and returned a moment later with two cups of tea. "I want you to drink your water, but I thought you might also appreciate something warm."

Silas grabbed the remote and turned on the television. He squinted at the couch, then approached cautiously and crawled among the pillows to sit next to Aaron.

The moment Aaron detected the warmth of another body, his heart skipped and his body flew through his entire index of emotion. Aaron's body decided to express these emotions by crossing his arms firmly over his chest, but leaning closer to Silas.

Silas made no attempt to hide the fact that he was now studying Aaron. After several minutes of staring at each other, Silas raised his arm and let it rest on the back of the couch behind Aaron's shoulders.

Aaron looked down at his lap and decided that, of all the feelings currently shouting for a voice, hope was the loudest.

Silas hit play and the movie began.

By the time the T-rex had broken free of its enclosure, Aaron and Silas were sitting shoulder to shoulder with Silas' arm wrapped firmly around Aaron.

When the frilled dinosaur spat poison from the front seat of the Jeep, Aaron's head was resting beneath Silas' chin.

Aaron let himself lean against Silas when the power came back on and the velociraptors were attacked by the T-rex. He felt himself falling asleep.

When Silas started the next movie, Aaron woke up, but only to wiggle closer to the doctor and mutter another "thank you," before drifting off.

Chapter Seven

The Video

Aaron woke up to his phone buzzing beside his face. He was sweating and still struggling to adjust to the reality beyond his latest dream. His phone was solid in his hand. It was one in the afternoon. He had thirteen missed calls, twenty new texts and five voice messages. He checked the missed calls. Daniel had called ten times. An unsaved number had called three times. Farley.

He checked his voicemail. The first message was from Farley.

"I'm sure you think you're clever, running out with my money and crying wolf all the way home. How fortunate for you that Silas has a soft heart and a small little walnut brain. Unfortunate, however, that I have a quick temper and I hate, *hate*, lazy workers who don't earn their pay. You have one hour to respond. Return the money and we'll forget this whole unpleasantness ever happened."

Farley had left the message at nine a.m. The next message was Farley again.

"You know, Aaron, I really didn't think you'd give us your real name. We had a little bet going. I bet against. I lost. Funny. Second time in twenty-four hours that I've lost money because of you. Anyway, this is a courtesy call. You have ten minutes remaining."

Farley had left another at ten-fifteen a.m.

"As luck would have it, I found another little Beaumont boy online. His name is Daniel. He is friends with an Aaron Beaumont, though poor Aaron doesn't seem to have a very active account. Daniel has tagged you in a few photos, though. 'Celebrating my sixteenth birthday with Dad and Aaron.' Sweet boy. I assume he's your brother? Point being, I messaged him an hour ago, just after I called you. I told him I had information about you. Gave him my number. He called right away. I didn't answer. I waited. I really wanted you to call — just so desperate to hear your voice. But, since you never called, I settled for Daniel. I did send him a video though. Now he won't stop calling. Oh, I think that's him beeping in now. Better go."

The next message was from Daniel. All of the texts were from Daniel. There was nothing from Robert and nothing else from Farley.

A snore from the other side of the couch made Aaron jump. He had to leave. He'd listen to the rest of the messages in the car. His hands shook as he slipped off the mattress. He snuck to the bathroom and dressed quickly in his old clothes. He couldn't risk showing up wearing another man's pajamas. He grabbed his keys and his wallet and finally, it clicked.

Silas had taken the money when they'd left. Silas had it. Aaron went back to the bedroom and saw the bag sitting on the edge of the bed. The cash was still in it. He left as quickly and quietly as he could, money in hand.

They kidnapped Daniel. I'm going to have to kill them. What do I know about hiding bodies?

Aaron shook the thoughts from his head as he got behind the wheel of his car. He held the phone up to his ear as he backed away from Silas' house. Listening to the messages was the only way to confirm Daniel was safe. Farley had said he'd sent Daniel a video. There was really only one way to interpret that. Silas had shot the camera, but that didn't mean he'd damaged the SD card or whatever. Aaron waited for Daniel's message to play. Even if Farley hadn't taken Daniel, Aaron still wouldn't see him again—not if Daniel saw what he'd done. His family would disown him.

Aaron decided to play Daniel's most recent message first. The message began with a deep inhalation.

"I don't know what's going on or why you won't answer your phone. Dad still won't let me call the cops. He's pissing me off. I don't know what to do. Please come home."

Aaron pulled over. His hands were shaking too much for him to get a good grip on the wheel. Daniel was safe, but Robert knew. How much did Robert know? He played Daniel's first voice message.

"Dude, this guy messaged me about an hour ago saying he knew stuff about you. I thought it was bullshit but he just sent me— He sent— Just call me, okay?"

Aaron swallowed hard and scrolled through the texts. He read fast, as though only half paying attention would somehow lessen the severity of his predicament. He played the rest of Daniel's messages. They confirmed his suspicions.

Farley had tried to call Aaron. Aaron had slept through the opportunity to make things right. Daniel had called Farley. Eventually, Farley had sent Daniel a video. Daniel was never able to articulate or type out what he saw. He just kept calling it 'the video'. After Daniel couldn't reach Aaron, he'd told Robert. Robert had told Daniel to wait, presumably for Aaron to come home. Daniel had kept trying to reach Aaron in the meantime.

His phone buzzed in his hand and he jumped. Daniel again. Aaron threw the phone into the seat beside him and steered his car onto the road. Home, then consequences, then he'd figure out how to move on.

Chapter Eight

Homecoming

When Aaron pulled into the driveway, the front door of the old white farmhouse flew open. A lanky teen with shaggy blond hair rushed to the car. Aaron barely had time to stand and shut the door before Daniel was standing in front of him, staring like Aaron's very existence was a surprise.

"Dude, I literally was about to call 911," said Daniel. He held up his phone. "What the fuck? Where have you been? I tried to look for you, but Dad wouldn't let me take the Jeep."

"Sorry," said Aaron. "I stayed out too late, drank too much. I crashed at a friend's house."

Daniel was already shaking his head. "But that weird guy... Did you get my messages? This guy sent me a private message saying he had information about you, then like an hour later he sent me this — this — uh — a thing, and I thought — I don't know. I thought you'd been kidnapped. Were you kidnapped?"

"No," answered Aaron. "Can I see your phone?"

Daniel raised his eyebrow.

"I want to see the video the guy sent you," said Aaron. "You can either describe it to me yourself or just let me look at it."

Daniel surrendered his phone without protest.

Aaron scrolled through Daniel's texts and found the thread from Farley. Aaron turned down the media volume before hitting play. Six seconds. That was it. It was six seconds of him sucking Silas' dick. It was a tight shot, too close for Aaron to claim it wasn't him. It didn't show anything else — didn't show Aaron screaming or struggling — didn't show him saying "no" over and over again. It was just six seconds of Aaron in a blindfold, very willingly sucking dick.

Aaron deleted the message thread then handed the phone to Daniel.

"I thought," began Daniel, voice cracking slightly, "I thought this was a hostage video or something." He bit his lip. "Was it? Were you —"

"No," snapped Aaron.

"Are you okay?"

"Yeah, Danny. Of course I'm okay." He crossed his arms over his chest to hide the shaking. He couldn't fucking stop shaking. His stomach turned.

"Then I don't understand," said Daniel.

"Someone was being an asshole," said Aaron.

"You said you drank too much," said Daniel. "Do you remember what happened last night?"

Aaron ran a hand over his face. "Nothing happened. That" — he pointed to the phone — "has nothing to do with last night."

Let the Lying Olympics begin.

"I don't know what that was," continued Aaron, "but it wasn't me and you don't need to be worried."

Daniel looked at his phone. "You deleted it," he said. "Aaron, that was evidence."

"Did Dad see it?"

Daniel rolled his eyes. "Yeah, but he wasn't any fucking help. He was three sheets to the wind last night and still pretty trashed when he got up. Hell, he's probably already drunk again."

"Where is he?"

"Inside," answered Daniel. "He went into work but Uncle Jack sent him home."

Jack Miller was their unofficial uncle and the only reason Aaron and Robert had jobs. He owned a garage in town. Aaron was a full-time mechanic and Robert worked part-time. Jack regularly sent Robert home. But if Robert had been sober, he would have been at work. If he'd been at work, maybe he wouldn't have seen the video. Then again, if Daniel had been left alone to figure this out, he would probably have called the cops and Robert would have found out anyway.

"He's not mad," said Daniel. "He just wasn't any help." Daniel shook his head and pushed his hair out of his eyes. "God, I'm glad you're all right."

"Guess I should tell Dad I'm back," said Aaron.

"I'll go with you."

It wouldn't matter. With Daniel at home and awake and in the loop, Robert wouldn't say anything. Aaron was a toxin to be disposed of once Daniel was safely contained somewhere else. Their mother had died in a car accident when Daniel was an infant, but Daniel still had nightmares about it. After June had died, Robert had devoted his life to keeping Daniel's world pure and clean and safe. Daniel hated it and told Aaron the reason he wanted to move so far away was to get away from Robert.

Aaron remembered the crash. Aaron was already stained. When Aaron was in high school, Robert had caught him making out with a boy, which had added a layer of grime. It had been his first and last encounter. It was also the first time Robert had hit him. He'd told Aaron he'd never be a real man. Aaron walked the line of being too dirty to be a part of Daniel's world and a necessary sentinel to keep Daniel safe.

Daniel, of course, had no idea.

Robert had promised that the day Aaron slipped up again would be the last day he saw Daniel. The definition of 'slip up' remained nebulous, because Aaron had always been too afraid to ask for clarification. But he didn't need clarification to know that what had happened yesterday counted as a slip up.

He followed Daniel into the house. Robert was sitting on the couch watching television. He nodded at Aaron when the boys entered.

"Told you," said Robert. "You were worried for nothing. Aaron, glad you're back."

"Thanks," said Aaron. "Sorry to worry you guys."

"I wasn't worried," said Robert.

Daniel rolled his eyes. "You should both be worried. That was weird."

Aaron faked a yawn. "You guys mind if I take a nap? I'm still a little hungover."

Robert didn't protest. He wouldn't look at Aaron. Daniel shook his head, clearly exasperated and clearly not buying the pathetic story Robert and Aaron were desperately trying to sell. Aaron was tainted and Daniel was too smart to stay pure forever. He already knew too much. But Robert was right to try to save him a little longer. Robert had wasted his life. Aaron's life was already beyond salvaging. Daniel was the last hope. If lying and hiding kept Daniel unburdened a little longer, long enough for him to make something of himself, it would be worth it.

* * * *

Aaron waited alone in his room until nightfall. He didn't change clothes. It didn't matter. He couldn't fall asleep. Half of him was forming an argument in favor of letting him stay. The other half knew he had to leave. Bad people were after him and the first thing they had done was reach out and scratch at Daniel's world. He sat on his bed with his head in his hands. Robert couldn't afford to let him stay.

He heard Daniel's bedroom door close around midnight. He heard Robert approach his room around one. He didn't knock. He opened the door, and when he saw Aaron was awake, he motioned for him. They couldn't talk upstairs. They might wake Daniel.

Aaron followed his father downstairs, through the living room, outside and into the front yard. It was dark, no moon, just bright stars.

"What did you do?" asked Robert.

Aaron couldn't look at him. His stomach flipped again.

"You've got to tell me so I can be prepared."

"I stole money," answered Aaron. The money, he realized, was still sitting in the trunk of his car.

"What was that video?

There was no point in lying and Aaron didn't quite understand the part of himself that had the audacity to try. "I don't know," he answered.

Robert hit him once, hard, in the side of the face. "What was that video?" he repeated.

"I agreed to do it for money," answered Aaron. He tasted blood. Robert had never been one to pull his punches. "I got scared at the last minute and ran. I took the money anyway. They want it back." Aaron also didn't understand the part of himself that had decided to leave Silas out of the story.

"Speak clearly, boy," said Robert. "They who? How many? Are they going to come after us?"

Aaron shook his head. "I've got the money," he said. "I'll give it to them and make it right. They won't hurt us."

Robert hit him again. "They who?" he repeated. "Numbers, Aaron. How many?"

"Two men and a woman," answered Aaron. "One of them is the person who contacted Daniel. But once I give them back the money, we'll be okay. I'll make it right."

Robert didn't speak and Aaron didn't look up. He stared down at his father's feet. It didn't escape his attention that Robert had led them to the car. Aaron heard himself talking before he understood what he was saying.

"I don't want to go," he said quietly.

"Don't make this harder than it needs to be," said Robert.

"Please," whispered Aaron. He knew he had to leave. He'd put Danny in danger. When June had died, they had been left with one good thing and that was Daniel. Aaron was dangerous. He had to leave.

He heard keys clank and knew Robert must have set them on the hood of the car. "I'm going to tell him we had a fight," said Robert. "I'll tell him you've got a boyfriend. You got drunk, took a video, your boyfriend sent it to Daniel as a joke."

Aaron nodded.

"You figured you could lie your way out," continued Robert. "You and I talked. I told you that shit was inappropriate. You were embarrassed. You got irrational. You left to live with your boyfriend. You're probably not going to speak to us for a while. That's how mad you are."

Aaron nodded again.

"Don't tell Jack. He's got a big mouth. He'll let something slip to Daniel and Daniel will think he needs to help you. But he doesn't, right?"

"Right," answered Aaron.

"You're going to handle this."

"Yes, sir."

"Take the money back. Do whatever you have to do. Don't come home."

Aaron felt something in him crack, like a bone but deeper. He closed his eyes and placed a hand over his stomach. "Please," he whispered.

"Don't," said Robert. "Don't do that."

Aaron bit his tongue.

"You've got the car," said Robert. "I put some stuff in the back seat for you — non-perishables and water. I'm sorry I can't give you more. Did you pack?"

Aaron shook his head.

"You should have packed. Don't act like you didn't know this was coming. I warned you."

"I know," said Aaron.

"You should leave now."

Wallet, keys, car. Aaron had everything. He didn't move.

Robert grabbed Aaron by the shirt collar, opened the door and shoved him into the car. He threw the keys into his lap. "Go," said Robert.

Aaron's hands were shaking again. He couldn't fucking stop shaking. Robert shut the door.

Aaron finally looked up and saw his father through the window. Robert was scowling at him and every now and then he'd glance at the house. When Aaron failed to drive away, Robert made a move toward the door.

Aaron cranked the car. If Robert had to beat him to make him leave, he would. Robert would never beat Daniel. Aaron closed his eyes and prayed that was true.

Aaron shook the thought away quickly. He gripped the steering wheel and threw the car into reverse. He didn't look back as he drove away from the house.

Chapter Nine

Semantics

He dug a cardboard box out of the dumpster behind the building where he'd last seen Farley. He folded it back together and put the money inside. He wrote "Farley" on the lid with a black marker. He put the box near the door and hurried to the car. He waited with the car doors locked, and sent Farley a text. It was four in the morning.

The woman from the shoot came out of the building. She stood under the lamplight. She glanced around the parking lot. When she saw the car, she nodded to Aaron and took the box. Several minutes later, Farley texted Aaron a quick *Pleasure doing business with you.*

Aaron drove away. He drove to the parking lot of a closed grocery store and parked in the back. He locked the doors and sat behind the wheel with his arms crossed over his chest.

The money was gone. The money that would have helped Daniel leave was gone. Robert wouldn't let Daniel leave. Daniel needed Aaron there to defend him, to help him escape.

You're justifying. You can't go home.

Aaron leaned against the door. Not telling Jack what had happened probably meant he couldn't go back and see Jack, which meant he couldn't work for Jack, which meant he didn't have a job. He hadn't packed, which meant he didn't have any clothes other than what he was already wearing. What he was wearing was dirty. His chest felt tight. His shirt smelled like Ralph, even though Ralph had never touched it. Or maybe he had. Aaron wouldn't have known.

Aaron wiped his hand over his forehead. He was too hot. He wanted to roll down the window, but it wasn't safe. He gritted his teeth and started stripping, doing the best he could while still seated. He tossed his clothes, shoes and socks into the back seat. He heard something crinkle and remembered Robert said he'd left Aaron *'some stuff'*.

Sadness gave way to fear, which gave way quickly to rage. Aaron understood rage. It made him strong. He didn't have to think when he was angry — he could just *be*.

Naked, he got out of the car and opened the back door. He swept his clothes and everything Robert had packed onto the ground beside the car. Satisfied, he slammed the door then got into the front seat.

The engine roared to life and Aaron hit the gas. Several minutes down the road, he took a quick inventory of his remaining belongings. The car was his. It had been a gift from Jack and Robert. His phone was his but Robert paid the bill. It would probably be disconnected soon. He'd need to get a new number. Of course he'd need a new number. Robert couldn't risk Daniel being able to call him. Aaron could ignore emails, but a phone call from his little brother... If

Aaron heard his voice again— He shook his head and focused.

His wallet had his license, debit card, some random crap and a twenty-dollar bill.

He kept the car clean to the point of compulsion. He knew every item in that car, and after kicking out Robert's contribution to his new life, nothing significant remained.

He'd have to steal new clothes—he couldn't shop naked. There was a blanket in the trunk. That would have to work for now. It was almost dawn. Aaron's phone rang. An unknown number appeared on the screen. It wasn't the one Farley had used, but something told Aaron not to answer it anyway. He ignored the feeling.

"Hello, darling," said Farley.

"I gave back the money," said Aaron. "What do you want?"

"No need to snap," said Farley. "I just wanted to tell you to tell Silas that if he doesn't press charges, he will still receive his last paycheck."

"What?"

"I assume you are in touch with him? He's not answering my calls and this is a somewhat urgent bit of business."

"No."

"Ah. Never mind then. Goodbye."

"Why would he press charges?" asked Aaron. He was met with silence. Farley had hung up. Aaron threw his phone onto the seat beside him. A bizarre form of fight or flight kicked in. He pulled over and retrieved the blanket from the trunk. He wrapped it around himself, returned to the car and headed back into town.

He pulled into Silas' driveway half an hour later. The sun was just beginning to rise. The porch light was out. Aaron could see glass on the ground. He gripped the blanket around his waist and got out. He approached the house. When he knocked on the door, it swung open. He went inside and shut the door behind him.

The house was trashed. The couch where he'd slept was ripped open, cushions gutted. The table was overturned. There were papers and broken bits of Silas' life strewn all over the floor.

"Silas," called Aaron. He stalked his way to the kitchen and found the broken leg of a chair. "Silas, you in here?" He clutched the blanket with one hand and held the chair leg like a bat.

He crept farther into the house. The bathroom door was shut. Aaron resituated the blanket so he could try the knob. It was locked. He banged on the door. "Silas? Are you in there?"

No answer.

He hit the door harder and called again. Still no answer.

He took a few steps back, hoping he could gain enough momentum in the hallway, and slammed his body, shoulder first, into the door.

The lock snapped from the frame and the door swung open. Aaron tumbled into the bathroom. He had one hand back on the blanket and a death grip on the chair leg. It took him a minute to process both what he'd done and what he was seeing.

The room reeked of pot and was filled with a combination of smoke and steam.

Silas sat up in his bathtub, eyebrows raised in alarm. He removed a large pair of headphones and let them fall on the tile floor. His phone sat on the edge of the tub, connected to the other end of the headset. He held a joint above the water.

"Hello, Aaron," said Silas. His face was various shades of blue and purple. His lip was split and one eye was almost swollen shut. He had a nasty cut across his shoulder and his chest was peppered with bruises. Despite his injuries, he frowned when he looked at Aaron. "Did Farley do that?"

"Do what?" asked Aaron.

"Your face," answered Silas.

"Oh," said Aaron, his memory kicking back into gear. "No, he didn't. What happened to you?"

Silas shrugged. "Farley was convinced I stole from him. Which is technically true, I suppose."

"I'm sorry," said Aaron. Farley had obviously beaten the shit out of Silas, convinced the money was with him. "I gave it back to him."

Silas tilted his head.

"I had to," said Aaron. "He contacted my family. He sent my brother a clip of us — of what we did." Aaron shook his head. "I'm sorry. I had to make it stop."

Silas blinked. "Aaron," he said slowly, "are you wearing a blanket?"

Aaron's face burned. "Oh. Um, yeah."

"Are you wearing anything else?"

Aaron shook his head.

"Aaron," said Silas again, "blankets are not clothes."

"Yeah, I know that," said Aaron. "How high are you? Did you hotbox your bathroom?"

Silas shook his head. "This is a bathroom, not a box." He held the joint out to Aaron. "Hit?"

Aaron sighed. "Sure." He approached the tub and took note of Silas' injuries. The bath water was clear with a slight pink tint. He was marked from head to toe. He took the joint and held it. "You're bleeding," he said.

"I've stopped bleeding," corrected Silas.

Aaron eyed the cut to his shoulder.

Silas followed his gaze. "It was that and my nose. It's broken. My nose, not my shoulder."

"Shouldn't you set it or something?" asked Aaron.

"I'll tend to it later." He squinted. "Who hit you?"

"My dad," muttered Aaron.

"Ah. Your father saw the clip Farley sent your brother?"

"So you are paying attention."

"Of course," said Silas. "This is very serious." He glanced around the room. "I suppose the setting is wrong." He frowned. "If you're not going to smoke it, give it back."

Aaron returned the joint.

Silas took another hit. "I'm going to get out of the bath. Turn around, or don't, but consider yourself warned either way."

Aaron turned around and stood in the doorway. He heard a splash, then the sound of the water draining.

"I'm covered," said Silas. "If that's what you're waiting for."

Aaron turned around. Silas had a towel wrapped around his waist and he'd put out the joint.

"Would you like to continue this conversation in the bedroom, living room or kitchen?" Silas asked. "May I suggest the living room, as it is the least fucked up at the moment?"

"Living room it is," said Aaron.

"After you."

When they reached the living room, Silas flopped down onto the ruined couch. Blood trickled from the inside of his nose.

Aaron headed to the bathroom and retrieved a box of tissues. He handed it to Silas.

Silas looked from Aaron to the tissues. "Thank you," he said. He held them in his lap.

Aaron rolled his eyes. "Your nose is bleeding again."

"Oh, right." Silas tilted his head forward and dabbed at this face. "So," he said, voice slightly muffled, "your father hit you."

"Yeah."

"Is there more to that story?"

"Not really."

"I assume then," said Silas, "there also isn't a story behind you breaking down my bathroom door wearing nothing but a blanket."

Aaron sighed. He took a seat next to Silas on the couch.

"You can tell me later," said Silas.

"Yeah," said Aaron. "Maybe later. What did they do to you?"

Silas half-shrugged. "Ralph seemed to think kicking me and destroying my belongings would magically produce the missing money. Shockingly, he was wrong."

Aaron held a hand over his stomach. "Did he — What did he do to you? Did he h-hurt you?" Hurt wasn't the right word. Yes, clearly Ralph had hurt him. Aaron couldn't ask his real question. He couldn't maintain eye contact. He pulled the blanket around his shoulders and stared at his lap.

"He threw a few punches," said Silas. "Farley and Regina searched the house. It was over quickly."

The amount of bruising on Silas' body told a different story.

"Why didn't you tell them I took the money when I left?" asked Aaron.

"Farley insisted he was looking for his money," answered Silas. "The money you took was yours. I have no idea why he thought he'd find *his* money at *my* house."

"Dude," said Aaron. "Semantics? Really? That's where you took your stand?"

"I've stood for less," answered Silas, the corner of his mouth twitching upward.

Aaron shook his head. "Where's your first-aid kit?"

"It's either on the dresser in my room or somewhere on the floor," he answered.

Aaron stood and went to Silas' room. The kit was on the floor, partially open. He collected the scattered contents and went back to Silas.

Chapter Ten

Guns 'n' Blankets

On his way back to the living room, he saw Silas had moved to the kitchen. "What are you doing?" asked Aaron.

Silas was rummaging through a cabinet above the microwave. He pulled a large plank of wood out, which looked suspiciously like the bottom of the cabinet. "Supplies," answered Silas. He retrieved a sizable rectangular black bag and shook it at Aaron. "If they'd spent less time bothering me and more time searching, they might have actually found something worthwhile."

"You're just all kinds of prepared, aren't you," said Aaron.

"The word you're looking for is paranoid," said Silas. He grabbed an ice pack and a bag of frozen peas from the freezer. He returned to the living room and Aaron followed. Silas began unpacking the contents of the bag. It was full of pill bottles. "Does your face hurt?" asked Silas.

"Not really," answered Aaron. It hurt, but it wasn't unfamiliar pain. Robert usually avoided hitting him in the face. The bruises were too visible. Marks sustained to his back and stomach usually cleared up after a week or two.

Silas grabbed a tube of something from the first-aid kit. "Come here," he said. "This will help."

"Let's patch you up first," said Aaron. "No offense, but you look like hell." He took the tube from Silas' hand and read the instructions. It was some kind of generic antibiotic. "This can go on your shoulder, right?" he asked.

"Yes."

Aaron took one of the disposable gloves from the kit, assuming it was necessary to avoid cross contamination or something. He found and opened a small packet containing an alcohol wipe, and dabbed at the wound. He gave it a moment to dry, then squeezed ointment onto his fingertips and rubbed it carefully over the cut.

Silas sat up straight, suddenly very still, and he watched Aaron with a look of amusement mixed with intrigue.

Aaron grabbed a gauze pad and taped it over the wound. He scanned Silas' body for other injuries he could treat.

"Just bruises," said Silas. "I'll heal."

"What about your nose?"

Silas held up the bag of peas. "These are for my face, and this"—he handed Aaron the ice pack—"is for yours." He grabbed a cotton swab from the box, and before Aaron could protest, Silas squeezed ointment onto the tip, smeared it quickly over Aaron's cheek and applied a bandage. He held the bag of vegetables against his nose.

"Thanks," muttered Aaron. He followed suit and held the ice pack against face.

"He hurt you often?" asked Silas.

"I don't want to talk about it," said Aaron. "Same way you don't want to talk about what really happened to you."

Silas sighed. "Please give me your hand."

"Why?"

"I want to say something and I'd like to sound as sincere as possible."

"It already sounds like a lie."

"All right, then I'll just say it," said Silas. "Farley, Ralph and Regina came into my home. Farley and Regina began searching my things. Ralph challenged me and I fought back. Obviously he won. He's larger than I am, but I like to think I did a decent amount of damage. I grabbed a knife. He took it from me, gave me the cut you just bandaged, broke my nose, then Farley called him off. That's it." He searched Aaron's eyes, presumably to see if he was listening. "We fought. It was unpleasant. But that's all that happened."

Aaron bit his lip. "I'm sorry I left without telling you." He should have told him. They were partners in crime. He should have left the money with Silas. He shouldn't have panicked. He always panicked first. Robert was right to keep him from Daniel. Aaron wasn't any use in a crisis. If he'd stopped, talked to Silas, called Daniel, they could probably have come up with a plan and Silas wouldn't have been attacked. If Aaron hadn't slept through Farley's calls, Silas wouldn't have been attacked.

"Aaron."

He looked up at Silas

"This wasn't your fault," said Silas. "I wasn't abused. I've looked better, that's certainly true, but this damage is cosmetic, I will heal, and it wasn't your fault."

Aaron shifted a little farther away from Silas. It was nice to hear that something wasn't his fault — too nice. He couldn't risk getting accustomed to hearing it or he'd crave absolution for all his mistakes.

"You're not responsible," said Silas. "Do you understand that?"

Of course I am.

"Yeah," answered Aaron.

"Are you, at any point, going to explain why you're not wearing any clothes?"

Aaron leaned against the couch. "I threw a fit in a grocery store parking lot. I don't know. It doesn't make sense. I just didn't want to wear those clothes anymore." He had no idea how much of the story Silas was piecing together. Aaron knew he wasn't giving him much to work with.

Silas didn't pry. He stretched and yawned. "I didn't get much sleep last night. I realize it's technically morning, but I don't have a schedule to adhere to. Can I assume you are also tired?"

Aaron nodded.

"My bedroom is a mess, as you may have noticed, but my mattress is still in good shape. I'll take the couch."

"*I'll* take the couch," said Aaron. "You're worse off than I am."

Sleep together. You've done it before. It doesn't have to be his idea.

"Thank you, but no. Although," he mused, "the air mattress might still be in one piece. I'll check." He stood, swayed, then wandered down the hall. He returned a moment later carrying an electric pump and an armful of deflated mattress. "I'll take this. You take the bed."

"It's not safe to sleep out here," muttered Aaron. "We can share a room. It's not a big deal."

"Are you comfortable with that?"

"I wouldn't offer if I wasn't comfortable with it."

"All right then." Silas retreated to the bedroom.

Aaron allowed himself a moment to settle the sudden flutter of nerves in his stomach, then followed. He examined the bedroom door. "This has a hollow core," he said.

"Is that significant?" asked Silas.

"It's easier to break down."

"They're not coming back," said Silas. "And if they do, I'll shoot them." He nodded to the gun sitting on the floor beside him. Aaron had never even seen him retrieve it. "I'll sleep between you and the door."

"Okay," said Aaron. "I'll watch the window."

"Or I could board up the window, sleep between you and the door, and you could sleep peacefully knowing we are well protected."

"We're not well protected," said Aaron. "We're targets. And if you were so well protected, how'd they manage to get the drop on you earlier?"

"Oh," said Silas. "I see. You think they broke in."

"Didn't they?"

"No, I let them in."

"Why the fuck would you do that?"

"Because I had nothing to hide," answered Silas. "And it's amusing to watch Farley bluster and make threats and still leave empty-handed."

"That's—" Aaron began. "I don't know. That's weird."

Silas shrugged and hooked the electric pump into the air mattress. He wandered over to the dresser while it inflated. He retrieved an armful of clothes from the drawers and picked up a few things that had been thrown on the floor. He handed the bundle to Aaron. "In case you want to change out of your blanket," he said.

He grabbed a few other articles of clothing from the floor and left. Aaron assumed it was to give him time to change. Aaron slipped into Silas' clothes for the second time. He felt cleaner, but weaker. He pulled his blanket around his shoulders. When Silas returned, he'd traded his towel for pajamas.

"I'll take the air mattress," said Aaron.

"No."

"Yes. I saw your bruises. Your ribs might be broken or cracked. I don't know, but it looked like he hit you pretty hard."

"No," repeated Silas. "Besides, I'll have a better vantage point from the floor." He nodded toward his gun. He was already curled up in the center of the air mattress, pillow tucked under his head, wrapped up in a fluffy comforter.

"Fine," muttered Aaron. He pulled the door shut and locked it.

"I appreciate your concern," said Silas. "But I am the one with the medical degree. I'm fairly certain I know what's best."

"You're also the one with a death wish," said Aaron.

"I don't have a death wish, Aaron."

"Sure you don't." Aaron crawled into bed above Silas. The mattress slowly gave way to his weight.

Silas rolled over, his back to Aaron. "If you wake up before me this time, I'd prefer it if you wouldn't leave without letting me know."

"Okay," answered Aaron. One day to rest, then he'd leave. He couldn't stay in town. Robert wouldn't want that. He just needed to rest, get some of his energy back, then he'd be ready to go. He fell asleep trying to remember how much money he had left in his bank account.

Chapter Eleven

Precipice

Aaron woke up to the smell of bacon and coffee sometime around noon. He checked his phone — no calls, no texts. He took a chance and tried calling the last number that called him. No service. Robert must not have wasted time in removing Aaron from the plan.

He sat up and rearranged his blanket so it draped over his shoulders. The air mattress was vacant, which meant the noise must be Silas cooking in the kitchen. After a minute, he convinced himself to get out of bed.

Silas was standing on a chair waving a dishtowel at a smoke detector when Aaron entered the kitchen.

Aaron coughed. "What did you do?"

Silas frowned and glanced over his shoulder. "Did I leave the stove on?"

Aaron rushed to the stove and turned off not one, but two forgotten burners. The bacon was already on a plate and appeared to be more or less edible. The coffee was still brewing on the counter. Aaron had no idea why the second burner was on.

Silas climbed down from the chair. He coughed and grabbed his side, wincing.

Aaron made a silent note about a possibly broken rib. "So this is how you make breakfast," he said.

"I'd intended to make eggs as well," said Silas.

"How about you sit down and I'll make eggs."

"Only if you feel like it," said Silas. He brushed past Aaron on the way to the coffee pot. Aaron's body decided to flinch without explaining why to his mind.

"Apologies," muttered Silas.

Aaron's mind decided to pretend it didn't happen. Aaron went to the refrigerator and pulled out eggs and butter. "Scrambled okay with you?" he asked.

"Yes," answered Silas. "Cream and sugar in your coffee?"

"Black," answered Aaron.

Silas made a face and poured a copious amount of sugar into a second mug. Aaron grabbed a pan and Silas handed him his untarnished cup of coffee.

The kitchen was in better shape than it had been the day before. Silas must have attempted to clean up before cooking. The table was standing. One chair had survived and Silas had replaced the other with a stool.

Aaron glanced over his shoulder. Silas was perched on the stool, sipping his coffee and watching Aaron.

"I'll help you clean things up after breakfast," said Aaron.

"No need," he said. "I've called in a favor. A cleaning crew will be here tomorrow morning."

"You called in a favor to a cleaning crew?"

"To my brother," said Silas. He shifted in his seat and winced. Then he seemed to realize Aaron was watching and tried to mask his expression with a curt smile. "He has the money to pay people to do the things he doesn't want to do himself."

"That's nice," said Aaron. He agitated the eggs with the spatula. "Does he know about Farley?"

"No," answered Silas. "I told him someone broke in and made a mess. He didn't ask for details."

"That's probably for the best," said Aaron. He watched Silas clutch his side as he lifted his coffee to drink. "What would I have to do to convince you to sit in the damn chair instead of trying to balance on the stool with your coffee and a broken rib?"

Silas blinked at him over the rim of his mug. He took too long to respond.

"Move," said Aaron. He gestured to the chair with his spatula.

"I'm perfectly com—"

"Save it," said Aaron. He removed the pan from the stove and plated the eggs. "We'll eat in the living room. Then we can both sit on the couch and you can stop being polite or whatever it is you're doing."

Silas blinked at him again.

"Dude, go," said Aaron. "Living room. I'll meet you there. I know where it is."

Silas squinted. He examined Aaron and seemed to have some kind of silent argument with himself. Finally, he acquiesced and took his coffee to the living room.

Aaron was pretty sure there was some rule somewhere about not bossing people around in their own homes, but he felt like an exception should be made for Silas.

Aaron served Silas first then made a plate for himself. "You want anything else?" he asked.

"No," answered Silas. "Thank you."

"Welcome," answered Aaron.

"Thank you for cooking, too," said Silas.

"Welcome."

"And I suppose I should thank you for arriving in the kitchen when you did." He was staring at Aaron again.

"Lucky I woke up when I did," said Aaron.

Silas nodded and tilted his head to the side. "I was thinking about tomorrow morning," he said. "I don't particularly want to be here while there are people wandering around the house. I have reserved a hotel room."

"That's a good idea." Aaron shoveled eggs into his mouth.

"I reserved a room with two beds," said Silas. "If you are inclined to come with me."

Aaron swallowed and looked to him.

"Of course, you're not obligated to stay with me," said Silas quickly. "I didn't mean to assume—I just thought—the way you arrived... I suppose I did assume." He frowned and his cheeks turned pink.

Something screamed inside Aaron. Something hot and dark told him not to accept the invitation. Something warned him against becoming indebted to this man. Something snapped when he realized he already owed Silas more than he could ever repay.

"Is that..." began Silas. "Was that wrong? Perhaps I shouldn't have mentioned it. But I think I'm right in guessing you have nowhere to go. Presumably your next move would be to sleep in your car and yes, I see you're capable of taking care of yourself, but you shouldn't have to. I'd rather you stay with me." Silas shook his head. "Not that you have to stay. I don't know how to say this without sounding 'creepy'." He actually put the last word in air-quotes, as though he'd been accused of being 'creepy' before.

Aaron must have taken too long to answer, because Silas spoke again.

"Please stay, but only if you want to," he said. His cheeks turned a darker shade of pink. "I hope I'm not overstepping."

"You, um," said Aaron, searching for the rest of his sentence, "you don't have to take care of me."

"I don't mean to insult your ability to care for yourself," said Silas.

"You didn't," said Aaron. "I guess I don't get why you care."

"I'd be a monster if I didn't."

Aaron saw a flicker of something, most likely pity, in Silas' eyes. He set his plate on the table, appetite gone. He held on to his coffee cup to keep himself from fidgeting. Why wouldn't Silas pity him? He'd only seen Aaron at his most vulnerable, most helpless. Silas thought he was responsible for him the way someone becomes responsible for an injured animal found alone in the cold. Aaron was helpless. Silas saw it.

Silas cleared his throat. "I understand if you're uncomfortable, of course. I'm gay. You're straight. I know you might have reservations—especially considering the circumstances—but you are safe with me. I would never hurt you."

Aaron saw something again behind Silas' eyes, but the emotion morphed. It was deeper than pity and it wasn't aimed at Aaron, and that fact alone made Aaron want to hunt it down and drag it into the light.

Silas broke away from his stare and took a sip of coffee.

"I believe that," said Aaron. It was like standing on a ledge with the wind whipping by so quickly he couldn't hear or feel or think. Silas wasn't asking him to take a step forward. He wasn't asking Aaron to jump. He wasn't behind Aaron waiting to push him. They were standing side by side on the precipice and Aaron knew that if Silas leaped, he would follow. They were doomed to fall together. The only way out was to leave now. Aaron could set his cup on the table, collect his few belongings, return what he'd borrowed, and leave. The only way to avoid the jump and subsequent fall was to leave Silas behind.

Silas glanced at him, a flicker of blue eyes, then they returned to the shadows of his lashes. Something in Aaron ached. His chest burned. His heart stopped beating.

He took a sip of coffee. "What time is check-in?" he asked.

"Three," answered Silas.

"Do you have a safe or something for your collection of illegal crap?" asked Aaron.

"I plan to take my illegal crap with me," said Silas. His face slowly regained some of its normal color.

"Let me pack my blanket and I'll be ready to go," said Aaron.

Silas grinned and finally looked at him again. "Would you like to take my car, yours or both?"

"Mine."

"All right." Silas picked up his plate and began eating again.

Aaron's stomach growled and he remembered he was hungry.

Chapter Twelve

Hotel and a Movie

It wasn't until Silas put his suitcases into the back seat of the car that Aaron realized he needed to buy clothes. They stopped at a store on the way to the hotel. Aaron bought a random assortment of clothing, some basic toiletries and a pair of boots. His feet were currently crammed into a pair of Silas' shoes.

Aaron carried his bag from the store and the suitcase containing Silas' clothes. Silas carried his bag of illegal crap. They took Silas' handgun just in case.

They took their belongings up to a room on the top floor of the building. Aaron claimed the bed by the window at the same time as Silas claimed the bed by the door. Silas pulled out his first-aid kit while Aaron placed the 'do not disturb' hanger on the door handle outside. Aaron locked the deadbolt then peered through the peephole to see how much visibility they had from inside the room. Satisfied, he returned to his bed, stretched out and closed his eyes.

* * * *

He must have fallen asleep. When he opened his eyes again, it was dark and Silas was asleep in the other bed.

Aaron rolled over. The room was too hot. He kicked away from the covers and lay exposed until he was suddenly shivering. He untangled his blanket from the hotel sheets and pulled it around himself. He sat up and glanced at the phone beside the bed.

Don't.

He looked at the alarm clock instead. It was late. He scrubbed a hand over his face. A shower. He needed a shower. He collected his things and crossed the room quietly. He shut the bathroom door and stared at the handle. He bit his lip. After a moment of inner debate, he locked it.

The water felt good, calming. He was in a small, bright room and he was clean, or at least he would be soon. More than cleanliness, he appreciated that no one could hide from him in here. The door was locked. There were no cabinets or closets or dark spaces where shadows could lurk and lunge.

He peered around the shower curtain every few minutes to make sure the door was still locked. He exhaled and hung his head under the spray of the shower. The water beat down against his neck and back. He closed his eyes.

He was with Silas now. Silas was too kind and responsible to turn him away. Aaron would have to leave eventually. He couldn't stay with Silas forever. He looked down at the floor of the shower and crossed his arms.

A few days might not be too long. Silas was injured and, despite his protests, he needed someone to look after him. Aaron could do that. It would justify his stay.

Silas couldn't cook. Once they returned to the house, Aaron could take over cooking. He owed Silas something.

Two or three days. He nodded to himself. Two or three days to find a job, pick a new city, do what he could repay Silas, and prepare for a new life.

He'd be more careful about job-hunting this time. He could do a few manual labor tasks to make ends meet until he found something steady. If it paid enough, he could set aside money and figure out a way to get it to Daniel.

Daniel would get to Stanford whether Robert wanted him to or not. Daniel had had his heart set on the university since he'd started high school, and Daniel was stubborn. He'd make it happen. If Daniel could leave Robert, Aaron could help him the rest of the way.

Anonymously. He can't know.

Aaron chewed on his bottom lip. Maybe there was a scholarship fund he could donate to, or create — something he could be sure Daniel would be awarded. Did it work like that?

He ran his hands through his hair and leaned against the shower wall. How much money would it take to support himself and secretly help Daniel? He needed to know how much rent would cost him first. He slid down and sat with his knees pulled into his chest, trying to keep as much of his body under the water as possible.

He knew a lot about cars, but he didn't have any certifications. Did he need that? Would someone hire him anyway? Could he use Jack as a reference? Would that count as contacting him?

He shook his head. Jack wouldn't work. Whoever called would give away Aaron's new location — wherever that happened to be.

He slumped forward and let his forehead fall against his knees.

Daniel had probably just gone to his room. He'd stay up and read for another hour or two.

He wondered what Daniel had done yesterday when he'd found out Aaron was gone. Was it yesterday? It seemed longer. He couldn't remember the last thing they'd said to each other. *Did I tell Daniel good night?*

It didn't matter. Daniel's last impression of Aaron had been cemented with the video from Farley. Daniel had seemed worried at first, but once he understood — once Robert explained his version of what happened — Daniel wouldn't care anymore.

Aaron was dirty now. He needed to remember that. He needed to remember what Ralph had done and that Aaron had let it happen, had asked for it to happen.

He stared at the white shower wall. He needed to remember. It was the only way to keep himself away from Daniel, and staying away was the only way to keep Daniel safe.

Unless Robert started hurting Daniel, too. Without Aaron, who would stand between them when Daniel was angry and Robert was drunk?

That's an excuse. You can't go back. Robert loves Daniel. He'll be fine. He'll be in college soon. He doesn't need you. No one needs you.

A loud thud shook Aaron's thoughts. Someone was banging on the door, calling his name. "I'll be out in a minute," he called. He stood and started to rinse the soap from his skin before remembering he'd never actually bathed.

Fuck it.

He turned the water off, stepped out of the shower and wrapped a towel around his waist. He opened the door to find Silas pacing in the small entryway of the room.

Silas' eyes snapped to Aaron's body as soon as the door opened and he stood still. "Are you all right?" He scanned Aaron from head to toe, frowning the entire time.

"Yeah, sorry," said Aaron. "I didn't mean to wake you up."

Silas released a breath and clutched his side.

"Hurts to breathe?" asked Aaron.

"Why didn't you answer me?" asked Silas.

"I did. I said give me a minute."

"Before that."

"Before when?"

"I was calling for you and I knocked. Didn't you hear me?"

"No." Aaron shrugged. "My bad."

"Your eyes are red. What happened?"

Aaron touched his face. Shit. Had he been crying again? "I got soap in my eyes," he said.

Silas clenched his jaw. "But you're all right?"

"Yeah." He felt his eyes stinging now.

Fucking bitch.

"Aaron." Silas stared at him.

There was something about the way Silas said his name. It wasn't a command or a threat or a warning. He said it like it was a spell that would grant him access to Aaron's soul.

It almost worked, but Aaron bit his tongue and screamed in his mind until it drowned out all other thoughts. He felt his emotions ebb away with each breath he took. He looked Silas in the eyes and shrugged again. "What?" he asked.

Silas' lip almost shivered. "Nothing," he answered. "I thought something was wrong. I panicked. I'm sorry. I didn't mean to interrupt your shower."

Aaron let it go. He couldn't chase whatever emotion Silas was trying to hide without losing grip on his own. "Do you need the bathroom?" he asked.

Silas shook his head. "No, thank you."

"Good. Pretty sure I still have shampoo in my hair."

"I'll go back to bed. I'm sorry, again, for disturbing you."

Silas left and Aaron shut the door. He turned the water on again and deliberately reminded himself to pick up the soap and bathe.

* * * *

They left the hotel in the afternoon. Silas had scheduled a late checkout. They ate at a café down the road. The cleaning crew would not be done until five. They had a few more hours to kill, so Silas suggested they go see a movie.

In line for popcorn, they apparently stood too close together, because a man behind them kept whispering to the woman standing with him. The second time Aaron heard the man say 'faggots', he spun around, grabbed Silas' hand and stepped into the man's space.

"Shut the fuck up," said Aaron, "or I will beat the ever-loving shit out of you in front of the whole fucking theater."

Silas squeezed his hand and moved closer to his side. "Alternatively," he said, "you could just shut up and we could end this without causing a scene and inevitably involving law enforcement."

The man had dark hair and a scruffy, haggard face. He appeared to be in his late forties. He glared at them. Just as he opened his mouth, Aaron made a fist and prepared to swing. Silas must have sensed the potential fight. He pulled his hand from Aaron's and slipped his arm around Aaron's waist.

"There are children present," said Silas, nodding to the families wandering through the lobby. "We should at least attempt the pretense of civility."

The man gritted his teeth and Aaron felt his mind teeter. How many times had Robert given him that look? The longer Aaron stared, the more the man in front of him began to change. He already resembled Robert. It wasn't hard to imagine. It wouldn't be hard to pretend the body he was attacking belonged to his father.

Silas pulled him closer, ever so slightly.

Finally, the woman tugged on the man's hand and moved him to stand in line at another cash register.

Aaron watched them leave. Silas had to force him to turn around. When he started to pull his arm away, Aaron slipped his arm around Silas' waist to stop him.

"Let's leave," whispered Silas.

"He can leave," snapped Aaron. "We're not going anywhere."

"Are you sure?"

"Yes."

Silas didn't argue. He ordered popcorn and drinks and moved Aaron's hand when he tried to pay. They had to release each other to carry their items and tickets, but Aaron stayed close to Silas, actively keeping less than a foot between them.

The man glared from the corner of his eye as they left the lobby and Aaron stared him down. Silas herded him toward the theater.

They took their seats, and as soon as Silas' hand was free again, Aaron grabbed it. He watched the entrance to the theater, but the man didn't appear during the previews. He was nowhere to be seen by the time the film began. *He must have picked a different movie.*

Silas' voice was soft and low when he leaned over and whispered to Aaron, "We can still leave."

"Fuck that," hissed Aaron. He was still glaring at the walkway, though he was suddenly aware that Silas was rubbing his thumb against the back of his hand.

Aaron's focus snapped and his need for vigilance subsided so quickly it made him woozy. He turned and saw Silas watching him in the dark. He finally registered the sound of the movie. He felt himself breathe again.

"You didn't have to do that, you know," whispered Silas. He leaned in close and Aaron could barely hear him.

"Do what?" whispered Aaron.

"Defend me. Pretend we were a couple."

Aaron opened his mouth, but nothing came out.

"The point is, I appreciate it," said Silas. "I thought you should know that."

Aaron couldn't find an appropriate response, so he nodded instead of speaking. He shifted in his seat to sit closer to Silas. They watched the rest of the movie in silence, still holding each other's hands.

Chapter Thirteen

Family

When they arrived home, the place was spotless. The cleaning company had left a card by the door and a note encouraging Silas to call if he needed them again.

The broken furniture was gone, and most of it had been replaced with new stuff. The crew had gotten rid of the pot smell. There was even a vase full of fresh flowers on the coffee table.

Aaron went to inspect the new couch, but Silas held him back. "Wait," he said softly.

Aaron tensed and immediately began searching for something to use as a weapon.

"What's wrong?"

"I didn't order furniture."

"That's not part of the service?"

Silas squinted at him again.

"I figured it was some kind of rich-guy cleaning deal," said Aaron. "Stop looking at me like that."

"People do not just give you furniture."

"I told you, I thought it was a rich-guy thing. You said your brother's got money, right?"

"Yes." Silas huffed. "I suppose you're not entirely wrong. I suspect this was his doing." He frowned at the room. "It seems he took a more hands-on approach than I'd anticipated."

Something clanked in the kitchen. Aaron flinched.

"Dammit," muttered Silas. He headed to the kitchen and Aaron followed quickly behind him.

A man stood at the sink. He was rinsing a cup. The room smelled like coffee. "You didn't even check to make sure it was me," said the man. "I could have been an intruder."

"You *are* an intruder," growled Silas.

The man resembled Silas, but was older, maybe in his late thirties, taller and slightly more muscular. His hair was cut much shorter than Silas', but it was also dark and they had the same permanent crease in the center of their forehead.

"Rude," said the man. "Especially considering all I've done for you today."

"I assume that's why you felt entitled to stick around," said Silas.

The man rolled his eyes. "I stuck around because you said someone broke into your home and I wanted to make sure you were all right." His eyes fell to Aaron. "I didn't know you had company."

Aaron straightened his back and stood a little taller. If one more person insulted Silas tonight, he wasn't sure he'd be able to restrain himself. The body language between the two men told him everything he needed to know. Silas didn't want this man in his house and the man had no intention of leaving. Potential brother or not, Aaron was ready to fight.

"I'm fine," said Silas. "You can go. Thank you for your help. I am no doubt forever in your debt."

"I thought we could chat," said the man. "It's been a while." He looked to Aaron again. "Unless your friend charges by the hour. Then I can understand the urgency."

Silas almost lost it. Aaron saw him lurch forward, recenter himself, clench his jaw and firmly plant both feet.

"I see your temper has marginally improved," said the man. "I'll be sure to tell Mom therapy paid off after all." He shook the water from the cup in his hand and dried it with a cloth from the counter. "I'm Max." This time deliberately addressing Aaron. "Since my brother has neglected to introduce us. I'm not sure if he's more reluctant for you to meet me or for me to meet you."

"I'm Aaron, and if Silas doesn't like you, I don't like you." He crossed his arms over his chest.

Max made a face and looked back at Silas. "He's not your boyfriend, is he? Please tell me this mess" — he gestured around the space — "wasn't because you fell for another junkie."

"He's not my boyfriend," growled Silas. "Nor is he a junkie. And none of that is any of your business."

Max shook his head. "Then you're the junkie. Again." He placed the cup in the cabinet above the counter. "I knew it as soon as you called. Who do you owe, for what and how much?"

"So you didn't stick around to check on me," said Silas. "You just wanted to make sure I wouldn't call again needing something else."

"You will always call again," said Max. "You will always need something else."

Silas' fists twitched at his sides.

Max sighed. "Come home. Let us help you."

"I don't want to discuss this right now," said Silas.

"You forfeited that right when you made this my problem."

"I just needed a loan," said Silas. "I told you I'd pay you back."

Aaron stepped forward and turned away from Max so only Silas could see his face. "I can make him leave," he said.

Silas shook his head. "He'll get tired and wander off eventually."

"Are you two conspiring over there?" asked Max. "Fine. I'll leave." He approached the doorway where they were standing.

Silas pulled Aaron to the side to let Max pass.

Max eyed Silas. "You look like shit," he said. "Both of you. I know you hate me — us — but we could help you. Remember, you're *choosing* to live this way."

"I'll repay the loan," said Silas.

"Don't bother," said Max. He took a last look at Aaron, then left, closing the front door a little harder than necessary.

Silas fumbled in his pockets and quickly withdrew a small metal capsule.

"What the fuck was that about?" asked Aaron.

Silas shook two blue pills into his hand. "Would you like one?"

Aaron shook his head, not entirely sure what Silas was offering, though it looked familiar.

Silas retrieved the cup Max had used and filled it with water. He took both pills, drank the water, then threw the cup in the garbage.

"Do I get to know what just happened?" asked Aaron.

"Only if you're ready to explain your naked blanket escapade," answered Silas.

Aaron considered the offer. "Not really," he said finally. It wasn't worth trading stories. Aaron would be gone in a few days. The more he knew, the harder it would be to leave. He realized he should probably share that information with Silas. He might want Aaron to leave sooner.

"On another note," said Aaron, "I was thinking I'd hang around for a few more days. Do some chores and stuff while you heal. I can cook and clean, and if your car needs work, I can take a look at it. Or I can leave sooner."

"How many days is a few?" asked Silas. "Is it fixed at two or do you mean that in a more nebulous sense?"

"Two," answered Aaron.

Silas turned away from him and opened the refrigerator. He retrieved a beer, opened it, handed it to Aaron then quickly brushed past him on the way to the living room.

Aaron followed him.

"Make yourself at home," said Silas. He went to a shelf full of DVDs.

Aaron shifted where he stood. He felt wrong. *Something* felt wrong. "I can leave sooner," said Aaron.

"Two days is soon enough," said Silas. He selected a movie and busied himself with the TV. "Try the couch. Let me know if it's comfortable."

Silas wasn't looking at him. Aaron hadn't realize how often Silas made eye contact until now. Maybe it was because of Max, or whatever pills Silas had taken. Maybe it didn't have anything to do with Aaron.

Silas turned around again. He glanced at Aaron, then turned his focus to the couch. He sat without commenting on the fact that Aaron was still standing.

He leaned against the armrest and stared at the TV as the movie began.

Aaron sat down at the opposite end of the couch. He decided to guess which movie Silas had chosen instead of guessing what Silas was thinking. He took a long drink from his beer.

When the title screen for the third *Jurassic Park* movie appeared, Silas spoke. "You mentioned chores," he said. "You don't have to earn your keep."

"I don't mind," said Aaron. "But like I said, if two days is too long—"

"It's not," said Silas. He still wasn't looking at Aaron.

Aaron sighed, took another drink and decided to push his luck. "Did I do something wrong? Things feel weird. Is it me or Max or something else?"

"No," he answered. "Things are not 'weird'."

"Come on, Silas. I'm dumb, but I'm not that dumb."

"You're not dumb."

"If you're still pissed about family stuff, I totally get that. I'll shut up," said Aaron. "But if it's me, if I did something, I want to fix it."

Silas huffed.

So it *was* Aaron's fault. "Did I overstep? I guess I shouldn't have assumed I could stay."

Silas finally turned to him. He closed his eyes, then opened them again slowly. "I'm sorry," he said. "Ignore me. I was being rude."

"Dude, talk to me," said Aaron. "I can leave now. It's no—"

"I don't want you to leave."

"Then what's wrong?"

"I don't want you to leave." He said it again, but slower.

Aaron was again on the cliff with the wind whipping around him. He knew he was too close to the edge. He felt the fall calling him.

"I'm sorry," said Silas. "I should have behaved better. Family visits have a habit of making me a generally unpleasant human being."

Aaron knew that what he was about to say was the wrong response, but his voice was faster than his brain. "I can't stay," he said.

It's not because of him. Tell him that. Tell him he's not the reason.

"Of course," said Silas. "I understand." He looked at the TV.

The truth was right there. He felt it like knot in the back of his throat. He couldn't say it. He couldn't elaborate. He didn't have enough control right now. If he started talking, he'd never be able to regain control. The truth would burst like a flood and Aaron couldn't stand the thought of breaking again, but Silas had yet to make him feel ashamed. Maybe he didn't have to feel ashamed about the truth either.

Chapter Fourteen

Like A Flood

"Would you like another beer?" asked Silas. His voice was back to that unnatural, clinical tone.

Aaron felt Silas step back from the ledge and suddenly he was alone. The knot in his throat dissolved into a silent scream. "Silas." His voice cracked and Silas' attention snapped to him.

Suddenly, Silas was beside him on the cliff, and just as suddenly, they began to fall.

"It's not you," said Aaron. "If I stay in town, I might run into my brother and I can't— Dad doesn't want me around him." He clutched the bottle in his hand. "It's not you. I want to stay, I really do, but I can't."

"Are you only staying away from your brother because your father asked you to?" asked Silas, the crease between his eyebrows deepening.

"Yeah," muttered Aaron. It was too hot again. His heart was racing and his chest was tight.

"Can I sit closer to you?" asked Silas. "Would that make you uncomfortable?"

It was too hard to breathe and talk at the same time, so Aaron motioned for him to come closer. Silas moved quickly, and the sudden warmth at Aaron's side reminded him that he was on a couch in a living room, not falling. He was dizzy. He leaned back against the couch.

Silas rested his hand on Aaron's shoulder. "It's all right," he said softly. "Nothing bad is going to happen if you talk about it."

Was he worried about that? Obviously nothing bad was going to happen. He was on a couch. In a living room. He closed his eyes and let his head lean against the cushion.

"I miss him so fucking much," whispered Aaron. His chest seized, ached and became numb all at once. "I don't even know if he's okay."

He felt himself being gently tugged to the side. He followed the pull and found himself wrapped in Silas' arms.

"It's okay," said Silas. "It's going to be okay."

Aaron almost shoved him away. He should have shoved him. He should have moved. He wouldn't survive the plunge. If he fell for kindness again, there wouldn't be enough of him left to put back together once he hit the ground. He wasn't strong enough. He wasn't strong—had never been strong.

Silas' voice called him back. He was running his fingers through Aaron's hair. Aaron was crying. He knew it without feeling it. But then Silas' voice cracked.

"You don't have to leave," said Silas. "You're safe here. I promise you."

Aaron looked up. Silas was crying too. He curled his fingers into Silas' shirt. "I can't stay," he whispered.

"Yes, you can," said Silas. "We'll figure it out. And if you want to see your brother again, we'll figure that out as well."

"He can't see me like this," said Aaron. He searched Silas' eyes, hoping he was making sense, hoping Silas understood. "He wouldn't want to see me now that he knows."

"Knows what?" asked Silas.

Aaron could almost feel Daniel's phone in his hand. He was standing outside his home. Daniel was watching him. Aaron was watching the video. But it wasn't just a video. Aaron remembered how it felt to touch Silas like that, how it felt to be touched.

There were too many hands on him. He was clammy, disgusting. He reeked of some unidentifiable odor. The stench consumed him. It was death and sweat and saliva—too many foul things rolled off his body in waves.

He pushed away from Silas. He was stupid for going back, for staying, for wanting to stay. It was going to happen again and he was going to let it happen.

Silas was calling his name.

Aaron knew better than to ignore him. "Sorry," he muttered.

"I need to know what you're thinking," said Silas. "Can you do that? Can you talk to me?"

"Yessir," muttered Aaron. He leaned farther away from Silas, eyes cast down to the floor.

"Dammit," muttered Silas. He was angry.

Aaron braced himself.

"What happened after you left to give Farley the money?" asked Silas.

"I went home."

"First? Or did you see Farley first?"

"Home first."

"It's all right," said Silas. "Remember you're safe here." He muttered something to himself, then got up from the couch. He returned a moment later. "You're shaking. Do you feel cold or hot?"

"Hot," answered Aaron. He glanced sideways and saw Silas had retrieved his coat.

"All right," said Silas. He held the coat across his lap. "What happened when you went home?"

Aaron couldn't answer. His voice didn't work. His chest was too tight. Something was wrapped around his lungs, squeezing the air out of them. Something gripped his heart and stopped it from beating. Instead of pounding against his ribs, it ached, hollow and hungry.

It was the last time he'd seen Daniel and he hadn't say goodbye. He'd never say goodbye. He'd never see him again.

"Does your family know what happened to you?" asked Silas.

Aaron shook his head. Mercifully, they didn't know. They had no idea how weak he really was.

"Remember when we did the breathing exercise in the bathroom?" asked Silas. "Can you do that again?"

No, he didn't remember.

Silas started counting and telling him when to inhale and exhale. It took him a minute or two to match Silas' pattern, but he eventually did it. He didn't remember leaning back into Silas' arms, or letting Silas hold his hand.

After a while, his heart started beating again, or maybe it stopped pounding. The sensation was too difficult to name. He remembered where he was. On a couch. In a living room.

Silas was running his fingers through Aaron's hair again, saying things like "you're doing very well" and "you're safe" and "take your time."

He was distantly aware that Silas was waiting for the rest of the story. He couldn't tell it. The rest of the story included Daniel.

"Farley sent your brother a clip of what happened, right?" asked Silas.

"Just of us," murmured Aaron. "Your face wasn't even in it." Silas was not Ralph or Farley or Regina. Aaron forced that thought to take priority.

"What did your brother say when he saw it?"

Aaron pulled away from Silas again, not because Silas was dangerous, but because he had to do this alone. He had to be able to remember Daniel on his own.

He covered his face with both hands. "He thought I was in trouble. He called me a bunch of times, left messages, texted me. I slept through it all." Aaron heard himself give Silas bits and pieces of the story, but not in the right order. He wasn't sure any of it made sense. He told him about Farley's deal, the deadline, the consequence for missing the deadline, about Daniel being worried and Robert knowing better than to be worried. Silas didn't interrupt him until he got to the part where he returned the money.

"You went back?" asked Silas. "Alone?"

"Yeah," answered Aaron. It was easier to talk with his eyes closed.

"Dammit, Aaron, they could have killed you," said Silas. "Did they hurt you? God dammit. I didn't even check you again. I didn't even ask."

"They didn't do anything," said Aaron.

"I'm so sorry," said Silas. "I was busy pitying myself instead of thinking about you. I should have made you talk to me when you came back. I wasn't thinking. I just knew you were with me again, so you were safe."

"You asked what happened," said Aaron. "I just didn't tell you."

"If I'd been sober, I would have known better. I'm so sorry." Aaron peered at Silas through his fingers.

"Jesus, what if you hadn't come back? I would never have found you. Why did you come back?"

Why had *he come back?*

"Oh," said Aaron, "I forgot. Farley called me before my phone got cut off. He wanted me to tell you if you didn't press charges he'd send you your last paycheck."

"That brought you here?"

"He said 'press charges'. That usually means shit went down."

Silas squinted at him. "Did you come here to check on me or to deliver the message?"

"To check on you," said Aaron. He let his hands slide from his face, felt himself coming around. "I should have relayed the message sooner, but I forgot. But that's not why I came back."

Silas shook his head. "I don't know what to say to that. I thought you came back because you needed a place to stay." He shook his head again. "But I had to convince you to stay. You were going to sleep in your car. I should have known better." He tilted his head to the side and looked at Aaron.

"I was worried about you," said Aaron. "You saved me. The least I could do was come here and check on you."

"Thank you," said Silas. "Wait, no, I don't want to get sidetracked again." He held up a hand. "You went home, your brother was worried, your father didn't care, he hit you and made you leave after your brother went to bed. You returned the money then came back here. Is that right?"

"Yeah."

"Where does your brother think you are now?" asked Silas. "If he thought you were in trouble before, won't your absence imply you are in trouble again?"

"Dad told him I had a boyfriend and we ran off together," muttered Aaron. "He said he'd tell Daniel the video was a joke or something."

"That is insane," said Silas. "Your father is a terrible person."

"He's just trying to protect Daniel. He wants to make sure he stays strong."

"No, Aaron, he's abusing you, not protecting Daniel."

Aaron crossed his arms over his chest.

"Has he ever hurt Daniel? Do you know?"

"Never." Aaron said it louder than he intended. If Robert hurt Daniel, it meant Aaron had failed.

"Is Daniel safe? When did your father start hurting you?"

"He didn't start hitting me until high school," answered Aaron. Silas' next line of questioning was predictable, so Aaron saved him the trouble. "He caught me making out with this kid—a guy. I'm not straight." He rubbed his face. "I knew better than to take the job with Farley. Dad warned me years ago that if he caught me with another guy he'd take Daniel away." He shrugged. "It's my fault. I did this to myself."

A small, distant part of him knew it was true. He'd known better than to get caught with another man. He'd known he'd be forced to leave. He'd known the only way he'd leave was if Robert made him, and a wretched, selfish part of him had wanted to leave for years, but he'd never leave Daniel. That was why Daniel had to get to Stanford. Daniel's way out was Aaron's way out. But Aaron had gotten impatient. He'd forced Robert's hand too soon and left Daniel behind.

Could Silas see that? If he could, surely he wouldn't comfort Aaron. He'd know Aaron was something terrible and greedy.

"Hey," said Silas. "Stay here." He waved a hand in front of Aaron's face.

He deserved to know the truth before he wasted more of his kindness.

"I think I wanted to get kicked out," said Aaron. "I mean, I know I did. I did it on purpose. I was too chickenshit to leave on my own and I didn't want to wait for Daniel. I left him on purpose."

"No," said Silas. "Do you realize how much of what happened you would have needed to control in order to make that true?"

"I knew the risk."

Silas shook his head. "You wanted to leave and get away from your father. I'm sure that's true, any sane person would. But you didn't orchestrate this elaborate catastrophe of coincidences to get kicked out. You are attempting to control a situation that is wild and unpredictable."

He set a hand on Aaron's shoulder again. "It makes sense that you'd want to leave. It also makes sense that you wouldn't want to wait for Daniel. It makes sense that you'd want to separate from Daniel—maybe not forever, but for a little while. Staying with Daniel ensured your suffering and put him in control of your relief."

The knot was back in Aaron's throat. He blinked at Silas.

"It even makes sense that you would resent him because you got hurt and he didn't."

Instead of his chest getting tight, it felt empty. Instead of lungs and a heart, there was a void. Silas saw it, the darkest part of him.

"All of that can be true," said Silas, "and it still doesn't make this your fault." He tilted his head. "Are you listening? Does that make sense?"

Silas was staring at him, seeing him for the coward he really was, and Silas wasn't leaving. He was still on the couch with his hand on Aaron's shoulder.

"When you start thinking this is your fault," said Silas, "you also need to think about all the details you would have needed to know in advance. You are smart, but you are not psychic."

Aaron nodded. He could agree with that much.

"You had no idea this would go wrong. You had no idea that Ralph and the others would attack you. You had no idea I'd start shooting at people. You had no idea Farley would contact your brother. You had no idea your family would see that video."

That was a surprisingly solid argument.

Silas gave a slight smile. "The most you could have planned," he said slowly, "was that your father would one day see that video. And that would mean he'd have to admit to watching gay porn before he could do anything to you. And would have been a fairly elegant revenge."

Aaron felt himself breathing. His chest was full again.

"Are you with me?" asked Silas.

"Yeah," answered Aaron.

"Good." Silas' features relaxed. "I have one more question."

"Okay," said Aaron.

"Do we need to go get Daniel?"

Chapter Fifteen

Hey, Danny

Aaron considered Silas' question carefully. "I don't know," he answered. "He's got Jack—our uncle, not our real uncle, but he's like our uncle... Never mind. Jack will look out for him."

"Why didn't Jack look out for you?"

"He didn't know."

"Your father beat you—how could he not know?"

"Dad was careful about where he hit me." Aaron licked his lips. "He'd be careful about where he hit Daniel, too. But Daniel's straight, I think. Unless he never told me. But he told me everything."

"It's all right," said Silas quickly, his voice soft and soothing. "So if Jack had known your father was hitting you or Daniel, he would have stopped him?" Silas shook his head. "No, forget that question. Jack would not be in favor of Robert hurting Daniel, is that right?"

"Right."

"Okay. How about," he said slowly, "and please consider before you protest, how about we call Jack and tell him just enough to let him know to watch out for Daniel?"

Aaron actively stopped himself from saying no.

"That way," continued Silas, "Daniel doesn't see you while you're feeling vulnerable. You don't have to see Robert, and we can relax knowing Daniel is safe."

"I don't know what to tell Jack," said Aaron.

"Do you want to practice?"

"No." Aaron leaned onto his knees and put his head in his hands. "Let's just do it. We should just do it now before I freak out again."

"I can speak on your behalf," said Silas. "Or we could see him in person, if that would be easier."

This was a shitty conversation to have over the phone, but Aaron couldn't trust himself to shut up if he saw Jack in person. Then again, if Jack decided he hated Aaron too, that might mean he wouldn't protect Daniel. That was something he needed to know. He needed to read Jack's face when he told him.

"Fuck," muttered Aaron. "In person. It's shitty to tell him over the phone."

"I'll drive," said Silas. He stood and handed Aaron the coat that had been sitting in his lap. "It seemed to help your first night with me."

Aaron nodded and took the coat. He didn't need to wear it, not yet, but it felt like a shield and it was good to have in his hand.

Silas grabbed his keys. He was again stepping into the way of danger on Aaron's behalf.

"I can go alone," said Aaron. "You've done enough."

"No," said Silas. "I—just no. I don't know if you're being polite or if you really don't want me to come with you, but I can't let you go alone. We can take separate cars, but that's the best I can offer."

"I was being polite," said Aaron.

"All right, well fuck that," said Silas. "Let's go."

Once in the car, Silas asked for directions and sped down the road. "Has no one attempted to contact you?" asked Silas. "Oh, no, your phone was disconnected." His eyes widened. "Aaron, what about email? I have a laptop. You could have checked. I didn't even offer." He scrambled to reach his pocket. "You can use my phone. I don't have any social media apps installed, but I assume you can still reach them online?"

"I'm not active on social media," said Aaron. "I probably don't have any emails. Jack hardly uses his computer and I don't know if Daniel would write to me yet."

Or, what if you check your email and no one has written you anything?

Aaron pinched the bridge of his nose. "Anyway. I don't need your phone. But thanks." He pointed to the stoplight ahead of them. "Take a left here."

They made it across town in record time. Silas was an angry, impatient driver. Jack lived just beyond the city limits. His house was at the center of what was essentially a ten-acre junkyard. He stored old cars and car parts on his land. Silas didn't lose speed when the asphalt turned to dirt and he broke another record reaching the other end of Jack's driveway.

Jack's car was parked near the front porch. Silas parked beside it. "Do you still want to do this?" asked Silas.

"Yeah."

"How are you feeling?"

"Itchy."

"That's not the symptom I was expecting," said Silas

Aaron shrugged. "I'm also pretty sweaty. I've been getting really hot lately."

"Probably due to your panic attacks." Silas got out of the car and pulled his metal pill capsule from his pocket.

"Panic attacks?" asked Aaron. He got out and met Silas at the front of the car.

"You've had several." He shook a blue pill into his hand. "Xanax? It should help to lessen the stress of the conversation we're about to have."

Aaron popped the pill into his mouth but failed to swallow it before it could leave a bitter, chalky taste on his tongue. He grimaced.

"I *was* going to offer you water," said Silas.

"Too late now." Aaron shook out his hands. "Let's do this."

The front door swung open. A balding, tired-looking man with a bushy beard squinted at them from under the porch light. Before Aaron could wave or say hello or offer any kind of greeting, Jack ran toward him.

Out of the corner of his eye, he saw Silas move to intercept. Jack shoved Silas aside and wrapped both arms around Aaron in what had to be the world's strongest hug.

Jack's cheek was wet as it brushed against the side of Aaron's face.

Holy shit, is he crying? Are we all crying now? Is this normal?

Jack finally pulled away and held Aaron by the shoulders. His lips were moving like he thought he was speaking. Finally he just sighed. "Thank God." He put his hand on Aaron's cheek, covering the spot where

Robert had punched him. "He cut your phone off, didn't he?" asked Jack.

"Yeah," answered Aaron.

"I'm so sorry, boy." His voice was rougher than usual. "I knew this day would come. I'm so sorry."

Aaron almost forgot Silas was with them until he spoke. "Is Daniel with their father?" he asked.

Jack glared, but then his face softened. "Is that your boyfriend?" asked Jack.

"Uh," answered Aaron. "Not exactly." What Silas was remained to be determined for sure, but as of that moment, he was the best friend Aaron had ever had.

Jack huffed. "I don't know how much of your daddy's story is true, but—"

"Probably none of it," said Silas. He moved to stand at Aaron's side. "But Daniel's location is the reason we're here."

Jack's face fell. "I was hoping he'd turn up with you," he said to Aaron.

"What do you mean 'turn up'?" asked Aaron.

"When Robert told him you were gone, he took the car and left," said Jack. "He came to see me, but"—he paused and couldn't quite seem to look Aaron in the eye anymore—"when he found out how much I knew, he took off again. We haven't been able to find him."

At that, Silas pulled Aaron away from Jack and stepped between them. "How much, exactly, do you know, and how long have you known it?"

"Don't blame him," said Aaron. He stepped around Silas.

Jack's eyes were watering again. "I'm so sorry."

"How long have you known?" growled Silas.

"Calm down," said Aaron. He grabbed Silas just above the elbow and hoped it would be enough.

"Sixteen years," answered Jack.

Silas turned to Aaron. "There is a discrepancy in the timeline."

"What?" asked Aaron and Jack in unison.

Silas leaned over to whisper to Aaron. "You said the abuse began in high school. You haven't been out of high school for that long. Is there more to the story? What happened sixteen years ago?"

"I have no idea," answered Aaron. "I was five. I don't remember."

"Are you sure?"

"We'll figure it out later. We need to find Daniel."

"What discrepancy?" asked Jack. "What are you two talking about?"

"Later," said Aaron. "Can you call Daniel and tell him I'm here?"

"Phone's in the house," said Jack.

They followed Jack inside and into the living room. His cell phone was sitting beside his computer. The browser was up on the computer and it looked like there were about thirty tabs open. Jack rubbed the back of his neck when he saw Aaron eyeing the screen.

"I didn't want to miss anything if one of you tried to contact me," said Jack. "But there are so many damn ways to get in touch with somebody these days, I didn't know where to start."

"Nothing from Daniel?"

"Radio silent. He's pretty pissed off." Jack wiped the remaining tears from his cheeks and nodded toward the kitchen. "He brought your laptop over, by the way. It's in the kitchen on the table. I think he was going to try to track your phone or something. I didn't touch it in case he has it doing something."

"Why is he mad?" asked Silas.

"He figured out Robert was full of shit pretty quick," answered Jack. "I think when he found out I already knew Aaron was gay, that was the last straw."

"Is that all you know?" asked Silas.

"Not helping," muttered Aaron. "And I'm not gay. I'm bi. I think. I guess. I don't know. I just want to talk to Daniel."

Jack dialed Daniel's number and held the phone up to his ear. "Is there more to that story?" he asked Silas.

"Later," snapped Aaron.

"He's not going to pick up," said Jack. "I'm gonna leave a message. I've left several already. Right now, the only call he'd answer is one from you."

Silas leaned over to whisper to Aaron again. "You should tell him about your father."

"Not now," hissed Aaron.

"What did he mean by sixteen years?"

"I don't know," answered Aaron. He shushed Silas when Jack started talking into the phone.

"Hey, Danny. I've got your brother here safe and sound," said Jack. "He wants to see you. We're at my house. You better get your ass over here ASAP. I've got a missing person's report filled out and I'm not afraid to file it."

He hung up and handed the phone to Aaron. "Text him for me, will you? My fingers are too slow and fat to deal with that crap."

Aaron's hand started shaking again as soon as he touched the phone.

Silas took it from him and narrated as he typed. "Hello, Daniel. Aaron is with Jack."

"You're using Jack's phone," said Aaron. "Just say 'with me'."

"Aaron is with me. He wants to see you." Silas clicked a button. "I sent it."

"How about fill me in while we wait?" said Jack. "I feel like I'm missing something."

"Where is Robert?" asked Silas.

"Probably drunk as a skunk passed out somewhere," he said. "He called me asking to drive him around to find Daniel. I said no. Don't know what happened after that and, forgive me, son, but I don't really give a shit. Daniel and I figured you wouldn't just run off without telling us. We figured he kicked you out and cut you off. That was reason enough for me to leave his ass out of the damn loop and I told him that when he called."

The phone rang and the room went silent. Jack grabbed it and answered. "Daniel? Yeah. He's right here. I swear. Yeah, hang on." Jack held the phone out to Aaron.

Aaron took a shaky breath and accepted the phone. "Hey, Danny," he said.

Chapter Sixteen

Co-Star

The conversation was short. Daniel said he was about twenty minutes away. Aaron told him not to talk on the phone and drive. Daniel was reluctant. Aaron hung up first. The important thing was that Daniel was all right.

They sat around the kitchen table. Aaron had a hand on his laptop, but hadn't opened it. Silas had moved his chair so he was almost touching knees with Aaron. Jack sat across from them, foot tapping nervously against the linoleum floor.

"We got a few minutes kill," said Jack. "When do I get to know what you two keep whispering about?"

Silas set his hand on Aaron's knee under the table.

"I thought since Dad hit me, he might hit Daniel," said Aaron. "I've never seen him that mad. I was worried Daniel wasn't safe."

"I'm sorry your dad's like that," said Jack. "He's not right. I should have taken you boys in when I had the chance."

"When did you have the chance?" asked Silas.

"Sixteen years ago," answered Jack. "Soon as I figured out Aaron might not be straight, Robert and I had a hell of a fight. I almost took him to court to get custody."

"Holy shit, I didn't know that," said Aaron.

"Why didn't you?" asked Silas.

"Because I'm a stupid old man," answered Jack. "I thought it would be worse to take you and Daniel away from your dad after you'd just lost your mom. I was wrong."

"Is that why Dad made us move?" asked Aaron.

"Yeah. Pretty much every time you boys had to pick up and leave was because of me. Y'all would stay gone, come back, I'd pick a fight with Robert, and he'd take off with you two again. I finally figured out if I wanted to be able to keep an eye on you two, I'd better keep my mouth shut."

Aaron decided he could never tell Jack the whole truth, not without Jack blaming himself. When Silas squeezed his knee, Aaron put his hand over Silas'.

"How did you figure out Aaron was not heterosexual?" asked Silas.

That was not the route Aaron would have chosen for the conversation, but it was better than the alternative.

"Just after he turned five, I got him a Batman figure for his birthday. He ran around telling people he was his boyfriend until Robert took it away."

Silas snorted, then glanced at Aaron. "Sorry," he said.

"Definitely don't remember that," muttered Aaron. Then again, he didn't remember much from the two or three years after his mother died.

Silas nudged him. "I always preferred Clark Kent."

Aaron rolled his eyes. "Oh my God, no. Over Batman?"

"He was kind," said Silas. "And I liked his glasses."

"Just plain Clark Kent? Not even Superman?"

Jack laughed. "How long have you two known each other?"

They gave their conflicting answers at the same time.

"About four days," said Silas.

"A few months," said Aaron.

They were saved from an interrogation when a car door slammed outside. "I'm gonna question you about that later," said Jack, pointing to Silas.

Aaron let Jack get ahead of them as they went to the door to greet Daniel. He pulled Silas back. "Don't tell them about Dad," he whispered. "They'll just feel bad."

"They'll find out eventually," whispered Silas. "But I'll yield to you. They're your family."

Daniel threw open the door just as they entered the living room. He rushed forward, and for the second time that night, Aaron found himself smothered in a hug. When he let go, he looked at Aaron's face.

"He hit you," snarled Daniel. "That motherfucker. I'm going to kill him."

"Take it easy, Hulk," said Aaron.

Daniel looked at Silas. "Who are *you*?" He glared. "Did Dad hit you too?"

Aaron kept forgetting that he and Silas looked like the tail end of a *Rocky* movie. He wondered why Jack hadn't mentioned anything about Silas' bruises.

"No, Robert didn't hit me," answered Silas. "I'm Silas Anderson. I'm Aaron's friend."

Aaron also realized he hadn't known Silas' last name until just now. Did Silas know his?

"He's your friend?" Daniel directed the question at Aaron.

"Yeah," answered Aaron.

Daniel's expression softened. He held his hand out shake Silas', and Silas accepted.

"Daniel Beaumont," he said. "I'm his brother."

"Baby brother," corrected Aaron.

"Younger brother," said Daniel.

"They're both idiots," said Jack. He clapped Daniel and Aaron on the shoulders and brought them into a hug. He released them, then lightly smacked the back of Daniel's head.

"Ow," said Daniel. "What was that for?"

"Running away," answered Jack. "You can ditch Robert, but you better not try to ditch me again, either one of you." He jabbed a finger at Daniel. "And no more grand theft auto."

"Sorry," muttered Daniel.

"I forgive you," said Jack, "but just barely. Take a seat. Silas and Aaron were just lying about how long they've known each other."

Jack claimed the recliner and Daniel claimed a chair, leaving Silas and Aaron to sit together on the couch. It felt deliberate.

"How'd you know they're lying?" asked Daniel.

"Silas said four days. Aaron said a couple months."

"Damn, guys," said Daniel, shaking his head.

"Aaron's estimate is the correct one," said Silas.

For all the skills Silas had proven to possess, he couldn't seem to lie. He didn't fidget or avoid eye contact or struggle to keep a straight face. He just sat there, staring down both Jack and Daniel, as though he had the power to will them to believe him.

"How about I tell you what doesn't make sense," said Jack. "And then you fill me in."

"All right," said Silas.

Fuck.

"Aaron's never mentioned you, but he's good at keeping secrets. Months is plausible. Days seems more likely. You've both taken a beating. Robert explains what happened to Aaron. We've got no idea what happened to you. He says you two aren't a couple, but you're damn sure in cahoots about something." Jack turned to Daniel. "You said Robert saw Aaron with a boy and that's what set the whole thing off, but if he" — Jack pointed to Silas — "isn't the boy Robert saw him with, then who the hell was it?"

Aaron shot Daniel a look. Jack didn't know about the video.

Yes, Virginia, there is a God.

"Guy I met at a bar," said Aaron quickly. Silas and Daniel were taking too long to respond.

"Where's he fit in?" Jack pointed to Silas.

"I met Aaron at a different bar," answered Silas.

Aaron had never wished for the power of telepathy more in his life than he did in that moment.

"And your face?" asked Jack.

"He doesn't remember," said Aaron.

Jack raised an eyebrow. Aaron had answered too fast. Jack turned to Daniel. "You want to shovel anything on top of this mountain of bullshit?"

Daniel glanced at Aaron, but Aaron couldn't help him. They were cornered. Everyone knew just enough to know they didn't know everything.

"Porn," blurted Aaron. He covered his eyes with one hand. "I was going to be in a porno. A big gay porno. For money." He laughed. "I guess I like sucking dick, so I might as well suck dick for money. Only I didn't finish the job and you can't half-ass gay porn, a-fucking-pparently. Anyway. Stole the money, ran like hell. Pissed off this guy — swear to God he's the Hans Gruber of gay porn. Hans sent Daniel a video." Aaron laughed again. "Sorry about that, bro, can't undo that kind of retinal scarring. Of course the video was me sucking dick, like I do, like a bitch."

He was vaguely aware of a hand on his shoulder.

"Of course, nobody knew I was a bitch until Hans outed me," continued Aaron. "His name's not Hans. It's Farley. Not like that's any better. Daniel thought I was in trouble because Farley is a cryptic dickwad, so he showed Dad and that's what set Dad off. That's when he hit me. That's when I left. And I stayed away for a few days, because who wants a bitch hanging around, right?"

Daniel and Jack were staring at him.

Aaron caught a whiff of the foul thing he'd smelled earlier and remembered that he was the source. His stomach lurched.

Silas grabbed his hand and pulled him to his feet. He nodded to Jack and Daniel. "Excuse us. We will be right back."

He led Aaron away from the living room. "Is there an extra bedroom here? Or somewhere you feel safe?"

"I'm fine," said Aaron. He swayed. The room spun. He laughed. It was too hot again.

Silas pulled him down the hallway. There were several spare rooms. It was an old, but decent-sized house. He and Daniel used to play in the attic. Aaron didn't know why he wasn't sharing any of this information with Silas.

It didn't matter. After opening the door to a bathroom and two closets, Silas found the extra downstairs bedroom. He pulled Aaron inside, shut the door and sat him down on the bed. He handed Aaron another blue pill and put two fingers on Aaron's neck.

"I'll handle this," said Silas. "Do you trust me?"

He couldn't even talk to his own fucking family. He was pathetic.

"Aaron."

"I trust you."

"It's going to be all right."

The door opened behind them. "What's wrong?" asked Daniel.

Jack pushed past him and went to Aaron's side. "What's going on?"

"He needs space," said Silas.

Aaron's chest was too tight again. He couldn't breathe — or maybe he was breathing too much.

"Who are you, really?" demanded Daniel.

"I'm his doctor and his co-star," snapped Silas.

That was the last thing Aaron heard before he blacked out.

Chapter Seventeen

The Truth

He heard their voices fading in and out. He considered trying to blink, but the darkness was warm and comfortable and there were no wide-eyed faces watching him. He focused on what he could hear and feel.

Someone had their fingers lightly pressed to his wrist. It was probably Silas. Silas was also talking.

"You do not need to know the specifics," said Silas. "I shot at Ralph and he released Aaron. We escaped and Aaron spent the night with me. I watched over him to make sure he was safe."

Sweet fucking Jesus, Silas was telling them everything. Aaron didn't move. He wanted Daniel and Jack to know. They deserved to know.

"When Aaron saw your messages the next day," said Silas, "he left to return the money to Farley."

Aaron tried to remember how to breathe and count. Silas kept talking. He told them about Farley trashing his house, how Aaron had showed up later, that he and Aaron had left and returned to find Max at the house.

He skipped some of the details and downplayed Max's visit, but for the most part, he told the truth.

"What is the address of that place?" asked Jack. "Where they assaulted him."

"I'll tell you later," answered Silas.

"I want to know, too," said Daniel.

"Jack can tell you, if he decides it's appropriate."

"I deserve to know," said Daniel. "He was there because of me. He knows I'm trying to move. He said he'd help."

"It doesn't matter why he was there," said Silas. "But, Daniel, you don't need to be involved in anything that happens next."

"I agree," said Jack.

"He will wake up soon," said Silas. "There's one more thing you should know. It will upset you. Daniel, if you've experienced something similar, please let us know."

He was going to tell them about Robert. Aaron could stop him. He felt the fingers on his wrist press down. Silas ran his thumb over the palm of Aaron's hand. He knew Aaron was awake. He was letting him have plausible deniability, letting him stay unconscious while he took on the burden of explaining. Aaron stayed still.

"Robert has been abusing him—" Aaron heard a sharp intake of breath. "Hitting him," clarified Silas. "Aaron says since high school. I assume he's telling the truth. Robert found out about Aaron's sexual preference and the beatings began. I do not know how frequently they occurred. Aaron said Robert hit him where the bruises wouldn't show— Jack, sit down. More violence won't help."

"That motherfucker," growled Jack. "Daniel, did he hit you too?"

"No," answered Daniel quietly. "I didn't know. I don't know how I didn't know. Aaron tells me everything."

"He has suffered a great deal of trauma," said Silas. "I'm sure he didn't want to share that burden with you."

"But he'll be okay," said Daniel. "You said he'd be okay."

"He's all right," said Silas. His thumb brushed over Aaron's palm again. "His physical injuries will heal. I'm not entirely qualified to treat the mental symptoms. I think he should see a psychiatrist at some point."

"He's never going to do that," said Daniel.

"He might," said Jack. "He talked to Silas."

"Silas shot people for him," said Daniel. "I can't think of a faster way to gain Aaron's trust. He's not going to trust a stranger."

"I didn't actually shoot anyone," said Silas. "I shot *at* people."

"Still," said Daniel, "it made him trust you."

"The important thing for you both to take away from this is that Aaron may need some time and space," said Silas. "It's also important that you don't take any of this personally. He's not angry with you. This wasn't your fault. Yes, it was terrible, but he is safe now, and I will make sure he recovers."

"We can help," said Daniel.

"Just be patient with him," said Silas. "Did Robert ever hurt you?"

"No," answered Daniel. "He loses his temper a lot, but he never hit me."

"Jack, I'll leave it to you to make sure he's telling the truth," said Silas.

"Roger that," said Jack.

Aaron felt the worst of the conversation was over and decided it was safe to pretend to wake up. He faked a groan and put a hand to his head. "What happened?"

"You fainted," answered Silas.

"What'd I miss?" he asked.

Silas pulled his fingers away from Aaron's wrist.

Aaron moved his hand up slightly, just enough to connect with Silas as he moved his hand away.

"I more or less told them what we discussed," said Silas. "Probably more, rather than less. But they are informed."

Aaron surveyed the room. Jack was standing over Aaron's bed and Daniel was standing near Silas with his arms folded over his chest. Silas was sitting on the edge of the bed.

Daniel was somewhere between angry and heartbroken. Jack was clearly trying to soften his expression, but Aaron could see a red-hot rage boiling just below the surface.

"How do you feel?" asked Daniel.

"Not too bad," answered Aaron. He sat up and swung his legs over the side to sit next to Silas. He braced himself for the onslaught of apologies from his family. Daniel cracked first—Jack probably let him. His little brother was visibly shaken and couldn't seem to say "I'm sorry," enough. He offered several forms of vengeance against their father and swore he'd never speak to Robert again unless Aaron needed or wanted him to.

Jack's apology was short, gruff, sincere, and it was the only time Aaron had ever seen Jack trip over his words. He ended with swearing to protect Aaron and to make sure Robert couldn't get to Daniel.

Silas sat quietly by Aaron's side through the whole ordeal. Aaron cried again, but so did everyone else. Aaron wasn't sure when the crying would stop — or if it would ever stop. He didn't mean to zone out. He didn't blame Jack or Daniel. He didn't really blame Robert, not yet anyway. However, the moment overwhelmed him and all he could do was wonder if this meant they'd treat him differently. Would they pity him or blame him for not speaking up? Would they think he was too stupid or weak to fight for himself? Would they walk on eggshells around him?

Silas must have sensed the start of another wave of panic, because he changed the conversation. "We should probably go back home," said Silas. "It's late. I'm sure we're all tired."

"Y'all stay put," said Jack. "As the oldest one here, I'm making an executive decision. We all stay here tonight. I've got plenty of rooms, and the couch isn't too uncomfortable if somebody wants to take the living room."

Jack rubbed his neck. "I'm going to run out and grab some stuff to make breakfast tomorrow. You boys can go ahead to bed, watch a movie, raid the kitchen. Make yourselves at home."

"Breakfast, my ass," said Aaron. "You're going to Dad's house."

"Breakfast," Jack said again. "That's it, I swear." He nodded to himself, turned to leave, then stopped. "Nobody go snooping around in my office while I'm gone."

Daniel rolled his eyes. "We know the rules."

Aaron leaned over to Silas. "He's ex-CIA, or so he says."

"One more thing," said Jack, pointing at Aaron. "I want to be clear that Daniel and I don't give a damn who you love, like, or hold hands with. We love you. Forever, no matter what."

"Yeah," said Daniel quickly. "Sorry. I thought that went without saying."

"Thanks," muttered Aaron.

"Okay," said Jack. "I'll be back. Any special requests? No? Good. Hang tight, and for the love of God, stay put." With that, he left.

"I have some of your stuff," said Daniel. "It's in the Jeep."

"Thanks, Danny."

"I didn't get everything. I couldn't tell if you'd packed or not, so I just grabbed a bunch of random stuff."

"Better than nothing," said Aaron. "I figured I wouldn't see any of my stuff again."

"It felt like the least I could do." He glanced behind him. "You think Jack really went to the store?"

"No," answered Aaron.

"I believe he took our keys," said Silas, searching his pockets. "I thought I heard a jingling sound a moment ago."

"Fuck," muttered Aaron.

Daniel was already on the way out of the room to check. Aaron heard him swear from down the hall. "Pretty sure you left your keys in the kitchen," said Aaron.

"I think you're right," said Silas. "That was foolish."

Aaron took Silas' hand and stood, pulling the other man up with him. "I'll never be able to repay you," he said. "I'll never be able to explain how much you've helped me. 'Thank you' doesn't begin to cover it."

Silas cocked his head to the side. "Remind me to tell you a story later," he said. "I've seen your demons. You have a right to know mine."

"I fucking knew you had secrets," said Aaron. "I want to know now."

"We should watch Daniel now," said Silas. "He might try to run away."

"That's a thin argument," said Aaron.

"I promise I'll tell you later," said Silas. "Tonight, if you want. But not now."

"Tonight," said Aaron. "I'll hold you to it."

* * * *

The Jeep was unlocked. Daniel and Silas helped Aaron carry his stuff inside and into the extra downstairs bedroom.

Aaron unofficially claimed the room and, without realizing it, expected Silas to stay with him. He didn't figure it out until Daniel said he'd sleep on the couch and Aaron told him that was dumb because no one was in the upstairs bedroom.

Silas didn't correct him and Daniel didn't make a big deal about it.

Unofficially, Daniel would stay upstairs and Silas and Aaron would stay downstairs, just down the hall from Jack's room. They didn't discuss it further.

Daniel found a deck of cards and convinced them to play poker until Jack came back. Aaron made a quiet bet with Daniel to see how long it would take Silas to figure out that Daniel was card counting.

Aaron bet three hands. Daniel bet ten. Silas figured it out after seven.

Jack came home three hours later, not carrying enough groceries to justify three hours of shopping.

"So," said Aaron. "How's Dad?"

"You never have quite grasped the concept of plausible deniability, have you?" asked Jack.

"What did you do to him?" asked Daniel.

"Nothing you need to worry about," said Jack.

"We know you did something," said Aaron.

"Plausible," said Jack slowly, "deniability. I didn't hurt him. I just needed to give him a piece of my mind and lay down some ground rules. Aaron, I got a buddy who'll help me move your stuff."

"I can get my stuff," said Aaron. "Or leave it. Daniel got everything I really care about."

"You don't need to go back there yet," said Jack. He cleared his throat and glanced at Silas. "I know some stuff can be triggers for bad thoughts. I figure that house is a trigger."

"I agree," said Silas. "Aaron, that's something to consider."

"Fine," said Aaron.

"We'll get you packed up and moved out tomorrow. You can keep your stuff here unless you have somewhere else in mind."

"Here," said Aaron. Hiding out with Silas was one thing—moving in with him was something different.

The four of them stayed up talking for a while longer, still coming down from the adrenaline rush of the day.

They parted ways around two in the morning. Daniel went upstairs. Jack went to his room. Silas followed Aaron to borrow pajamas.

When Silas came back after changing, Aaron tried to act casual. "You want to sleep in my room?" he asked. "The bed's big enough to share."

"Are you comfort—"

"Wouldn't offer if I wasn't comfortable with it," said Aaron.

"All right."

"Is that a yes?" asked Aaron.

"Yes."

"Shut the door." Silas did and Aaron patted a spot on the bed. "Good. Now tell me about your demons."

Chapter Eighteen

A Brother

Silas sat beside him on the bed with his head bowed. "I don't know where to begin," he said.

"That's okay, I'm not above asking stupid questions," said Aaron. He frowned. "Plus there's a lot about you I don't know, so maybe I *should* ask questions."

"All right."

"How old are you?"

"Twenty-seven."

"What the fuck?" said Aaron. "How have you had time to become a doctor, join the military and lose your license? *If* you lost your license. I guess I don't know that either."

"I did lose it," answered Silas. "And I was dishonorably discharged. It all happened rather quickly."

"And how about becoming a doctor? Doesn't that take like a hundred years, or something? Are you Doogie Howser?"

Silas squinted at him. "What is Doogie Howser?"

"It's a show about this super young doctor — Point is, you're pretty young, aren't you? For all of that?"

"My family is in the healthcare industry. They've always wanted one of us — my siblings and me — to become a doctor and another to become a pharmacist. They thought it would be useful to have us on staff," answered Silas. "I developed an obsessive need to learn and I desperately wanted to be a doctor. My family paid for anything and everything to expedite my education. My sister had the same opportunity and became a pharmacist." He sighed. "School was a welcome escape from the family, which helped fuel our progress." He paused. "That and Adderall."

"How does the military fit in?"

"My father died not long after I completed my residency. Instead of attending his funeral, I enlisted. I'm still not entirely sure what I was trying to accomplish."

"How'd you get discharged?"

"Drug abuse." Silas glanced at him before lowering his head to look at the floor. "And attempting to shoot my superior."

"Well, I guess that would do it. Do you usually solve problems by shooting at them?"

"It's become an accidental trend. Honestly, I'm not sure what provoked me. I don't remember much about the incident."

"Because you were blind with fury or because you were high?"

"Both. Mostly high." He sighed again. "So, after that, I lost my medical license and was discharged. My family tried to send me to rehab. It helped me, but they never did see a return on their investment in my education."

"So that's what Max meant with the junkie comments?"

"Yes," answered Silas. "I'm sorry about that. They know I'm a junkie. He assumed you were one as well because I moved in with an addict after leaving rehab. He and I were not romantically involved, but I also chose that moment to come out to my family. I suppose that didn't help. They cut all ties to me after that, except for Sara."

"Wait, how do you have a gun if you were dishon—oh—it's not registered, is it?"

"It's not. It's part of my 'illegal crap' collection, as you called it."

"Is that it?"

"Is what it?"

"Are those all of your demons?"

"More or less."

"Silas, you made it sound like you'd done something terrible. I thought you had a body buried in your backyard or something."

"No, no bodies." He bit his lip.

"Is there more?"

When Silas spoke again, he was quieter. "My older brothers, Max and Zach, are similar. You met Max. You can imagine how Zach behaves. Sara and I are similar. We had a middle sibling. His name was Joshua. He was the reason we went into medicine. It wasn't for our family."

"What happened to Joshua?"

"He died."

"Shit, Silas. I'm sorry."

"I was young. I don't remember much about it, but I do remember him. He was…" Silas paused again. "I don't know how to describe him in a way worthy of his memory. He was wonderful, smart, kind. He was gay. The family hated that and tried to push him away. He must have suspected I was gay, too. He watched out for me, and defended me on more than one occasion."

Aaron draped his arm over Silas' shoulders and pulled him closer.

"He was murdered," said Silas weakly. "It was brutal. A hate crime. A group of men tortured and killed him." His voice cracked. "And the family tried to cover it up. They told people he was in an accident."

"Come here," said Aaron. He pushed himself farther back on the bed and pulled Silas into his lap. Silas trembled against his chest. Aaron didn't push for more answers. He could figure out the rest.

Joshua's death had made his younger siblings want to help people. It had made Silas become a doctor. It explained his excessive drug use. It explained why he'd saved Aaron. It explained why he had been so quick to reunite Aaron with Daniel.

"I can't imagine what he must have felt," breathed Silas. "I read the report. The things they did to him. He died alone. He shouldn't have been alone."

Aaron ran his fingers through Silas' hair.

"That's why I—" His voice faltered. "That was why—when I saw you—"

"I know," said Aaron. "It's okay."

"It's why you don't need to thank me," he said. "You don't have to thank people for being humane."

"I understand," said Aaron. He rocked Silas slowly from side to side.

Silas clutched Aaron's shirt and hid his face against Aaron's chest. He fell silent. Eventually Aaron encouraged Silas to lie down. Aaron got up to turn off the lights. He crawled back into bed and wrapped himself around Silas' shivering form. Aaron could feel Silas' pain, but it made him feel strong. Strong because he was able to take some of Silas' pain away, strong because he could hold Silas and be his shield, if only for a night. Strong because in that moment, he knew he and Silas had fallen together and survived.

* * * *

Silas did not sleep peacefully, if he slept at all. Aaron faded in and out of consciousness throughout the night. Sometimes he woke up to readjust his position and move closer to Silas.

In the morning, he awoke to find Silas pillowed against his chest with his eyes closed. Aaron brushed Silas' hair away from his forehead.

"Good morning," rumbled Silas.

"Morning," said Aaron. "How are you feeling?"

"Better. I'm sorry for my behavior last night."

"There's nothing to be sorry about. I'm glad you told me."

Silas was quiet for a beat, as if searching for something to say. He settled on, "Thank you."

Aaron glanced at the clock on the wall. It was still early. "You want coffee, or do you want to keep lying here?"

"Lying here is an option?"

"Yeah."

"Then I pick that."

Aaron laughed. His chest felt heavy and warm beneath the weight of Silas' body.

"How are you feeling?" asked Silas.

"Better than I've been in a while."

Silas nuzzled against him and ran a hand up his chest, resting it just below Aaron's shoulder. Aaron covered Silas' hand with his own, his other hand creating patters against Silas' back.

"So," mumbled Silas, "you're not heterosexual."

"Nope," answered Aaron. At first the question seemed random, but then he remembered he was curled up in bed with a man who'd previously believed Aaron to be straight.

Aaron wanted to follow his reply with something more committed. Maybe he could roll Silas onto his back and kiss him. Maybe he could start with leaning down to kiss Silas' forehead. Maybe he could roll Silas onto his back and grind his hips against him and suck and bite at his neck until he left a mark that said, 'This man is mine.'

The thoughts made him dizzy. He took a deep breath and squeezed Silas' hand a little tighter. Silas looked up. He wiggled an arm free to prop under his chin. He frowned for a moment. "You look pale," he said.

Aaron laughed, because he couldn't think of a better way to respond.

"Are you all right?"

"Yeah."

Silas raised an eyebrow and cocked his head to the side.

Aaron cleared his throat. "I guess it's that this is kind of new for me. I've never, um, cuddled with a guy."

Silas' lips turned slightly upward. "That makes two of us. There isn't much post-coital cuddling in porn."

"What about before porn?" asked Aaron. "You've had sex other than porn sex, right?"

"Before Farley hired me, I'd only had one sexual encounter. It was nice, but brief. I had an exam the next morning, so I left somewhat abruptly."

"One?" asked Aaron. "How did you go from one to porn?"

"I enjoyed it," answered Silas. "Porn seemed like a logical career move."

"I don't know if that's genius or naïve."

"It was stupid," said Silas. "Clearly, it was a stupid decision. Porn is to sex what lip-syncing is to singing."

"That's adorable."

Silas grinned.

Aaron heard clanging coming from down the hall. "Bet that's Jack starting breakfast," he said.

"Should we assist?"

Aaron sighed, and watched Silas rise and fall with his breath. "Yeah, I guess." They changed out of their sleep clothes and went to find Jack.

Chapter Nineteen

Something Different

Jack left the three of them after breakfast. His friend, a man named Liam, stopped by with a large truck and picked him up. They took off, presumably to retrieve the remainder of Aaron's belongings. Aaron wanted to go with them. It felt wrong to have someone else clean up his mess, but Jack refused.

Daniel volunteered to help Aaron tidy the kitchen while Silas went to take a shower. He was fidgety and kept shooting nervous glances at Aaron.

"Out with it," said Aaron.

"What?"

"You've got something you're dying to say."

Daniel looked down at the dish he was drying. "I don't know how to say it," he mumbled.

"Just spit it out. Don't hold back."

"I'm sorry," said Daniel.

"You already apologized. You don't need to do it again."

"No. I—I'm sorry you got hurt trying to take care of me. I'm sorry I made you feel like you had to take care of me."

Aaron stopped what he was doing and grabbed Daniel's shoulder. He forced his little brother to look at him. "Don't do that," he said. "Don't start down that road. What happened to me isn't anywhere near your fault. I try to take care of you, that's true. But it's because you're my brother and that's what brothers do."

Daniel's eyes were watering. "But I know you did it for me. I know you wanted the money to help me."

"It's not your fault, Danny. My stupid decisions are my own. Besides, I was going to use the money to fix the car, not give it to you. No offense."

"I don't believe you."

"You should."

Daniel shook his head. "I don't want you to make sacrifices for me anymore. I want a future beyond this town and I want you to want that for yourself, too."

Aaron bit his lip and went back to the dishes.

"I don't want to lose you because you were too busy taking care of me to take care of yourself," said Daniel.

"I'm fine, Danny. I swear."

"You're not fine. And the shit you've been through isn't okay. I'll never be able to thank you for everything you've done to keep me happy and safe. But I can give you permission to look out for yourself."

"I can look out for both of us," said Aaron. "I'm a pretty damn good multitasker."

Daniel sighed and brushed his hair out of his face, a sign that he was agitated. "I don't want a future without you in it."

"I'm not going anywhere."

"Aaron."

"What, Danny?" He turned to inspect his baby brother.

Daniel's eyes were red and he suddenly looked like he was five years old again. "Please."

Aaron dried his hands on a rag. He pulled Daniel into a hug. "It's all right, buddy. I understand."

Daniel pulled away to wipe his eyes. "When I find that Ralph fuck, I'm going to kill him."

"You've got to stop saying you're going to kill people," said Aaron. "I'm pretty sure that will ruin any chance you have of getting into law school."

"I can make it look like self-defense."

"No. Hard no. If you don't want me getting into trouble on your behalf, you can't get into trouble on mine."

A voice from the doorway startled them.

"What trouble?" Silas' hair was still wet and stuck out haphazardly.

"Daniel's plotting murder," said Aaron.

"Vengeance," corrected Daniel. "Technically, justice."

"Don't worry about vengeance," said Silas. "The wicked will get what's coming to them."

"Well that's cryptic," said Aaron. "Do I have to worry about you murdering people, too?"

"I heal people," said Silas. "I don't kill them."

Aaron raised an eyebrow.

Silas looked away. He went to help Daniel with the dishes.

Aaron wondered briefly what it would be like to stand behind Silas and wrap his arms around his waist, to kiss his neck, to have Silas turn and smile. He shook his head, clearing the thoughts from his mind. He needed to stop letting himself drift into fantasies, especially ones he knew he'd never be able to satisfy.

After cleaning up, Daniel excused himself to study. He'd graduated in the spring and had already been accepted into Stanford. At this point he was just being a nerd for fun. Aaron teased him and told him not to hide in his room all day.

With nothing else to do, he decided to take Silas on a tour of the property. There wasn't much to see other than old cars, but it was an excuse to leave the house and stretch his legs. It also gave him a good reason to spend time alone with Silas.

There was a barrier between them. Silas stayed about an arm's length away from Aaron unless Aaron drifted into his space. If Aaron were braver, he'd walk closer and let his hand brush against Silas'. But he wasn't brave. When he drifted, Silas would glance at him and Aaron would self-correct.

They reached a spot beneath an old tree where he and Daniel had played when they were children.

"There used to be a tire swing," said Aaron. "Daniel broke it a couple years ago."

"How?" asked Silas. He shifted his weight and moved about an inch closer.

"He was spinning around like an idiot and the rope snapped."

"It sounds like the structural integrity of the rope failed," said Silas.

"Yeah, but it's more fun to blame Daniel." Aaron stole a glance. He wanted to lie back in the grass with Silas in his arms, but he couldn't even verbalize his desire, much less follow through. Besides, something told him Silas would leave soon. There was no reason to get attached. Silas had saved him and taken care of him because of what had happened to Joshua. This was about redemption, not romance. He was safe now. Silas had no reason to stick around.

He realized Silas was staring at him. "What?" he asked.

"You have freckles," answered Silas.

Aaron felt his cheeks flush. "Yeah," he said.

"I like them," said Silas. He looked away and suddenly became intensely focused on the tree. "Um, how old is it?"

"I don't know," answered Aaron. "It's been here as long as I can remember." He eyed Silas, puzzling over the freckles comment.

"It's a nice tree," said Silas. He cleared his throat and walked away from Aaron, apparently engrossed in studying the bark.

They'd shared so much already. Aaron didn't understand the rising awkwardness between them. Maybe it was because Silas had feelings for him, too. Maybe it was because Silas *didn't* have feelings for him and was worried about sending the wrong message now that he knew Aaron was bi.

Aaron decided it didn't matter. They'd met a few days ago. They didn't know enough about each other to justify a relationship. Aaron wasn't sure he could even be in a relationship. He'd never been in anything serious before, and certainly nothing serious with another man. If he started something with Silas, it would probably end with them resenting each other. Aaron would fuck up something, hurt Silas and ruin whatever they had now. It was better this way. They were friends, friends who occasionally shared a bed, held hands, saw each other naked and had been in a porno together.

Aaron sighed. Something deep in the center of him began to blossom and a warm sensation crept slowly outward, a prelude to destruction. He tried to push it back, resist the intoxicating feeling. It was a losing battle. When Silas finally looked at him again, Aaron reluctantly surrendered. The sensation spread like a tidal wave, drowning him. He was in love.

He was in love and the feeling was so terribly wrong he almost couldn't stomach it. Silas watched him and Aaron swayed.

Silas noticed and moved closer, eyes already scanning Aaron's body for any other signs of weakness. "What's wrong?" he asked.

"Tired," said Aaron.

Silas frowned. "You're sweating." He stepped closer, hand slightly raised. "Do you remember our breathing exercise?"

Silas was going to touch him, and God, Aaron wanted Silas to touch him. He wanted that moment of contact where it was just the two of them alone in the world, happy, calm and quiet. But it was wrong to want that. It was wrong to stand still while Silas approached. It was wrong to lead Silas into doing something Aaron would enjoy without warning Silas first. It was wrong, but he did it.

Silas took Aaron's hand and placed it in the center of his chest. He kept his hand over Aaron's as they began to breathe together.

Aaron couldn't make his breathing match Silas'. He tried, but the air felt heavy and thick. His throat was too tight.

"Aaron," said Silas softly, "stop thinking, and count with me."

Aaron nodded.

"Out loud," said Silas. He started counting, telling Aaron when to inhale and exhale.

Aaron counted with him, his lungs stuttering as he struggled to copy Silas. It was bizarrely intimate, Silas watching him closely while he tried to calm down. Everything they did was bizarrely intimate. After a minute or two, his thoughts stopped spiraling. The wind blew lightly against his skin. It was cool and soft.

"Good," said Silas. "That was good."

"Thanks for that," said Aaron. "I'm sorry, I don't know what happened."

"Did I do something wrong?"

"No," answered Aaron quickly.

"You can tell me if I did something," said Silas. "I want to know any time I make you uncomfortable."

"It wasn't you," said Aaron.

It was me and my stupid brain. I scared myself.

"Do you remember what you were thinking about?" asked Silas. He was holding Aaron's hand against his chest.

"I don't know," said Aaron. He was enjoying the feeling. He still didn't tell Silas. It still wasn't fair. Silas would give him anything he asked for because Aaron reminded him of Joshua. He had no way of knowing what these moments of contact meant to Aaron.

He heard a car approaching. He pulled his hand away and stepped back from Silas. The sound faded. It was just someone passing Jack's property on the main road.

Silas looked down at his feet, blushing again. "I'm sorry," he said. "I should have let go sooner."

"It's okay," said Aaron. He needed to add to that. Silas wouldn't want to touch him anymore if he thought it upset Aaron. But that was probably for the best. It didn't make sense for either of them to indulge in something that couldn't be.

Aaron faked a yawn. "I might take a nap," he said.

"All right," said Silas. He walked with Aaron to the house. Silas was once again careful to keep his distance.

When they reached the house, Silas stopped in the living room and let Aaron continue to the bedroom alone. Aaron flopped down on the bed and stared up at the ceiling. He was relieved to have time alone, but his brain kept wishing for stupid things, like that Silas had come with him.

He didn't sleep. He heard footsteps around the house. Later, he heard Daniel and Silas talking, heard Daniel laughing. After a while someone knocked lightly on the door. Aaron sat up as Silas slowly opened the door and poked his head around the corner.

"Oh," he said. "I was just coming to check on you. I didn't wake you, did I?"

"No, I was up."

"May I come in?"

"Yeah," said Aaron, then after a moment he added, "It's your room too."

Silas entered and shut the door. He made it to the center of the room and stopped. "How are you feeling?" he asked.

All the thoughts Aaron worked so hard to wrangle back into submission broke loose as soon as the door closed. Wishes and wants ran free without fear. They were safe in this little room.

"Better," answered Aaron.

"Did you sleep?"

"Yeah."

"Good," said Silas. He frowned slightly. "I think I will return home this evening. I want you to have time to catch up with your family."

Silas was leaving. Aaron wasn't invited. His heart sank. He didn't realize he'd missed his cue to say something until Silas spoke again.

"I can tell you're uncomfortable again, but I don't know why," said Silas.

He needed to tell Silas to stay. He enjoyed having Silas around. Silas made him feel safe. He banished that thought quickly. He was a grown man. He didn't need someone else around to protect him and take care of him. Besides, what did Silas get out of that?

"I, uh," began Aaron. "I must still be tired."

"I think it's me," said Silas.

"No," said Aaron, "it's not you."

"It is, and that's all right. I'm not offended. I sort of expected it, actually. I think I represent a part of your life you've had to keep separate. If I leave, it will allow you to establish a routine with Daniel and Jack and make it easier for you to merge the two worlds."

"That makes sense, I guess." It didn't. Aaron hid from Robert, and he wasn't there. Technically he hid things from Jack and Daniel, but that was for their own best interest. The only person he was completely truthful with was Silas.

Some tiny part of him got brave. Silas had seen him at his very lowest and had yet to judge. What he had with Silas might be the only honest relationship in his life. He licked his lips. He didn't want to lose that.

"Stay," breathed Aaron. Silas tilted his head.

"You don't have to," said Aaron, "but I don't want you to think I don't want you here. I want you to stay.

Unless you want to leave. I mean you should stay because you want to stay."

"I'll stay," said Silas.

"Yeah?"

"Yes," said Silas. He furrowed his forehead. "Aaron, I—" He seemed to struggle with the rest of the thought. "Never mind."

"Wait, what?" asked Aaron. "What were you going to say?"

"Nothing," answered Silas.

"Come on. You can't start something like that then leave me hanging. Now I'm curious."

Silas opened his mouth then closed it, frowning. "I'm happy you want me to stay," he said.

"You don't look happy."

"I am. I'm just concerned about you."

"I'm fine," said Aaron.

"All right," said Silas. "Daniel is going to teach me how to count cards. Would you like to join us?"

"Sure," answered Aaron.

He followed Silas out to the living room, acutely aware of the change between them.

Chapter Twenty

Listen

Liam and Jack returned in the evening. They unloaded the truck and Silas volunteered to help. Aaron announced that Silas had a broken rib, and Liam and Jack made an executive decision to unload the truck on their own. Daniel and Aaron carried things from the drop point in the living room back to his bedroom. Aaron gave Silas small things so the weight wouldn't aggravate his injury. Silas kept insisting he could do more.

It didn't take long to unpack. Aaron didn't have a lot of stuff. He wasn't sure why it had taken Jack all day to collect his things, but he suspected it had something to do with Robert. Aaron still hadn't heard from his father.

Liam didn't stay for dinner. He shook Aaron's hand, said it was nice to see him and Daniel. He and Jack shared a cryptic glance, then he got back in his truck and took off.

They looked at Jack, waiting for an update.

"So," said Jack, "what's for dinner? I'm starving."

"Pizza," answered Daniel. "It just got here. What did you and Liam do all day?"

"Pack," answered Jack.

"You were gone a long time," said Aaron. "Considering I don't have that much crap."

"Beaumonts," muttered Jack. He looked at Silas. "Do they give you this much trouble?"

"No," answered Silas.

Aaron laughed.

Jack rolled his eyes. "Daniel, we packed your stuff too, but we didn't have room to fit everything in the truck. We'll go back tomorrow for the rest of it."

"I'm moving out?" asked Daniel.

"Yep," answered Jack.

"Dad's going to be pissed," said Aaron.

"It took some convincing, but he eventually warmed up to the idea," said Jack.

"Before or after you kicked his ass?" asked Daniel.

"No ass kicking necessary," answered Jack. "Shouting, yeah. But we reached an understanding, and you boys are going to stay with me and he's not going to give us any trouble." He scratched his beard. "Daniel, I assume you're okay staying here. I don't mean to kidnap you, but I'll rest easier knowing you're safe."

Daniel shrugged. "Fine with me. Thanks for packing my stuff."

"You're welcome. I'll take the Jeep to Robert tomorrow. I've got a car you can use. It ain't sporty, but it's safe and reliable."

Aaron knew exactly which car Jack was talking about. He and Jack had worked on it together. It was a going-away present for Daniel.

"Why can't I just keep Dad's car? It's not like he's sober enough to drive it."

"That's true, but the car's in his name and it's easier if we just give it back. It's bad enough I took both his kids. I don't need to take his car too."

"Fine," muttered Daniel.

"Good," said Jack. "Enough bellyaching. Let's eat."

They followed Jack inside and gathered around the table for dinner.

"I'll be late again tomorrow," said Jack. "I'm going to go into the shop for a while, get some work done. I'll be back with Daniel's stuff around dinnertime."

"I'll go in with you," said Aaron. He assumed he still had a job. He hadn't been a terribly reliable employee lately, but Jack probably wouldn't hold that against him, considering the circumstances.

"No," said Jack. "You're out on sick leave for a while."

"I'm not sick," said Aaron.

"Boy, I'm offering you paid leave. Don't argue, just take it."

"But I can work," said Aaron. He wondered if this was a punishment.

Jack turned to Silas. "You're his doctor. Is he sick?"

"Yes," answered Silas.

"There you go," said Jack. "Your doctor and your boss recommend time off. Quit fussing about it."

"Am I fired?" asked Aaron.

"Of course not," answered Jack. "As long as I'm breathing, you've got a job."

Aaron nodded and looked down at his plate.

"It's not a punishment," said Jack. "Shit. I should probably just tell you."

Aaron looked up and Daniel's attention snapped to Jack as well.

"I haven't fired Robert yet. I'm letting him throw one fit at a time. Yesterday he was mad about you leaving, today he was mad about Daniel leaving, tomorrow he's gonna be mad about being fired."

"No one else will hire him," said Aaron quickly. His dad wasn't exactly easy to employ. He'd still need income. He relied on Jack to survive. The whole damn Beaumont family relied on Jack.

"Who gives a shit?" said Daniel.

"But it's my fault," said Aaron. "And I can work somewhere else. I can find another job. He can't."

Silas didn't say anything, but he reached over and laid a hand on Aaron's knee under the table.

"It's not your fault," said Jack. "I'll take care of him. You don't need to worry."

"You've got enough to deal with," said Aaron. "I can fix this. I can actually help here."

"Let Jack handle it," said Silas. His hand was still on Aaron's leg. "He owns the business. It makes sense that he gets to decide who stays and who goes."

Aaron looked down at the table again. They didn't understand. Jack clearly felt obligated to fire Robert now that he knew the truth. That was Aaron's fault. It was Aaron's fault Robert was losing his family, his job, his friend. Yes, Robert had hurt him, but only because he'd thought he was protecting Daniel. He shouldn't be punished for trying to protect his son. Robert had turned out to be right anyway. Aaron's first foray into being gay had been a disaster. Aaron had led Farley right to Daniel.

"Hey," said Daniel. "Silas is right. This is Jack's call."

"Yeah, okay," said Aaron. He couldn't argue. He'd never be able to explain what he was thinking, and he knew that if he started talking he'd just get upset again. He couldn't do that. He needed one day without a fucking breakdown. He'd stopped himself earlier, with Silas outside, but only barely, and even then Silas had known he was upset. Once upon a time, he had been master of hiding in plain sight. Now he had to cower in a room because he couldn't control his feelings. Still, it was better than crying.

Emotions somewhat in check, he looked up from the table. Everyone was watching him. Silas pulled his hand away from Aaron's knee. He reached into his pocket, fiddled with something, then set a blue pill beside Aaron's plate. Aaron was taking them like candy now.

"What kind of business do you run, Jack?" asked Silas.

Jack blinked, and looked away from Aaron. "Auto repair," he answered.

"Interesting," said Silas. "Aaron said you used to be in the CIA. What work did you do there?"

"Classified," answered Jack.

"Was it mechanical work?" asked Silas.

"I can't answer that," said Jack.

"Good luck getting anything out of him," said Daniel.

"How did you learn to fix vehicles?" asked Silas.

Jack sighed. "It was the family business."

Aaron popped the Xanax into his mouth and swallowed it. He focused on the conversation. Silas had saved him. Again.

"So you grew up around cars?" asked Silas.

"Yep," answered Jack.

"So you have a predilection for mechanics," mused Silas. "And you learned from your family. Assuming you were not motivated to break from family tradition, your CIA work was probably tangentially related to mechanics."

Jack sat back and crossed his arms.

"Or," continued Silas, "the 'family business' story is a cover and you learned a new skill once you left the CIA."

Aaron laughed. He'd never seen anyone outside their family interrogate Jack.

Daniel was leaning forward in his chair, watching. "I think it's true," said Daniel. "Jack's last name is Miller and his shop has always been called Miller Auto."

"How do you know?" asked Silas.

"I was curious," answered Daniel. "I looked it up, but it's been Miller Auto since it was built in the 70s."

"What if Miller isn't really his last name?" asked Aaron.

Daniel gasped.

"That's enough speculating for one night," said Jack. "You boys can sit here and gossip about me. I'm going to grab a beer and see what's on the TV." He stood and went to the refrigerator.

"I'll join you," said Aaron. He followed Jack and reached out his hand for a beer. Jack hesitated. He glanced at Silas before handing Aaron a drink.

"Can I have one?" asked Daniel.

Jack sighed. "Yes. One. Only tonight."

"I've had beer before," said Daniel.

"God help me," muttered Jack. He grabbed two more bottles from the refrigerator. He popped them open and handed one to Daniel and slid the other across the table to Silas. "You boys go find something for us to watch. I want to ask the doctor a question."

"About what?" asked Aaron. He knew it was about him, but he wanted to know how Jack would lie.

"I got an oozing rash on my back," he answered. "You want to stand here and see it?"

Daniel made a face. "Gross, no." He tugged Aaron's arm and pulled him into the living room. Once they were out of earshot, he leaned closer. "You eavesdrop," he whispered. "I'll put in a movie and you tell me what I missed."

Aaron grinned. "I'm on it."

Daniel picked over the DVDs and Aaron crept to the kitchen. He stood against the wall and listened.

"It was Xanax," said Silas. "It helps with his anxiety."

"Can he have alcohol with it?" asked Jack. "He's a grown man. I hate to tell him he can't have something, but I don't want him doing anything dangerous."

"You're not supposed to have alcohol when you take it," answered Silas. "But I frequently mix the two. He can have one drink. I'll watch him and monitor his intake after that."

"All right," said Jack. "Thanks. It's damn convenient having a doctor on hand."

"I'm happy to help."

The movie started playing in the living room. Aaron pressed closer to the wall. Daniel snuck up and joined Aaron in spying.

"You're good with him," said Jack. "I'm real glad you two found each other."

"Um, yes," said Silas. "Me too."

"Have you mentioned filing a report to him?"

"Not yet. I think we're better off handling this on our own. The law isn't terribly helpful in these situations."

"That might be true, but he needs to know it's an option," said Jack. "I'll talk to him if you don't want to."

"I'll do it. I can read him better than you can."

"That's not—" began Jack. He stopped. "Touché. You talk to him. You know what you're doing."

Silas was silent.

"We should go before those two wander back," said Jack.

Aaron pulled Daniel away from the wall and they hurried to the living room. They each took a seat and assumed a pose Aaron hoped looked comfortable and natural. Jack and Silas entered the room seconds later.

Silas sat next to Aaron and blushed as soon as they made eye contact.

After the movie, Jack went to bed and Aaron went to take a shower. His thoughts kept drifting back to Silas.

Chapter Twenty-One

We're A Mess

Aaron sat on the edge of the bed and Silas hovered in the doorway. Aaron wanted to sleep curled up next to him again, but had no idea how to vocalize that desire. Instead, he made awkward eye contact.

"I need to ask you something," said Silas.

Please ask if you can stay with me.

"Go for it," said Aaron.

Silas closed the door. "Do you want to report Ralph and the others? I can assist, and I'm certain Jack can too."

"No," answered Aaron. Instead of reaching out to the other man, he felt himself curl inward, defenses suddenly on high alert.

"They should pay for what they did," said Silas.

"No." Aaron crossed his arms firmly over his chest. He couldn't imagine repeating the story again, especially not to the police. They'd need details, evidence. Would they examine him? How many old scars did he have? Would he have to explain them, clarify that they were from his father, not his attacker?

Thinking about it made him sick again. What if he needed a lawyer? What if the case went to court? What if everyone found out what happened? He couldn't live that life. He couldn't live with his frailty exposed to strangers and his failures made public. He was already on camera, his humiliation immortalized in a convenient sharable format.

"All right," said Silas. "If you change your mind, I can help."

Aaron nodded, half listening. He wondered how much was on film. How much could people see? How much would they want to see? It was technically porn. He'd technically agreed to it.

The smell was back, that awful stench of weakness. He imagined faceless people sitting in dark rooms, their bodies illuminated by the soft blue glow of a screen. They watched him, touched themselves, came as the man on the screen begged and cried out.

Aaron clutched his stomach. He felt hands ghosting over his skin, rough, sticky fingers pressing against him as they touched, then grabbed, then hit... And God, why wouldn't they stop hitting him? Everything hurt so much already—his back, his chest, his head. Everything ached.

Then suddenly Silas was there. Not in his mind, but actually there in the room. He was on the floor kneeling in front of Aaron and looking up at him with the sincerest expression of concern.

And God dammit, Aaron had promised himself one day without a breakdown, one day without crying and leaking his problems into the rest of the world. He was a gaping wound of a human being, bleeding and oozing onto the nice things around him.

And Silas was so close, so fucking close, closer than anyone else. He was stained with Aaron's mess. Every time Aaron bled, Silas stepped forward to stem the flow with his bare hands. Aaron let him, because ultimately Silas was a stranger and it was easier to bloody a stranger than family. He was too kind, too empathetic. Aaron was using him.

Hesitantly, Silas placed his hand on Aaron's knee. That was all it took for Aaron to break. He felt the tears, heard himself choke and sob, felt himself slide from the bed and onto the floor in a pathetic, desperate search for comfort.

Silas obliged, of course, and pulled him into his chest. Aaron wished he'd met Silas under different circumstances. He wished he'd been braver sooner, had more faith in his family, broken away from Robert on his own.

Love couldn't live like this. He wanted Silas to hold him and lie next to him and touch him, not because Aaron needed comfort but because Silas loved him. He wanted to close his eyes and believe the way Silas was slowly rocking him in his arms was something Silas wanted as much as Aaron did.

Aaron couldn't confess. It was too soon and he had nothing to offer Silas other than nights spent cautiously holding each other. Maybe he'd kiss him again, one day, but not any time soon. Silas would certainly want more, and he was entitled to want more.

Silas was running his fingers through Aaron's hair. The touch sent shivers down Aaron's spine and left his body aching for something sweet and more substantial.

Silas pressed a light kiss to his forehead. "Are you all right?" he asked softly.

"Yeah," muttered Aaron.

"Is this all right?"

"Yeah." He heard Silas' heartbeat, felt the rise and fall of his chest. He wanted more — he wanted so much more. He clutched the T-shirt Silas was wearing. He couldn't remember the last time someone had treated him with this kind of tenderness. If he gave Silas more, sex would replace gentle touches. Grabbing would replace holding. Taking would replace asking.

He looked up at Silas from where he was cradled against him. Silas looked down, eyes wide with worry as he licked his lips. He ran a thumb over Aaron's cheek, again wiping his tears with a familiar touch that almost felt ritualistic.

"I'm sorry," muttered Aaron.

"For?" asked Silas quietly.

"I'm not like this, not really," he said. He'd meant to say he was sorry Silas had met him like this. He was sorry Silas never got to see him be strong. He was sorry Silas was left holding the mangled remains of his psyche. He was sorry he'd missed his chance to be something Silas could love instead of pity. He raised his hand to cup Silas' cheek. He closed his eyes and imagined they weren't burdened with the ugliness of reality.

Silas' thumb brushed over Aaron's lower lip and Aaron's breath hitched. The air was hot and thick between them. Aaron's hand moved to Silas' hair. He knew better. He knew exactly what message he was sending.

In an attempt to prove himself to his father, he'd made a point of seducing as many women as would have him. As a side effect, sex had become something like a reflex. He knew exactly which moves encouraged and which moves defused, and he normally took the lead instead of trembling like a virgin.

Silas kissed his forehead again and a silent scream ripped through him. He was suddenly overwhelmed. His fingers tightened in Silas' hair and he surged forward, his lips crushing against Silas'. He licked his way into Silas' mouth, desperate, hungry and delirious. He broke from Silas' arms, stood and tugged Silas to his feet.

He fell back into the bed, pulling Silas down on top of him without any real thought behind his actions, and thrust his hips upward. Silas gasped against his open mouth and pressed himself down against Aaron.

Aaron barely had time to catch his breath before Silas was kissing him. Aaron rocked upward, searching for friction. When his erection pressed against Silas', something like ice water rippled through his veins and he froze.

Silas moved lower, teeth grazing Aaron's neck. He stopped suddenly and looked up. "Your heart is pounding," he said.

For whatever reason, the voice Aaron heard was not Silas'. He blinked at the man lying on top of him and waited for the pain. Logically, he knew it was Silas pressing against him, petting his hair, asking him to respond, but his mind was struggling to reconcile fact with fear.

Silas moved above him. He shifted and slid from the bed back to the floor, kneeling and staring at him with one hand still running through Aaron's hair.

Aaron followed him with his eyes. He was pretty sure his lips were moving, but he was also pretty sure he wasn't actually saying anything. Finally, he managed to breathe out a quiet apology.

"It's all right," said Silas. "Do you know where you are?"

"Yeah," muttered Aaron.

"I'm so sorry," said Silas. "I shouldn't have — "

"It's okay."

"It's very clearly not okay," said Silas.

Aaron sighed. "I don't know what's wrong with me."

"Can you tell me what you're thinking?"

"I'm not thinking anything," answered Aaron. That was only partially true. He was thinking a lot of things, but he wasn't thinking anything clearly enough to explain himself. He sighed again. "Sorry I pulled you around like that. Forgot about your rib. Did I hurt you?"

"Not at all," answered Silas. His fingers were still tangled in Aaron's hair. "Quite the opposite, actually." His cheeks turned pink and he bit his lip.

Aaron stared at him, searching his face. He knew how to show his thanks. He knew how he could repay his debt. He knew, now, exactly what Silas wanted.

He felt the muscles in his body go limp. He wasn't relaxed — he just didn't have the strength to move. "Can you come back up here?" he asked. He had to ask. Silas wanted him to ask.

"You're very pale," said Silas. "How are you feeling? Do you feel queasy?"

Yes.

Generally speaking, he'd been queasy for the past week, if not longer. Silas pulled his hand away and sat on his heels.

"Just come to bed," said Aaron.

"Do you want me to turn off the light first?" asked Silas.

It felt like he was stalling, but darkness was too tempting an offer to resist. "Yeah," muttered Aaron.

A moment later the room went black. The bed dipped as Silas settled beside him. Aaron wiggled closer to the wall to give Silas room. The movement exhausted him.

"You want to pick up where we left off?" asked Aaron. He did his best to seem inviting, but his voice sounded hollow, even to him.

"No," answered Silas. "I want you to sleep, and if anything bothers you, I want you to wake me up."

No, because Aaron was fragile and broken. No, because Aaron wasn't convincing. No, because the stench rolling off Aaron's body was disgusting and Silas could smell it too. No, because Silas was yet again doing him a favor and his weakness was unappealing.

"I'm sorry," muttered Aaron.

"You didn't do anything wrong," said Silas.

"I'm a mess."

"No, you're not." Silas rolled onto his side, and through the darkness, Aaron saw him wince.

"Be careful," said Aaron.

Silas froze. "Sorry," he said quickly. "Did I hurt you?"

"No, your rib," said Aaron. "I meant don't hurt yourself. And don't think I haven't noticed that you only wince when you think I'm not looking, by the way."

"I'm fine," said Silas.

"Then so am I," said Aaron.

Silas huffed.

Aaron's ribs had been broken before. He knew what hurt Silas. Moving probably hurt. The deep breathing exercise he did with Aaron probably hurt. Silas' shoulder was still injured as well. Everything he did for Aaron probably hurt.

"All right," said Silas. He winced again as he sat up. "I'm sore, that's true. I'm worried you'll feel guilty if you're constantly reminded of my injuries, so I've been trying to hide them. That's also true. But none of this — of anything you've been through — is your fault. I want you to feel safe and comfortable, no matter what that takes."

Aaron scrubbed a hand over his face. It was too difficult to crave and fear and ache all at the same time. Love couldn't survive this. The best thing he could do at this point was let Silas go. Silas wouldn't go on his own, not as long as he thought he was saving Joshua by taking care of Aaron. So Aaron had to release him. He had to set him free.

"You should leave," said Aaron.

"All right," said Silas. "I'll be on the couch if —"

"I meant go home," said Aaron. He was a hurricane. Anyone nearby was doomed to get captured in his storm. Their freedom was his responsibility.

"No," said Silas.

"Yes."

"No."

Aaron sat up and glared. "Go home, Silas."

"Tell me what I did wrong," he said, scowling back at Aaron.

"For fuck's sake."

"If you tell me what I did wrong, I'll leave," said Silas. "I don't want to repeat my mistake the next time we see each other."

"Next time?"

Silas' expression relaxed. He started to say something, then stopped. He seemed lost for a moment.

"Yes," he said finally. "I—" He looked down at his knees.

Aaron looked at him, equally lost.

"I would like to see you again," said Silas quietly. He looked at Aaron, eyebrows creased together.

Suddenly, the urge to pull him in and kiss him returned. Aaron wanted to take it back, to tell Silas to stay, to tell him it was a lie. At the same time, he wanted to push Silas away, leave Jack and Daniel behind, run as far away as he could until his legs gave out or his lungs stopped taking in air.

"Honestly," said Silas slowly, "I don't want to leave. That's selfish, I know, but it's the truth." Aaron slumped to the side and rested his forehead against Silas' shoulder. He wondered how many mixed signals he'd sent in the past thirty minutes. Enough for Silas to be angry, or at the very least confused. Aaron had successfully confused himself. His brain was too tangled up with itself to understand.

But Silas didn't get angry—instead, he wrapped an arm loosely around Aaron's shoulders.

"I'm a fuck-up," said Aaron.

"So am I," said Silas.

"I don't want you to leave."

"Then I won't."

"You didn't do anything wrong," said Aaron. "I just freaked out. I don't know why."

"That's all right."

"I don't want you to sleep on the couch, either," said Aaron.

"Then I won't," said Silas.

"Sorry for all the mixed signals," said Aaron.

Silas sighed. "You're not sending mixed signals," he said.

"Yeah, I am. You're just a really nice guy."

"Being 'nice' is not synonymous with 'not being an asshole'," said Silas.

Aaron felt numb, possibly a reaction to suddenly feeling so much at once. It happened slowly, a creeping realization that parts of him were shutting down until he was too weak to stay upright. His mind was the first thing to go. His head slipped from Silas' shoulder back down to his pillow. Silas followed him down. Aaron fell asleep against his chest. The last thing he heard was Silas whispering good night.

Chapter Twenty-Two

Dad

Aaron was still numb the next day, and the day after that. He was numb when Silas left to check on things at his house. He was numb when Silas returned. He was numb when he showed Daniel how to change the oil on his new car. He was numb at night when Silas held him and they fell asleep. He was numb and he didn't break down anymore.

Things shifted and morphed around him, and staying with Jack turned into living with Jack. Daniel unpacked. Aaron didn't. Silas brought a suitcase over because Jack asked him to stay for a while. No one heard from Robert, but Jack swore he was doing fine, just learning to cope.

Aaron thought about his father constantly. He couldn't decide if he cared or not. He couldn't decide if what he felt was rage or grief. His body was hollow, detached. The tattered, surviving fragments of who he was had retreated somewhere deep inside him. They hid behind his eyes, tucked safely in the back of his mind where his feelings couldn't reach and where his thoughts couldn't see them.

He watched the world, touched it and interacted with it without actually feeling anything. He didn't remember when he had decided to sequester himself, but as the days went on his body became less of a sanctuary and more of a tomb.

Aaron had a new phone and a new number and a new set of contacts. But Jack had been right when he'd said there were many ways to contact someone. He didn't remember exactly when two cars in Jack's driveway became four cars. Jack's car was gone during the day. Daniel's car was gone whenever he got the urge to leave the house and be social. Silas' car stayed parked beside Aaron's. They hardly left.

Still, Aaron made a habit of checking on his car every morning. It wasn't a job and there wasn't a good reason, but it gave him the illusion of purpose and that was something he desperately needed.

He'd checked his car that morning. He'd been surprised to find an envelope and the spare car key waiting for him in the driver's seat. His name was scrawled across the paper in Robert's messy handwriting. Aaron knew what his father had done before he opened the letter. He knew because Robert didn't have his family anymore. He knew because he'd have done the exact same thing. Robert was lonely and lost, had been since the day their lives had crashed and June had died.

Aaron took the letter and keys and wandered to a place where prying eyes couldn't see him. Jack was at work, but Daniel and Silas were inside.

Aaron made sure no one was watching, and went to hide by the tree that had guarded him through his childhood. The letter was three lines long.

I'm sorry for everything, son. Take care of Daniel. I know you will.

He read the words once, then folded the letter back into the envelope. He tucked it and the spare key into his pocket, then headed to the house.

He didn't say a word about it to Daniel or Silas. They spent the day hanging out. Aaron laughed and joked. He made passing glances at Silas, who predictably blushed. He made dinner for everyone when Jack came home.

That night, he curled up next to Silas and waited for him to fall asleep. In the quiet, early hours of the morning, after Silas had rolled away in his sleep, Aaron slipped out of bed.

He took his keys, put the car in neutral and rolled it away from the house. Once he was far enough that the sound of the engine starting wouldn't wake anyone, he got behind the wheel and shifted into drive.

* * * *

The farmhouse wasn't a trigger. Pulling into the driveway wasn't disturbing. Instead of remembering it as the last place he'd seen his father alive, he remembered it as it was, just a driveway. Opening the door and turning on the lights in the living room wasn't a trigger, and neither was going to the back of the house.

He checked Robert's bedroom first. It was dark and empty. He checked his room and Daniel's. Both rooms were spotless, probably thanks to Jack and Liam. The rest of the house was as he remembered it, with the addition of a few more empty bottles.

Aaron turned on the light in the kitchen. There were two coffee mugs on the counter and a pamphlet for a local Alcoholics Anonymous group. The room still smelled like coffee. Jack must have stopped by after work. He was probably the source of the AA pamphlet.

Robert must have dropped the letter and key off last night. He must have had a plan.

Aaron went through the rooms and turned off the lights. He walked to the back of the dark house again and stood outside of the downstairs bathroom. He pushed the door open and waited for his eyes to adjust.

The shower curtain was closed. Robert was going to make him get close. Aaron paused for a moment. He imagined his father going through the house, turning off all of the lights, then standing in the darkness right where Aaron was standing now.

He knew he should feel a sense of urgency. He knew he should have felt a sense of dread when he'd seen the envelope that morning. He knew he should feel guilty now for not feeling anything.

He pulled back the curtain. Robert's body was crumpled in the bottom of the tub, a .45 in his lap. The wall behind him was stained and patches of blood were still wet. Even in the darkness, Aaron knew the mess was contained to the shower.

He sat down on the tiled floor and waited to feel something.

* * * *

Silas texted him around four a.m., wanting to know where he'd gone. Aaron should have told him he'd gone for a drive and would be back soon. He didn't. His fingers typed out the words *At the house. Dad's dead.* and hit send. He didn't even feel guilty, even though he knew his text would pull Silas out of bed and send him, panicking, straight to Aaron.

His phone rang and he answered.

"Are you all right?" asked Silas. His voice was measured and even.

"I'm fine," answered Aaron.

"I'll be there in a few minutes," said Silas. "Don't touch anything."

"All right," said Aaron.

Silas hung up. True to his word, he arrived at the house ten minutes later. How he'd known the address was a question for another day.

"Aaron?" Silas' voice rang through the hall.

"Here," he answered.

Silas found him. "Can I turn on the light?" he asked.

"Sure," answered Aaron. "But it's gross." His eyes had adjusted hours ago. He saw the mess in shades of blue and black. He didn't need light to know Robert was dead.

Silas flipped the switch and the blood screamed to life. It covered the shower area, but the spatter didn't touch the rest of the room. It would be easy to clean later.

Silas knelt and took Aaron's hand. "Come on," he said. Aaron couldn't. He wasn't sure he wanted to.

After a few moments of silence, Silas surrendered and sat beside him. "I left a note for Jack and Daniel," he said. "I told them we went out for breakfast, then were going back to my house to check on things. I indicated we would return later."

"Okay," said Aaron.

"I will take care of this," said Silas. "You can wait here or at my house, whichever you prefer."

"There's nothing to take care of," said Aaron. "He's dead."

Silas took a shaky breath. "I don't mean to be insensitive," he said, "but how thorough were you? Did you wipe your fingerprints from the gun?"

Aaron looked at him. Silas stared, wide-eyed and serious as ever. Aaron couldn't control the manic part of himself that started to laugh. Logically, it wasn't funny. A reasonable man wouldn't laugh because his friend thought he was a murderer. A reasonable man would clarify the misunderstanding. Aaron was not a reasonable man. He was only able to stop laughing when Silas' expression morphed from concern to fear.

"He shot himself," said Aaron, catching his breath.

"All right," said Silas. "How did you know to check on him?"

Aaron rolled his eyes and retrieved the letter from his pocket. He handed it to Silas. "I didn't kill him," he said.

Silas read the note. "When did he give this to you? And how? There isn't any postage on the envelope."

"I found it in the car this morning." He frowned and realized it was technically a new day. "Yesterday morning, I guess."

Silas sat up straighter and peered at the body in the tub.

"If you're thinking his body looks too fresh to have died yesterday, you're right," said Aaron. "He probably did it an hour or so before I got here."

Silas frowned and looked between Aaron and the body.

"Have you put it together yet?" asked Aaron.

Silas was smart. He'd figured it out. It wasn't hard to guess exactly what Robert's plan had been.

"He left me the letter yesterday," said Aaron. "Didn't tell anyone else and kept my note vague but cryptic. Then he waited. I had all damn day to mention it and check on him."

Silas' lips parted and he reached his hand out.

Aaron waved him away. "He even waited for Jack to drop by. Poor bastard probably sat here thinking Jack was going to talk to him. Tell him not to do it. I bet he sat here thinking we were all going to show up and see if he was all right. Bet he thought we'd beg him not to do it."

"You can't start thinking that way," said Silas.

Aaron raised an eyebrow. "I knew what he was going to do. Granted, I figured he was dead already when I got the letter, so I don't really feel bad."

"I think you're in shock," said Silas.

"I'm not," said Aaron. "I just don't care."

"We need to go ahead and call the police. I don't think you should be here — Aaron, stop."

Aaron dialed 911 before Silas could snatch the phone from his hand. "I need to report a death," he said.

Silas was right. They needed to call it in before things became any more suspicious. It was already strange that he'd waited so long to tell anyone. The woman on the phone was calm as she asked for the address. That made Aaron calm and it made it easier to lie. He relaxed, let his brain shut down and switch to autopilot.

Time blurred together after that. He let himself cry so that his eyes would be red when the police arrived. He needed to look the part of the grieving son. He took the letter from Silas and crumpled it so it would look like he'd read it over and over, like his father's last words were a treasured thing, like those three lines were words he'd never forget.

He let himself collapse against Silas' shoulder, and by the time the police arrived, he was appropriately distraught. He changed the time that he'd found the letter. He said it was much later, setting the discovery back to after Jack had come home from work. The police took statements. An ambulance arrived. Robert was pronounced dead. Silas called Jack, who showed up with Daniel just as the EMTs were hauling the body out in a bag.

Daniel was a wreck. He was heartbroken and angry. Aaron still didn't come back to himself. Sometime after sunrise, Jack herded everyone to his house. Aaron let himself calm down, end the show. The living room was quiet. Daniel finally stilled after the initial shock. A new reality settled in among them.

Silas stayed by Aaron's side through the entire ordeal. He didn't question or contradict. He was the only one who'd seen Aaron turn from ice to something warm, something feeling. Continuing the trend of their relationship, Silas knew the ugly truth.

Silas made everyone try to eat something. When appetites failed, he insisted on rest.

Before they parted, Aaron found his voice again. He had to tell his family what they needed to hear. He needed to ease their pain. "I found that letter this morning," he said. Jack probably felt the guiltiest and needed to hear it the most, but Aaron spoke directly to

Daniel. "I had all day to check on him. I knew what it meant and I didn't tell anybody."

Jack cursed under his breath.

Daniel stared at him wide-eyed, like a child. Daniel would always be innocent.

"I lied to the police," Aaron continued. "I figured it would be less suspicious that way." He sighed, exhaustion finally kicking in. "Point is, I don't want either of you to think this is your fault. Dad left me the note because he wanted me to be the one to stop him. I didn't. I'm okay with that."

"It's not —" began Jack.

Aaron cut him off. "You went above and beyond for us," he said. "You did everything you could for Dad, but he's been a lost cause since Mom died."

He turned back to his brother. "Danny, I don't know if he told you, but you were the best thing to ever happen to him. He was so proud of you, how smart you are, what you've accomplished. He talked about you all the damn time when —"

Daniel crossed the room quickly and threw his arms around Aaron. "Shut up," he muttered. "He was an asshole."

Suddenly Jack was right beside them. "It's nobody's fault," he said. "It's not your job to clean up his mess and it's not your job to patch up his legacy. We're in this together."

Somewhere deep in his chest, Aaron felt something crack. He felt it, if only for a second. Daniel squeezed him tight before letting go. "Together," he said.

Aaron nodded.

Jack pulled Silas into the huddle and draped an arm over his shoulders. "We're all going to get some sleep," he said. "You boys take care of each other and I'll take care of everything else."

They went their separate ways, with Silas following dutifully behind Aaron.

Chapter Twenty-Three

Starting Over

His father was cremated. Robert's ashes were spread along the river, where June's ashes had been spread years before. There was a short service for him at Jack's. A surprising number of people showed up to pay their respects. It was a relatively painless ordeal.

Daniel seemed to experience the full range of emotions. Jack seemed disappointed. Aaron was still numb.

He found a moment of peace the day after the service. He sat beneath the tree in Jack's yard, eyes closed against the bright sun. Silas sat beside him in silence.

He still loved Silas. He sensed the emotion moving in his heart. It called to him like a ghost in the night, but stayed just out of reach. The feeling existed without Aaron experiencing it or touching it. Aaron wished he could feel again.

* * * *

Days drifted by, persistent and unremarkable. The world was unmoved by the death of Robert Beaumont and so was Aaron.

Silas found a job and was gone during most of the day. Daniel got a part-time job to save money before school started. Aaron was home alone for the first part of the day. Jack wouldn't let him return to the shop. He seemed to think it was in Aaron's best interest to stay home.

Aaron set a schedule for himself. He made breakfast for everyone in the morning, cleaned the kitchen, vacuumed every other day and kept the house in general working order. When Daniel came home, Aaron made lunch. They'd talk for an hour or so, then Aaron would retreat to the garage to work on any car or part he could find.

He'd rebuilt two cars and was working on a third. He heard whispers and saw worried looks from his family in the evenings. He soldiered on, undisturbed.

He was distracting himself with an engine in the garage when Jack interrupted. "Silas went to check on his place," he said. "Told me to tell you he'd be back soon."

"Okay," said Aaron, not bothering to look away from the metal in front of him.

Jack sat on the workbench. "Boy, I need to talk to you about something."

"Go for it."

"Put the pliers down first."

Aaron sighed and set the tool beside him. He looked at Jack, but did nothing to hide his annoyance.

"I'm worried about you," said Jack. "You don't seem like yourself."

"I'm bored," said Aaron. "If you'd let me go back to working at the shop, that might help."

"That might help, but that's not why I'm here," said Jack. "I actually wanted to talk to you while Silas was gone. Is he bothering you? I wanted to keep him around at first because y'all seemed like — uh — you got along real well. It felt right having him here. But if he's bothering you, I'll send him on his way."

"Silas doesn't bother me," said Aaron. They still shared a bed and laughed and joked together, but the thought of Silas leaving didn't terrify Aaron like it once had. Silas went to his house several times a week and his absence had become a fact of life. One day, Aaron suspected Silas wouldn't come back.

"You can be honest," said Jack. "Nobody can hear us. Daniel's in his room. It's just us."

"I am being honest."

Jack sighed and clasped his hands together. "Well, something's wrong. I'd like to know what it is. I think — " He stopped and licked his lips nervously. He sighed again. "I noticed a change before we lost your daddy."

Aaron thought he'd done a better job of masking his indifference in the beginning.

"Do you feel different? Have you noticed any changes in yourself?"

"What are you getting at?" asked Aaron.

"You've been through a lot of — um — trauma and I — "

"*Trauma?*" asked Aaron, picking up on Jack's word choice.

"Yeah."

"You've been talking to Silas." He wasn't surprised. He knew they talked.

Jack ran a hand over his face. "Yeah, I have."

"About me."

"Yes."

"About how to take care of me."

184

"We just—I just want to make sure you're okay."

"I'm fine."

"You're not fine," said Jack.

Aaron rolled his eyes. He would be fine if they'd stop poking at his bruises. "Clearly you came out here with a mission. Quit dicking around and get to the point."

"Don't snap at me," said Jack. "I'm trying to help."

"Gee, thanks."

"Boy, I'm warning you."

"What?" demanded Aaron. He was on his feet staring down at Jack before either of them registered the movement. "What are you going to do? I better behave or else you'll what?"

"I wasn't threatening you."

"It sure as hell sounded like it."

"I don't want to fight," said Jack, holding up his hands.

Aaron huffed. "Don't hold back on my account. I'm not scared of you."

Jack's face fell.

Aaron heard it as soon as he said it, the little boy arguing with a father he didn't have—never had. The prospect of a fight fueled him. Anger was safe. He trusted it and it made him strong. But he'd let the emotion go too far too fast and it got lost in the dark, haunted edges of his thoughts. As quickly as the anger had strengthened him, it turned on him and cut him down.

"I don't want to fight," Jack said again, more quietly this time. "I told myself, if you got pissed, I'd walk away and leave you be. I'd really rather not do that."

Aaron scrubbed his hands over his face.

"I won't drag this out," continued Jack. "I came out here to tell you that if you want to talk to someone — a professional — I can make you an appointment."

Aaron frowned.

"Like a shrink," said Jack.

Aaron sat down again, his head in his hands.

"We don't think you're crazy. We just don't want to overestimate our ability to help you. We want you to know there's no shame in seeing someone if you want to."

We. He'd buried his problems, but apparently not deep enough. His family had found the scent and, like bloodhounds, tracked the emotions to their graves. He wasn't fooling anyone. They knew he was broken, but they cared about him. That meant they were going to spend their time putting him back together. They'd waste the rest of their lives on him — Daniel and Jack out of love, and Silas out of guilt. He was a burden, just like Robert.

He was vaguely aware that Jack had moved and was now sitting beside him.

"I think," said Jack slowly, "if you'd gotten the chance to hit Robert once, as hard as you fucking could, I think that would have been really therapeutic." Jack put a hand on his shoulder. "But he took that away from you."

Aaron's vision blurred and he felt tears on his cheeks. A breakdown was inevitable. He should have known he wasn't strong enough to be stoic forever. He'd always been soft, overly sensitive. Robert had wanted to make him stronger, better. Robert had hit him in hopes Aaron would build up a resistance to pain, but it hadn't worked. Aaron would always feel, always hurt, always bleed.

"It's all right if you don't miss him," said Jack. "And it's all right if you *do* miss him."

Aaron closed his eyes. A tremor ran through him and another little piece of him fractured.

Jack tightened his hand against Aaron's shoulder. "It's all right."

It wasn't. It couldn't be all right. Aaron opened his eyes. The tremor shook through him again. He felt himself crack. He swallowed hard and forced the leaking emotion behind the barrier. For the first time in weeks, he realized he didn't really want to feel anything. He wanted to be numb.

Aaron couldn't find the words to respond. His hands began shaking again. He tried to fight it. He wasn't ready to break so soon. Something burst inside of him. He felt himself shatter. Emotions erupted in a fit of chaotic glee. They consumed him, too many to name and too quick to grasp. He choked and clutched at his chest.

He cried. He couldn't make himself stop. Helpless and weak, he let Jack pull him into a hug. His body shook. He couldn't control himself, couldn't get a grip. Jack just kept telling him it was all right, but it wasn't. So much was wrong.

It was true, what Jack had said about hitting Robert. That might have fixed the whole problem in some Freudian sense, but it wasn't an option anymore. The only shield Aaron had was indifference, but Robert had died and taken that with him, too.

It mattered. Everything that happened to him mattered in a huge, insurmountable, significant way. He was broken, but he didn't want to shatter and leave behind pieces for other people to collect and put back into place. He wanted to be better. His family wanted to fix him. The least he could do was make their efforts a luxury and not an obligation.

"I don't know any therapists," said Aaron quietly.

"Silas does."

"Of course he does."

"You don't have to go," said Jack.

"I think I need help," said Aaron. He needed to be someone else's problem. Therapists were paid to clean up people like Aaron.

"I'll do anything you need me to do."

Aaron nodded. "Thanks."

Jack clapped him on the shoulder. "We're going to get through this."

He knew Jack meant it. They'd stick by him until the bitter end. He couldn't make them wait that long. He had to get better so they could be free.

* * * *

Silas lay next to Aaron, eyebrows knitted in a way that told Aaron he was deep in thought. Their nights were always like this, pressed together and teetering on the edge of something more.

Silas pursed his lips, then finally spoke. "Would you like to move in with me?" he asked.

Aaron laughed. "Way to jump right in."

"Feel free to say no," said Silas. "But I have to return home eventually. We are essentially living together right now. It made sense to extend an offer."

"Aren't you tired of me yet?" asked Aaron.

Silas frowned. "If I was tired of you, why would I ask you to live with me?"

Aaron sighed and let his forehead rest against Silas'. "Because you're kind," he muttered.

Silas cupped his cheek. "I like you," he said. "Isn't this what people do when they like each other? Assuming you also like me, of course."

"I like you," said Aaron quickly.

I love you.

"I suppose I don't know the correct protocol," said Silas. "I'm not sure I've done anything that would qualify as 'dating', but this feels like the next logical step."

Aaron couldn't help the grin that spread across his lips. "You want to date me, Silas?"

"Obviously," he answered. "Do you want to date me?"

"Yeah," answered Aaron. His emotions were still raw from talking to Jack. He felt his heart beat a little louder, felt something warm in his chest. He bit his lip. Loving Silas meant feeling everything, the good and the bad.

"So is that a yes to moving in? Or is it too soon?" asked Silas. "I think this is traditionally a much larger step in a relationship, but we haven't really been traditional thus far."

"Yeah," muttered Aaron. "We didn't exactly meet in a coffee shop." He sighed again. Living with Silas sounded perfect. It was exactly what he wanted. It was what he'd wanted since the first night they'd spent together. But living with Silas was a commitment he wasn't sure he wanted to make. It meant they'd stay together forever or eventually break apart. Forever felt too long and breaking up felt too painful, and being together implied other intimate things Aaron wasn't sure he could promise.

"You can say no," said Silas. "I've never wooed anyone before. If this is wrong, you can tell me."

"I want to say yes," said Aaron. "But I'm still a little fucked up. I don't know if it's a good idea."

"Are you trying to tell me it's not me, it's you?" asked Silas.

"No," Aaron answered quickly. "I mean, it is me, I'm definitely the problem, but I want—um—more, you know?" His heart was pounding and his throat was tight for no discernible reason. He felt his internal wall repairing itself, blocking out Silas and Jack and Daniel. The words *I want you,* dangled from the tip of his tongue before he was able to swallow them back. It wasn't the relationship that terrified him—it was something else, something he wasn't ready to name.

"I don't mean to rush you," said Silas.

"You're not," said Aaron. He felt Silas' disappointment, knew he'd pull away if he didn't get what he wanted, if Aaron didn't behave.

"I can slow down," said Silas. "I suppose I was being a bit selfish. I was trying to find a way to return to my home but still wake up beside you in the morning."

No, Silas wouldn't pull away. He'd stay until Aaron forced him to leave, because Silas was loyal to a fault. Aaron closed his eyes. His thoughts never made sense. He wanted to believe people stayed with him because he made them happy, not because they were afraid to leave him alone with himself. Jack was right. He needed a shrink, or someone objective to talk to and set his head on straight.

He realized this wasn't the first time he'd withdrawn from the world—it was just the first time he'd noticed it. When Robert had sent him away, Aaron had been shocked back into his feelings. He was safe with Silas and his emotions took advantage of their new freedom. The numbness wasn't the change. He was back to himself, back to normal. He hated it.

"Two things," said Aaron, finally finding his voice. "Thing one, Jack says you know some shrinks or therapists or whatever. Can you give me their numbers?"

"Of course," answered Silas, surprise evident in his voice. "I'll check with Sara and see if she still recommends them. I know of a counselor with a very good reputation. I can see if we can get you in soon."

"Thanks," said Aaron.

"What is thing two?"

"Let's date."

Silas laughed. "I am very much in favor of that."

"I mean like normal people date, like dinner and movies and shit."

"All right."

"Like, fucked-up shit aside," said Aaron. "We'll start over, clean slate. I'll buy you flowers and pick you up and open your car door and stuff."

And you can love me instead of pity me, he thought. He needed to know if he made Silas happy or if he was just a project.

Silas grinned at him, cheeks bright pink. "And I'll learn to cook and give you a dedicated drawer in my dresser."

"We'll be totally normal."

"I doubt we'll be normal," said Silas. "But I think we'll be happy."

"I can settle for happy," said Aaron. He took Silas' hand and pressed it to his lips. It wasn't much, but it was all he could offer. He hoped it could be enough.

Chapter Twenty-Four

First Date

Silas knew a counselor and two psychiatrists. He said Sara recommended the counselor, so that was who Aaron went to see. His first appointment arrived and he couldn't stop fidgeting while he waited for his name to be called.

Silas had officially moved back to his house yesterday. Their first date was tonight and Aaron insisted on planning it despite not actually having a plan. He'd searched the web for first-date ideas, but the articles were written for straight couples and the fact that he wasn't going out with a woman was impossible to ignore.

It shouldn't matter. He shouldn't care. He shouldn't wonder if the world would watch them or if people would shy away from them. Their love shouldn't be treated like a sickness and Aaron shouldn't want to quarantine himself.

He told himself over and over again that he was not contagious, not infecting the good, clean people around him. He told himself that wanting to be with Silas, to touch him and hold him, was normal and not the product of something dirty and shameful.

His stomach turned and he leaned back in his chair. He told himself to breathe.

"Aaron?" A woman with light brown hair smiled at him from the doorway.

He stood and followed her to her office. "I'm Ava," she said, holding out her hand.

Aaron accepted the handshake. "Nice to meet you," he said.

She closed the office door behind them. "Make yourself comfortable." She pulled out a sheet of paper and a notepad. "What brings you in today?"

"I think I'm kind of fucked up," he said. "Maybe depressed? I don't really know."

"What makes you think that?" she asked.

He shrugged. "I'm not sure." Suddenly he felt silly. Surely there were people with bigger problems. Surely Ava had better ways to spend her time. "I don't hear voices or hallucinate or anything," said Aaron. He half expected her to tell him to leave.

"You don't have to hear or see things to feel fucked up," said Ava.

She said 'feel fucked up' instead of 'be fucked up'. Maybe she didn't think he actually needed to be there. Maybe he was overreacting.

"I guess," he said.

"Why don't you tell me what's been going on?" she said.

He nodded. He could start with the facts. "I tried to get into porn," he said. "I went to this shoot, but it kind of went tits up. I guess I got assaulted." He looked at the ground instead of looking at her. "I'm bi—I just figured that out, or accepted it or whatever. My dad killed himself about two weeks ago. It might have been because I came out." He felt ridiculous, confessing these things to a stranger.

"That's certainly a lot to deal with," she said.

Aaron nodded again. "I guess I'm here because I don't feel things. Or, I mean, I feel things but I can't really touch the feeling. I don't want to touch it." He huffed. "So the obvious answer is to just feel the feeling and stop being afraid of it." He shook his head and stood. "I'm sorry, I'm wasting your time. I know I need to nut up and deal with my shit."

Ava held up a hand. "Hold your horses," she said. "You've paid me for an hour, so even if we sit here and say nothing, you're not wasting my time. If you want to leave, that's up to you, but it just means I get an early lunch break."

Aaron chewed on his lower lip. Hesitantly, he returned to his seat.

Ava smiled at him.

"I don't really know what to do," said Aaron.

"We can just talk," said Ava. "Or we can sit here quietly. I have music if you want to listen to something."

"I should talk," said Aaron. It was the whole reason for the appointment.

"But?" asked Ava.

"But I don't really want to," he answered. "Like, yeah, a lot of crap has happened lately but I'm sick of thinking about it."

"We don't have to talk about the bad stuff," said Ava. "We can discuss anything you want."

Aaron knew exactly what he wanted to talk about, but again it felt like a waste of time.

Ava waited patiently for him to make a decision.

"What if I just want to talk about dumb stuff?" he asked.

"It's your appointment," she answered. "We can talk about anything."

"I've got a date tonight," said Aaron. "What if I want to talk about that?"

"Sounds good," said Ava. "Let's talk about it."

"It's a date with a guy."

Ava nodded and seemed to be waiting for the rest of the story. She wasn't taking notes at the moment. She wasn't writing down that Aaron liked men and that was the source of his problems.

"He kind of saved me," continued Aaron. "I was—I couldn't move and—" He couldn't finish that sentence. "The point is, there was this other guy and he was—um—attacking me—and Silas stopped him. His name is Silas, by the way." He felt heat rising in his cheeks.

"And Silas is the man you're going out with tonight?" asked Ava.

"Yeah," answered Aaron. He couldn't give more details without telling her personal and potentially incriminating information about Silas. "I was living with my dad, but he kicked me out. I stayed with Silas for a while, then we kind of moved in with my uncle. Not my real uncle. He's an old friend of my dad's. His name's Jack."

There were too many things to tell her. He needed to start from the beginning. He knew he wasn't making sense.

"Are you two still living with Jack?" she asked.

"No," answered Aaron, pulling away from his thoughts. "Silas moved back to his place. We're starting over since we met under weird circumstances."

Ava nodded and Aaron kept babbling. Thirty minutes later, he was feeling less like an idiot and a little more comfortable. He told her he was taking Silas to the natural history museum, since he seemed to like dinosaurs. After that, he'd made dinner reservations. He told her he was nervous and that he'd never been out with a man before. He confessed that the museum was about forty minutes out of town but the restaurant was local and he was worried people he knew would see him.

He knew it was wrong to be afraid, and he told her being afraid felt like he was betraying Silas. He wanted to be brave. Silas deserved someone brave.

Ava was kind and understanding without being overly saccharine. By the end of the session, he'd cried once but managed to keep himself together. This was a safe place to be weak. No one was at risk if he broke down or couldn't handle himself.

Her office was built for blood. It was a place where strangers came to rid themselves of problems and leave the mess behind. He wondered if Ava got to leave her problems behind as well, or if they followed her home?

She waited for him to dry his eyes and blink away the evidence of his tears before she walked him back to the waiting room. She hugged him gently and spoke quietly before letting him go.

"I hope to see you again," she said.

Aaron couldn't commit to coming back, so he just nodded and gave her a half smile. He wasn't fixed, but he did feel better. He made another appointment for the following week, just in case he decided to return.

* * * *

Aaron stood in front of Silas' door. He ran his hands along the front of his button-down shirt and hoped he looked respectable. He knocked.

Silas answered the door immediately. He was wearing a full suit. His hair was a mess and his face was bright red. "I bought flowers," he said quickly.

"For what?"

"I have no idea." Silas disappeared behind the door and returned with a dozen roses wrapped in brown paper. "They were for you," he said. "You mentioned buying flowers the other day, but then I realized you were probably making a joke, but I bought them anyway. I don't know why. I suppose they're still for you."

Aaron took the flowers and suppressed a laugh. Silas sighed and ran a hand through his hair. "Come on, Romeo," said Aaron. He took Silas' hand and led him to the car. Silas being nervous made Aaron weirdly calm. He opened the car door and grinned as his date settled inside.

"Am I overdressed?" asked Silas.

"I don't know," answered Aaron. He backed out of the driveway and set a course for the museum. "Am I overdressed?"

"No," answered Silas. "You look very nice."

"So do you," said Aaron.

Silas fidgeted with his tie.

"Dude," said Aaron. He grabbed the other man's hand and squeezed it. "Relax. It's me."

Silas almost smiled. "Right," he said. "Where are we going?"

"It's a surprise," answered Aaron. "It's kind of lame, but it's still a surprise. I made a dinner reservation for later."

"You made a reservation?"

"Yeah."

For some reason, that made Silas blush harder.

"Did you miss me this morning?" asked Aaron.

"Yes," answered Silas. After a moment, he frowned. "Are we pretending like we don't know each other or are we just continuing our narrative?"

Aaron laughed. "I'm up for whichever option will make you relax."

"Sorry," muttered Silas.

Aaron cleared his throat. "So, where are you from?"

"New York. Where are you from?"

"Here. What do you like to do for fun?"

Silas looked at him before the realization dawned. "Oh," he said, sitting up a little taller. "I am training for my black belt."

"That's pretty cool," said Aaron. "Is that job related, or just for kicks and giggles?"

Silas pursed his lips. "It's a hobby, but I suppose it could be beneficial to my line of work."

"Where do you work?"

"Home," answered Silas, then he shrugged. "I can work anywhere. I sell illicit narcotics."

"Wait, really?" asked Aaron, breaking character. He should have guessed, but it was still surprising.

"Yes," answered Silas. "Are we still pretending we don't know each other?"

"No," answered Aaron. "I legitimately didn't know that about you."

Silas finally smiled. "Tell me something I don't know about you."

"Daniel and I got lost in the woods for a couple hours when we were in elementary school."

"Why?"

"Daniel thought he saw Bigfoot," answered Aaron. "Dad had just given us these crappy little slingshots and we thought we could hunt it down and trap it."

Silas snorted.

"Your turn," said Aaron. "Tell me something else about you."

"I don't know how to swim."

"How is that possible?" asked Aaron. "You're a grown-ass man."

Silas shrugged. "I never wanted to learn."

Aaron shook his head. "I'm going to teach you," he said. Without realizing it, he'd planned their third date. Silas had suggested they switch off date-planning to keep either of them from feeling too much pressure.

They continued swapping tidbits of information until Aaron pulled into the museum parking lot.

Silas' face lit up. "I love this place," he said.

"Yeah? I've never been, but I thought it might be fun."

"You've never been here?" Silas was already out of the car. The door shutting muffled the rest of his sentence.

Aaron hurried to follow him into the building. He barely beat his date to the front desk. Silas made a quiet noise of protest when Aaron paid for their admission.

"You get the next one," said Aaron. "This date is mine."

"Fine," muttered Silas. He pointed to a corner where a group was forming. "Do you want to do the official tour or the unofficial tour?"

"Which one is better?"

"I'm not sure if one is better than the other," he mused. "But the official tour guide is that nice woman over there and the unofficial tour guide is me."

"Unofficial it is," said Aaron. "Lead the way."

Without hesitating, Silas grabbed his hand and pulled him toward the first exhibit. He was explaining something about eons, but Aaron was suddenly very distracted by their entwined fingers.

"There is a larger graphic of the geologic time scale down the hall," said Silas. "It's much easier to read." At the next exhibit, Silas released his hand and began pointing to different parts of a large mural. "We're in the Cenozoic era," he said.

Aaron listened until Silas took his hand again and pulled him to the next exhibit. He asked questions and made comments to prove he was paying attention, but he couldn't ignore the fact that he was out in public with his very obvious and very oblivious boyfriend.

Silas made sure they saw everything and led Aaron through the exhibits in chronological order, only skipping the T-rex statue because he wanted to "save the best for last".

They stayed in close contact for the entire two hours it took to explore the museum. Aaron let Silas lead him around and every time Silas grabbed his hand, his heart beat a little faster. He didn't drop his guard. At any moment someone could decide to pick a fight or endanger the moment of normalcy. Aaron kept silent watch, prepared to defend them on the off chance someone posed a threat.

By the time they reached the T-rex, Aaron realized how willing he was to fight for the man enthusiastically pointing out the size of the dinosaur's head.

"New evidence suggests the tyrannosaurus had feathers," said Silas.

"Like bird feathers?"

Silas nodded and launched into an explanation. Aaron grinned, and for a moment the other people disappeared and it was just the two of them in the room.

They left the museum and Aaron was in a daze. Silas owned him. During the drive back, Silas continued to babble, talking more than Aaron had ever heard him talk before. With every word Aaron fell a little more in love.

At the restaurant, Aaron made a point to take Silas' hand again, daring anyone to challenge their relationship. He caught a few raised eyebrows, but no one said anything.

Silas nudged his shoulder as they followed the waitress to their table. "You don't need to worry," he said.

"I'm not worried," said Aaron.

"Your vise-like grip on my hand says otherwise."

"Sorry."

They took their seats and placed drink orders. When the waitress left, Silas leaned forward to speak quietly across the table. "No matter what happens," he said, "I've had a wonderful time with you."

"That's cryptic," said Aaron.

"I know, but I thought it should be said. It's not that I think something bad is going to happen. I just want you to know I don't regret anything and that I enjoy my time with you."

Aaron tried to snuff out his automatic sense of impending doom and just appreciate what Silas was saying.

"Of course, I wish we'd met under different circumstances," added Silas.

"Yeah, but you made a hell of an impression," said Aaron. "On me and those other assholes."

"About that..." said Silas.

The waitress returned with their drinks. She said she'd be back to take their orders. Aaron waited for her to leave. "About what?" he asked.

"It just so happens Farley and his associates were also drug trafficking," said Silas. "They were arrested last week and are being held without bail."

Aaron almost choked on his drink. "Seriously?" he asked.

"Yes," answered Silas. "There is some bad news, but I'm reluctant to bring it up during our date."

"Out with it," said Aaron.

"As far as I can tell, they haven't arrested Ralph. I saw an article about it this morning. Police are searching for someone who fits his description but they haven't released a name."

"That's great news," said Aaron.

Silas tilted his head.

"I didn't expect any of them to do time. I just accepted they'd joined the world's free-roaming herd of douchebags. I can't believe they got—" He frowned, catching himself before crediting some karmic force. "You didn't have anything to do with them getting caught, did you?"

"Not at all."

Aaron crossed his arms over his chest. "Was it Jack?"

Silas stared at him and very deliberately shook his head. "No."

"You're a terrible liar," said Aaron. "Why do you even try to lie to me? I can tell when you're bluffing. What did Jack do?"

Silas shrugged. "I don't know anything for sure," he said. "He asked where he could obtain Schedule I drugs. I gave him some names, then Farley and his nefarious cohorts just happened to get caught with the same drugs Jack was searching for."

"That sneaky bastard," muttered Aaron.

"It's possible he intervened."

"Yeah, you think?" Aaron ran a hand through his hair and wondered how far Jack's vigilante streak went.

"The waitress will be back soon," said Silas. "We should decide what to order."

Aaron agreed. He quickly decided on some gourmet dish that sounded suspiciously like a cheeseburger. Silas ordered pasta. The waitress returned and took their orders, and Aaron went back to questioning his boyfriend.

"What exactly did you sell Jack?" he asked.

"I didn't sell him anything," said Silas. "I simply provided him with information. He specifically said he didn't want to buy anything from me."

"Probably to keep your hands as clean as possible. What else did he say?"

"He told me not to ask any questions, so I didn't."

Aaron put his face in his hands. "Oh my God," he muttered. "He set them up."

Silas shushed him. "I don't think we're supposed to know that and I'm positive we aren't supposed to say anything."

"How long ago did he ask you?"

"A few weeks."

"And you didn't tell me?"

"There was nothing to tell until now," said Silas.

"Does Daniel know?"

"I doubt it."

"Is Ralph missing or is he *missing*?"

Silas tilted his head to the side. "What are you implying?"

Aaron leaned closer. "Do you think the cops can't find him because he took off, or do you think Jack's holding him in a shed somewhere?"

"Oh," answered Silas. He shrugged. "You know him better than I do. Is he capable of holding someone hostage?"

Aaron frowned. "I legitimately don't know the answer to that."

"I don't think we should worry about it either way."

"Then why'd you say it was 'bad news' that he hasn't been caught yet?"

"Because he's a terrible person and he should be locked away somewhere," answered Silas. "He doesn't deserve to be free."

"Jesus," muttered Aaron.

"It didn't occur to me that Jack could have 'taken care' of him."

"I'll ask him," said Aaron.

"He won't tell you, and he shouldn't. You don't need to know." Silas cleared his throat. "On a different subject, when can I schedule our next date?"

Aaron raised an eyebrow. "Real smooth."

"Or we can continue to discuss crimes your uncle may or may not have committed."

Aaron rolled his eyes. "I'm free whenever," he said. "Tomorrow?"

"Yeah. Isn't that kind of soon after this date? Aren't we supposed to wait?"

Silas huffed. "Aaron, I don't know where you get your rules for dating and relationships, but I really don't care what we are 'supposed to do'. I know what I want to do. Do you know what you want to do?"

Aaron thought for a moment. "Yeah," he answered.

"Do you want to go out again tomorrow or do you want to wait?"

"Tomorrow. Do you already have a plan?"

"Yes."

"What is it?"

"I'm not going to tell you," said Silas. "You didn't tell me, so that seems fair. But there's no need to dress up."

"You gonna buy me flowers again?" teased Aaron.

Silas blushed and covered his face with his hands. "I panicked."

Aaron grinned. They talked through dinner and dessert. Aaron took Silas home and awkwardly walked him to his door. He kissed Silas on the cheek, dropped his keys and nearly tripped going back to the car. Silas was still giggling when he backed out of the driveway.

When he got home, he set the flowers on the kitchen table then retreated to his room. To their credit, Daniel and Jack didn't press him for details.

He woke up before anyone else the next morning. He told himself it was because he'd gone to bed early, not because he already missed Silas. Bleary-eyed, he wandered into the kitchen to find the flowers from last night neatly arranged in a vase in the center of the table.

Chapter Twenty-Five

Second Date

Aaron carried two car batteries back to the garage. His current project was almost finished. It wasn't pretty or exciting—an old Toyota with body damage and dead or dying parts under the hood—but it kept his hands busy.

He set the batteries on the ground near the car and searched for the multimeter. He could have sworn he left it on the hood.

Silas was due to arrive in about an hour. Aaron should have been taking a shower and scrubbing oil stains from his hands instead of crawling around the garage searching for gadgets. He hadn't slept much last night. There was a knot in his stomach and he had to actively remind himself he was going to do something he enjoyed. He wanted to see Silas. Silas was his boyfriend. Aaron had a boyfriend.

He flinched as phantom pain struck the center of his back. He had to sit down.

He crawled into the back seat of the Toyota. The air inside was heavy and stale. He lay down across the seats, knees scrunched up against the door. Everything hurt. His body was exhausted and sleep-starved. His hands started shaking, a reaction that didn't surprise him anymore. He clenched his fists and waited for the feeling to pass. It didn't help. He needed to get ready. Silas couldn't see him like this again.

He'd done so well yesterday. He had been strong yesterday — a little paranoid, but overall he had been good and Silas had had fun and no one had had to take care of him.

No, that wasn't true. He'd talked to Ava yesterday, spread his sickness to an innocent stranger. But he'd paid her for her trouble. It was part of her job. It had been an honest transaction.

He forced himself to inhale and exhale. He needed to at least take a shower, clear his head.

He spent the next half hour on autopilot. Daniel was out with friends and Jack was working late at the shop. There was no one around to witness Aaron's vacant stare or the few panicked seconds when he came back to himself.

When he finally managed to settle back into his body, he was dressed and pacing in front of the door. A car pulled up and he wondered if it would seem overeager to go outside. He decided he didn't care. He opened the door then froze like he'd never seen another human before.

Silas approached him instead of waiting for Aaron to go to the car. He examined Aaron and, when he got closer, reached out to brush damp hair from his forehead. His brow furrowed. "Good to know I'm not the only one with control problems," he said.

"What?"

"You were in charge yesterday and I was somewhat terrified. I'm in charge today and you — well, you don't seem comfortable."

Without thinking, Aaron grabbed Silas by the hand and pulled him into the house. He kicked the door closed behind them and pulled him into a kiss. He felt fear, panic and shame, but he also felt how warm Silas' body was against him. He felt the way Silas' hands gripped at his shirt, the way his tongue licked at his lips and his heart beat through his chest and into Aaron's.

They stumbled backward until Silas was pinned between Aaron and the wall. Silas wrapped a hand around the back of Aaron's neck then threaded his fingers in his hair and pulled him closer. His other hand settled on Aaron's chest over his heart.

Aaron pulled back to gasp for air and Silas quickly released his grip. His mind was racing and a thousand voices were screaming at him. Instead of listening, he looked into the wide, blue eyes staring back at him.

He leaned in again and gently pressed his lips to Silas'. He had no explanation for himself. Silas ran his fingers through Aaron's hair, touched his cheek and hummed softly. Aaron wondered what life would be like when Silas was gone.

"I hate to ruin the moment," said Silas. "But your brother is due to return shortly."

"How do you know?"

Silas smirked. "He may or may not have been my accomplice for the better part of the afternoon."

"Why?"

"I needed insider information." He frowned, glanced down at Aaron's lips, then paused before leaning to kiss him quickly. "Come on," he said. "We're sort of on a schedule."

Aaron followed Silas to the car and failed to nag any information out of him. When they pulled into the driveway of Silas' house, Aaron raised an eyebrow and waited for an explanation. Silas remained tight-lipped. He followed him into the house, feeling as if he was missing something obvious.

Halfway through the living room, Silas stopped and suddenly seemed nervous. "I had an idea of how I would present this to you, but now it seems somewhat idiotic," he said.

"I'm up for idiotic ideas," said Aaron.

"Would you mind—um—would you close your eyes and follow me?"

Aaron closed his eyes. "I don't really get why I need to. I mean, I know where we are."

Silas took his hands and led him carefully through the house. Aaron knew they'd entered the kitchen when the feel of the floor changed from carpet to tile.

"Wait here," said Silas. "And don't peek. Please."

Aaron waited and moments later Silas returned. He slipped something soft over Aaron's head and it hung around his neck. Then something tugged on either side of his waist and Aaron realized Silas was tying an apron around him. He grinned, thoroughly entertained by Silas' specific brand of weird.

"All right," said Silas. "Open your eyes."

Aaron opened his eyes and confirmed his own suspicions. They were in the kitchen and he was wearing an apron. Silas was beet red and chewing on his lower lip. The table was set and two unlit candles had been placed in the center.

"I thought you could teach me to cook," said Silas. "I bought steaks. Daniel said that's your favorite thing to cook."

Aaron glanced at the stove. A familiar-looking cast-iron skillet was sitting beside it.

"Daniel brought it over here before we went shopping," said Silas.

"Shopping?" asked Aaron, still putting the pieces together.

"Yes," he answered. "I wanted to make sure I got everything right." He eyed Aaron and shifted his weight nervously. "This is stupid. It seemed like a better idea in my head."

"This is awesome," said Aaron. He went to the refrigerator to see what Silas and his brother had purchased. "What are we having for sides?"

Silas approached and pointed to the counter. "We got baking potatoes and snow peas and carrots. Daniel said that's what you usually make."

"Did you guys get honey?"

"Yes."

"Chives?"

"Yes."

"Unsalted butter?"

"Yes," said Silas. "We double-checked to make sure it was unsalted. Is that the right brand? We weren't sure. We also weren't sure about the steaks. We had to enlist the help of someone from the meat counter."

Everything was right. Of course it was right. It was perfect. Aaron closed the refrigerator and turned to Silas, mouth open but suddenly at a loss for words. Silas had spent the entire day hanging out with his little brother. Daniel liked Silas enough to keep it a secret. They must have planned it together. The skillet was Jack's, so he was probably in on it as well. Silas wasn't just trying to win over Aaron—he was winning over his whole damn family.

"Your expression is making me nervous," said Silas. "Is this good or bad?"

"Does Jack know you took his pan?" asked Aaron.

"Of course," answered Silas. "He volunteered it." He tilted his head, probably still waiting for Aaron to elaborate. "I paid for everything — if you're wondering. I only took Daniel with me as a consultant." He shifted his feet again. "You don't have to cook, if you don't want to. I just — I find it very — um — well, frankly it's a very 'sexy' quality." His cheeks somehow turned redder.

Aaron grinned. He crossed the kitchen and pulled Silas into his arms, still unable to find the right words for the moment.

"So this is a good thing?" asked Silas, nuzzling against Aaron's neck.

"It's a very good thing," answered Aaron. He cupped Silas' cheek and kissed him.

Silas relaxed in his arms. When they broke apart, his cheeks were light pink and he was smiling.

'I love you' buzzed on the tip of Aaron's tongue. He kissed Silas' cheek to keep himself from saying it. For some inexplicable reason, all he wanted to do was hold on to the other man, keep him close, feel the rise and fall of his chest, touch him, taste him.

The muscles in his chest clenched around his heart and he had to keep himself from pushing Silas away. Aaron wanted this and that wasn't a bad thing.

"Screw cooking," mumbled Silas. "Let's just stay here and do this."

Aaron laughed. "We can do this after we cook," he said. "Come on, I'm going to teach you how to use the stove without starting a fire."

While Aaron prepared the meal, Silas more or less impeded the process. Aaron found himself either distracting Silas or being distracted by Silas. He'd changed the dynamic when he'd pinned Silas against the wall earlier. There was less tension between them and more 'accidental' touches. At one point, while he was watching Aaron sauté the vegetables, Silas wrapped an arm around his waist and absentmindedly created patterns against Aaron's shirt with his fingertips. Later, while he stood behind Silas and showed him how to ladle butter onto the meat, Aaron leaned down and kissed his neck. Silas became so flustered he nearly dropped the spoon.

It was strange, interacting with another man without the threat of consequence. He didn't flinch when Silas touched him, but he didn't relax either. Silas' house was a sanctuary, but the world outside was cruel and predatory. It lay in wait for now, but one day it would pass judgment and one day there would be repercussions for their stolen peace.

* * * *

After dinner, Silas revealed a second surprise in the form of a cake from a local bakery Aaron hadn't even known existed.

"Daniel said of all desserts, you love cake the most," said Silas, "And of all cakes, you love chocolate the most."

"Daniel's right," said Aaron. They sat side by side on the couch. When he leaned over to kiss Silas, he tasted like butter and sweet, dark chocolate. He kissed him again to quell another urge to confess his feelings.

Love, as it turned out, was a persistent and impatient emotion.

After dessert, Aaron insisted on cleaning up the kitchen. Silas helped, but only to speed the process along, and spent most of the time declaring the room clean when it clearly wasn't.

With nothing left to distract them, Silas pulled Aaron back to the couch. They picked a movie, then curled together, quiet and content. As the movie progressed, they slid into a more relaxed position with Aaron settled against Silas' chest. He didn't want to be comfortable tucked into Silas' arms, but he was.

First he scolded himself for taking the woman's position, then he scolded himself for comparing their relationship to something it wasn't. He reminded himself he wasn't dirty and what they were doing wasn't something shameful.

His thoughts stopped spiraling when Silas pressed a kiss to the top of his head and began running his fingers through Aaron's hair. His eyelids fluttered and he lost himself in the sound of Silas' heartbeat.

"Will you stay with me tonight?" asked Silas.

"Yeah," answered Aaron.

"Good," said Silas. "You are welcome to use anything here you need."

Aaron had a bag packed — technically a go-bag, but it was tucked away in the trunk of the car. He'd packed it after settling in at Jack's. He never wanted to be caught without a backup plan again.

"Aaron," said Silas, a subtle hesitation in his tone.

"Yeah?"

"I may have overstepped."

Aaron craned his head back to look up at Silas. "What'd you do?"

"Technically Daniel did it, but I was complicit in the plan."

"Out with it."

"He—I made you a drawer."

Aaron sat up and turned to face Silas. "A drawer?"

Silas shifted in his seat. "Yes. Daniel stole a few of your things and I bought a few things and now you have a drawer. Well, technically two drawers, one in the bathroom and one in my room."

Aaron couldn't explain why his initial reaction wasn't something joyful. He couldn't explain why his throat closed and his mind went blank. He loved Silas. He wanted to stay with him. He wanted to curl up beside him every night and wake up to him every morning. He was beyond thrilled that Daniel approved. He was relieved Silas wanted him as much as he wanted Silas. He should be happy.

Instead, the news of two drawers sent a jolt of adrenaline through his veins. He stood.

"Is that—was that wrong?" asked Silas. "I don't mean to pressure you or anything. I suppose I got carried away."

"It's okay," said Aaron.

"It clearly isn't."

"I need to think about this for a second."

Silas stood too. "I didn't mean anything by it. I just wanted to be prepared. I thought since Daniel approved—"

"Quit blaming Daniel," snapped Aaron.

"I'm not blaming anyone," said Silas, brow furrowed. "I didn't realize this was such an offense that it constituted blame."

Aaron shook his head. This was it. This was where Silas would see how truly broken Aaron was. This was the moment Silas would regret caring about him. This was the end because Aaron was damaged, unstable and unreliable.

"Talk to me," said Silas. "I was more or less joking when I said I'd overstepped. I didn't think this would actually be a problem. Please tell me what went wrong."

"I need to get some air," said Aaron. "Don't follow me." He went to the door, but Silas blocked him.

"Don't leave like this," he said.

"I'm not leaving, I just need some air."

"Bullshit. You're going to walk out that door and you're going to run."

That was exactly what he was going to do. "Move, Silas," he said.

"No."

"I don't want to fight with you. Let me go."

"We're already fighting," said Silas. He crossed his arms over his chest and glared. "I think I deserve to know what we're fighting about."

"I don't know," snapped Aaron. "I'm crazy. I don't have a reason. You and Daniel put some of my stuff over here. Cool. No big deal. Good for you guys."

"Are you mad because we took your things?"

"No. Just let me out of this fucking house. I need some air."

"You're going to run."

"So you're going to force me to stay here?"

Silas rubbed his temples. "Fine," he spat, stepping aside. "Leave."

Aaron brushed past him without another word. He kept walking, mind blank and body numb. An hour later, he wasn't any closer to figuring out why he was so angry.

At some point, he'd turned around and begun walking back to the house. He wasn't sure if it was intentional or by accident, but he didn't change course. When he got back, there was an unfamiliar car in the driveway. As he approached the house, he heard a woman's voice.

The sound was muffled. Aaron crept to a side window. Dark shadows hid him from neighborhood onlookers and he could clearly hear the people talking inside.

"Fuck him," said the woman. "You didn't do anything wrong."

"I need to look for him," said Silas. "I should have called his brother."

"You're not his keeper," she said. "I don't care how broken he is, he's not your responsibility. He's a big boy. He can fend for himself."

"He's had a fucked-up life."

"So have you. You got your shit together. You figured it out."

"He doesn't have the same resources I have."

"He's got a brother and an uncle, right? And they both love him?"

"Yes, very much."

"Then fuck him. That's more than we ever had. You can't save the world, Silas. Just because you've had a little bit of good luck doesn't mean you have to be a saint and take on every charity case that comes your way."

"He's not a charity case," growled Silas.

"Then why the fuck are you trying to rehabilitate him?"

"I'm not."

"Then what are you doing?"

"I enjoy his company and I want to help him."

The woman was quiet for a moment. Aaron risked stretching taller to peer into the window. Silas was pacing. The woman was standing across the room with her feet firmly planted. She had light brown hair, blue eyes and a scowl that must have been hereditary. Aaron had seen it many times on Silas, once on Max and now on the woman. She had to be Sara. Aaron ducked back down.

She said something, but it was too quiet for him to make out. The exchange continued at a low volume for about a minute, then Silas must have said something to ignite her rage.

"He's not Joshua," she shouted. "Joshua is dead and there's nothing we can do about it. Saving him won't bring our brother back."

"Fuck you," shouted Silas. His voice shook and Aaron couldn't remember hearing him use that tone before. "Not everything I do is because of Joshua."

"You shot your commanding officer because he called somebody a fag," snapped Sara.

"I was high."

"Because of Joshua."

"No, because I like being high."

Aaron risked looking in the window again. They weren't facing him and he was partially concealed by the curtain.

Sara threw her hands up. "What the fuck, Silas? What are you doing? You're dealing again. You're using again. You fucking whipped your gun out again. You moved in with another crazy asshole and didn't even tell me."

"It's not like that."

"Then what is this? It sounds like Aaron needs professional help. You've got enough on your plate."

"I love him," said Silas.

"Do you? Or do you love feeling like you're useful to him?"

At that Silas crumpled back onto the couch, his face hidden in his hands.

Sara knelt on the floor in front of him. "Let him go," she said. "He's just another David. Neither of them meant to be assholes, but they're too broken to stand without a crutch. People like that will use you as long as they can. They'll use anybody."

"Aaron is different."

"He's not," said Sara. She pulled Silas' hands away from his face and held them in her own.

"You are the kindest, most honest, loyal person I've ever known. You have a grace about you and people gravitate to it. That's not your fault, but you do need to set boundaries."

"I love him," said Silas again.

"Does he love you?"

"I think so."

"Then why did he lose his shit over a damn dresser drawer? Why is he dragging his feet with your relationship? Why did he try to kick you out of his uncle's house?"

"He's afraid."

"He's *guilty*."

Silas didn't answer. He closed his eyes and pulled his hands away from Sara.

She stood and sat next to him on the couch. "I won't let anyone else hurt you," she said, wrapping her arms around him. "Fuck the world. It's cold and lonely and people are assholes, but we're strong. You can count on me and I can count on you."

Silas nodded.

Aaron backed away from the window. He crept from Silas' house without looking back. His mind was quiet except for the echo of Sara's words. She'd stripped him, seen the nastiest parts of him without even meeting him in person. He was needy and selfish. It was a shameful secret he thought only Robert had known. He'd been wrong. If Sara saw it, maybe everyone else did, too. Maybe Jack and Daniel were blind. Maybe he'd tricked them, convinced them he was something good. Or maybe they knew and pitied him.

He walked until his feet hurt, but by then he was too close to Jack's to justify calling someone to pick him up. He reached the house and quietly went inside. It was late and everyone else was asleep. He went to his room and got into bed without bothering to change.

Chapter Twenty-Six

Out Loud

Aaron sat at the table in the kitchen with his arms crossed over his chest. They'd lured him in with bacon and pancakes then trapped him with the very conversation he wanted to avoid.

Silas had texted Daniel last night. He'd told him he and Aaron had had a fight and that Aaron had left. He'd apparently been checking to make sure Aaron got home safely.

"You don't have to tell us what the fight was about," said Jack, "but you've got to give me something. Did you walk all the way back here?"

"I got a cab," lied Aaron. He didn't need to lie. He was a fucking adult, but Jack was overcompensating for years of missed parenting opportunities and he'd probably find fault with Aaron wandering across town at night.

"You should have called me," said Daniel.

"It was late," said Aaron.

"Did he do something to hurt you?" asked Jack. "Just say the word and I'll take care of it."

Daniel raised an eyebrow at him. "Did you find your drawer?" he asked.

"I don't want to talk about it, Danny."

"I knew it," said Daniel.

"What?" asked Jack.

"I was being helpful," said Daniel. "I took some of his stuff over to Silas' because I knew he'd be too stubborn to do it himself."

Jack looked between the two of them. "Is that what your fight was about?"

"No," answered Aaron. "Kind of. I wasn't mad about it. I'm glad you guys are bonding, but I wasn't immediately thrilled and Silas took it the wrong way, then I got pissed and it just went to hell from there. I can't tell you what the fight was about because I honestly don't know."

Jack sighed. "Okay. At least that's a start. First things first." He jabbed a finger at Daniel. "Don't meddle with your brother's relationship."

"I'm being supportive," said Daniel.

"I don't care," said Jack. "Don't do it."

"Silas asked for my help."

"With *dinner*," said Aaron.

"You're a smart boy," said Jack, still eyeing Daniel. "You know the difference between helping and meddling. This is a delicate kind of thing we're dealing with."

"I'm not delicate," snapped Aaron.

"I didn't say you were," said Jack.

Aaron pushed away from the table and stood.

"Oh hell no," said Jack. "You can run from Silas, but you can't run from us. Something's got you in a twist and I want to know what it is."

"I'll save it for therapy," spat Aaron. Jack ran a hand over his face.

"Why are you being such a jerk?" asked Daniel

"Why are you being such an ass?" asked Aaron.

"Both of you sit down," said Jack. "Now." He glared until they relented and took seats at the table. "Daniel, behave."

"But they love each other and Aaron's being dumb about it," said Daniel.

"Well fuck you very much," said Aaron.

"Knock it off," said Jack. "You're not mad at each other."

"He's mad at me," said Daniel.

"He's not," said Jack. "He can huff and puff all he wants, but I got news for you — Aaron's never really mad at you. He's mad at Silas. Their fight isn't our business, but I want to make sure Silas didn't cross a line. You can shut up or you can leave. Take your pick."

"I'll shut up," muttered Daniel.

"I'm not mad at you," grumbled Aaron.

Daniel huffed, but true to his word, he didn't say anything.

"Aaron," said Jack. "Did Silas hurt you?"

"No."

"Do I need to kick his ass?"

"No," he answered.

"Did you feel unsafe at any point?"

Aaron rolled his eyes. "It was just the stupid drawer. I swear."

"Okay," said Jack, nodding slowly. "Second thing, then. You can't fall off the radar. Check in with me or Daniel — actually, that goes for everybody at this table. Nobody goes off the radar. I check in with you two and you two check in with each other or me."

"I didn't go off the radar," said Aaron. "I came home."

"We didn't know that until Daniel checked your room. You don't want to talk to Silas, fine. But don't run away and not keep us in the loop. Family gets to stay one step ahead of everybody else."

"Yeah, okay," muttered Aaron.

Jack turned to Daniel. "Fine by me," he said.

"Okay," said Jack. "Problem sort of solved."

"Can I go work on the car?" asked Aaron.

Jack sighed. "Go ahead."

Aaron hurried away from the table and retreated to the garage. He managed to savor a half hour of solitude before Daniel invaded.

His brother leaned against the side of the car, arms folded and clearly pouting.

"Hand me that wrench," said Aaron.

"He loves you," said Daniel.

Aaron huffed and grabbed the wrench himself.

"And you love him," said Daniel. "And he wants you to move in with him. He said you're not sure if that's 'right', whatever that fucking means."

Aaron slammed the hood shut with more force than necessary. "Jack told you not to meddle."

"Fuck that," said Daniel. "You're my brother. I know you best and I know when you're being dumb."

Aaron bit his tongue. Daniel was trying to help. He didn't know everything, but he knew Aaron.

"After all the shit you guys have been through, a drawer crosses the line? Seriously?"

"It's not about that," said Aaron.

"Then enlighten me. What's it about?"

"I don't know."

"Are you scared?"

Aaron glared at him. "You're on thin ice."

"I don't care. You deserve to be happy. Silas makes you happy."

"For now," said Aaron.

"What's that mean?"

Aaron shook his head. "Nothing."

"Dude, I'm trying to be—"

"Supportive, I know. Thanks. I get it. But I don't need it."

"You hurt his feelings."

Aaron threw his hands in the air. "Are you two best friends now or something?"

"I thought being his friend would make it easier for you. You know? Like, so you know I approve and stuff."

"Well maybe he hurt my feelings," snapped Aaron.

"Did he?" asked Daniel. "Because I'll kill him. I'm bigger than he is."

"No," muttered Aaron. "I hurt him." Sara was the one who had ripped the truth from Aaron's chest and presented it to Silas. Daniel didn't need to know that. No one needed to know that.

"So apologize."

"It's not—I can't—it's not that easy."

"Yeah, it is. Just say you're sorry for being an ass. You have commitment issues, but you know Silas wasn't trying to freak you out—he was just doing what I told him to."

Aaron sighed. "Yeah, you're right."

"Call him."

"Danny."

"What? What are you waiting for?"

"I need some time."

Daniel rolled his eyes. "Look, I'm sorry. You guys had a good thing and I fucked it up and I want to fix it."

"It's not your fault," said Aaron.

"Feels like my fault."

"I swear it's not."

"It was my idea to take your stuff over. He didn't even know until I showed up with a bag. But that's a thing people do, isn't it? Isn't that normal couple stuff?"

"It's not your fault," said Aaron again.

Daniel ducked his head. "I'm sorry."

"Look," began Aaron. "I'm glad you like Silas. I know we've got a weird kind of 'damsel in distress' kind of story, but we're not a permanent thing. You don't need to worry about supporting me or us or whatever. This is my first big gay thing, and I'm happy as hell you don't judge me, but don't get invested. We're not looking at forever."

"Oh," said Daniel. He looked down at his feet.

"I'm sorry to disappoint you," said Aaron. He wasn't sure how much of what he'd said was true and how much was a bluff to distract Daniel.

"That's okay," said Daniel. "As long as you know what you're doing."

"I do," said Aaron. He decided it was half true. Whatever he had with Silas wasn't going to last, especially not now that Silas knew what Aaron really was. It was pointless to get invested, pointless to keep their things at each other's homes. It would only make things messier in the end.

"Then I'm sorry for meddling."

"Don't worry about it. You didn't know."

"How do I treat him?" asked Daniel. "Are we mad at him?"

"No," answered Aaron. "You can treat him like you always have. It's just—he's not a big deal, okay?"

"Okay," answered Daniel.

"Okay," echoed Aaron.

Daniel kicked at the dust on the floor. "I'll let you get back to your car. Thanks for looping me in."

"Thanks for giving a shit," said Aaron.

Daniel returned to the house and Aaron focused on his project, mind blissfully quiet.

* * * *

A week went by without contact. Aaron found himself in Ava's office again. When she smiled and asked if he was all right, he cracked.

He told her about the fight, that he'd come back and heard Sara explaining to Silas what he would never have been able to see on his own. He told Ava he was relieved because at least Silas knew the truth and Aaron didn't have to pretend anymore. Finally, someone had said the truth and exposed Aaron for the fraud he was.

Ava listened quietly, through the rambling confessions. When Aaron was finished, she only had a few questions.

"You've never met Sara, right?" she asked.

"Right," answered Aaron.

"She only knows about you through her brother, Silas?"

"Yeah."

"Why do you believe this person, who is essentially a stranger, knows you better than anyone else? How does she know you better than your family? Or better than your boyfriend?"

"She's not invested in me. I—" He licked his lips, trying to find the best way to explain. "I've never met her, so I haven't been able to trick her, so what she says is honest."

"Do you think you tricked your family into thinking some way about you that isn't true?"

"They think I'm better than I am."

"Jack and Daniel, right?" she asked. "What about your father? What did he think?"

Aaron scowled and sat back against his chair. Ava didn't know everything, but she knew enough. He'd babbled enough for her to know how Robert had seen him.

"Do you think it's possible," asked Ava slowly, "that you are looking for a critical voice to replace the one you lost? To replace your father?"

"I don't know," muttered Aaron. "I guess."

"Do you think you're giving Sara's words priority because it sounds like something your father would say?"

Aaron closed his eyes. His throat was too tight to talk, so he just nodded.

"Why do you think Sara would say those things about someone she doesn't know and has never met?" asked Ava.

Aaron stared down at the floor. "Because she loves Silas," he answered.

"So," continued Ava, "what do you think her goal was when she was talking to her brother?"

"I don't know."

"What would your goal be if you were talking to your brother about a fight he had with a significant other?"

"Make him feel better."

"Could that be what Sara was doing?"

Aaron looked up. Of course that was what Sara had been doing. She didn't know Aaron. She wasn't psychic. She'd just known Silas was hurt and Aaron was the one who'd hurt him, therefore Aaron was bad.

"I'm so fucked up," he muttered.

"It's all right to be fucked up," said Ava.

"I've got to talk to Silas. He probably thinks I hate him."

"That sounds like a good plan, if it's what you want."

"It is," said Aaron. "Fuck. I should talk to Sara, too. Silas has been so nice. He's friends with my brother now, probably because he knows how much Daniel means to me."

"Do what makes you happy," said Ava. "And stop punishing yourself when you feel happy. You've been conditioned to think it's wrong that you feel good."

Aaron snorted. "Dad would get suspicious if I was too happy. He always thought it meant I'd met some guy or something."

Ava made a note on her paper.

"If I came home from work or from just hanging out, if he wasn't one hundred percent sure where I'd been and I came home looking a little too happy, he'd beat the shit out of me until he got an answer he liked."

Aaron ran a hand through his hair. "He'd wait until Daniel was asleep or gone or whatever, then just lay into me. He'd do it if he saw me crying too — thought it meant I was turning gay or something."

Ava scribbled something else on her paper. She looked at Aaron and something fiery and honest flickered across her face. "How old were you?" she asked. "How long did he treat you that way?"

"High school," answered Aaron. "I told you he saw me kiss that kid and got mad? He didn't just get mad. He cracked two of my fucking ribs. He took me home and dragged me out into the backyard and beat the shit out of me. He got me a few times in the face, but he wised up a few swings in. Then he stuck to my back and my stomach. Sometimes he'd use his belt."

"Aaron," breathed Ava. "I'm so sorry that happened."

"He took me to the doctor that first time," said Aaron. "He'd always been pretty rough with me. He was a son of a bitch when he was drunk. But that time — I guess he wasn't sure how bad he'd hurt me. I wouldn't stand up without help. We went to the ER. Danny was staying late at school. I think he was in a computer club or something. He didn't know."

Aaron licked his lips and took a breath. He'd relived that day so many times, but he'd never heard himself say it out loud. "We told the doctor I got into a fight at school. I had a busted lip and my eye was pretty swollen. Of course, we didn't tell anybody what the doctor said or how bad it was. We told Daniel I got hurt during gym. We didn't see Jack until my face was healed. I think Dad knew he'd ask too many questions."

"I can't imagine what that was like," said Ava.

"It's over now," said Aaron. He wiped his eyes and took a steady breath. "I don't think I want to talk any more today."

"All right," said Ava. "Thank you for sharing that with me. Will I see you again next week?"

"Probably," answered Aaron.

Ava made another note on her paper. She stood and hugged Aaron, squeezing him a little tighter than last time. "I look forward to our next appointment," she said.

She walked him to the front desk with one hand on his back, between his shoulder blades. She told the receptionist to schedule him for one week out.

Aaron left and went back to his car feeling a little lighter. He drummed his fingers on the steering wheel. Silas made him happy. Maybe that was all he needed to know.

Chapter Twenty-Seven

Take Two

Aaron stood on the porch, a clumsily wrapped package held in front of him as both an offering and a shield. He hit the doorbell with his elbow and waited.

Silas didn't make him wait long. Footsteps approached the door, paused, then the knob turned and there he was. His eyes moved from Aaron to the gift he was holding. He stepped back and let Aaron enter the house. "Nice of you to show up," he said.

"This is for you," said Aaron, offering the package. "I know I've been radio silent for a week and I just now realized that was probably torturing you, so I figured you deserved something."

"I need to ask you something," said Silas.

"I'll answer honestly," said Aaron.

"Do you want to be with me or are you just here because you think you owe me something?"

"I want to be with you," answered Aaron. "This past week was fucking awful. I missed you. I thought about you so much I forgot how to change the oil on the goddamn car. I had to look it up. I went to therapy today and all I did was talk about you. Granted, that's what I did last time, too. Point is, I want you. I want to be with you and I want you to open this stupid present." He held the gift out.

Silas accepted it. "You talk about me in therapy?" he asked.

Aaron rubbed the back of his neck. "Yeah. It's nothing bad," he said quickly. "I just— I don't know. I guess I like talking about you. You're always on my mind, so it's hard not to talk about you."

"You're always on my mind as well," said Silas. He blinked and looked down at the gift in his hands.

He was crying. Aaron had made him cry. Silas wiped his eyes and began tearing the paper away.

Aaron had emptied a drawer from the dresser in his room. He'd made a quick adjustment to it and wrapped it.

When Silas had unwrapped it, he stared at it quietly.

"It's got a secret compartment," said Aaron. He'd added a false bottom with a short leather strap to pull it out. He'd bought an eighth of weed and hidden it in the drawer. "If you pull this," said Aaron, "this panel pops up and you can hide your stuff." He pointed to the baggie. "I thought I'd get you started."

Silas looked up, tears still in his eyes. "You bought weed?"

"Yeah. One of the guys from Jack's shop is stoned pretty much 24/7," explained Aaron. "I got it from him."

Silas looked back down at the drawer.

"It's from the dresser in my room," said Aaron. "I— um—it's yours. Not to keep here. I figured we could put stuff in it here and I'd take it back." He licked his lips, mouth suddenly very dry. "I'm so sorry, Silas. I shouldn't have freaked out like that and I shouldn't have kept you waiting."

Silas set his present on the table by the door and Aaron suddenly found himself wrapped tightly in his arms.

"I'm sorry," Aaron said again.

"I forgive you," said Silas. "And if you don't want to have your things here—"

"No, I do," said Aaron. "That's why I got you a drawer. I want this. I want this so much. I want you. This is a real thing and I don't want to fuck it up." He deliberately left out eavesdropping on the conversation with Sara. It wasn't her fault he'd run and Silas didn't need to know every tiny detail.

"I don't know what I'm doing," said Silas. "Relationships are not my forte."

Aaron threaded his fingers through Silas' hair. "That goes double for me, but I'm willing to figure it out."

Silas nuzzled closer. "For what it's worth, I tried to return your things, but Daniel refused to take them back and I didn't want to go to Jack's uninvited."

"That fucking kid," muttered Aaron. "I guess he approves."

"Good," said Silas. He tilted his head back and looked up. "I missed you."

"I missed you too," said Aaron. He cupped his cheek and pressed a tentative kiss to his lips. "Want to show me the stuff Daniel stole?"

"Yes," answered Silas. "Want to help me pick out things to take back with you?"

"Hell yeah," answered Aaron.

* * * *

Later that night, Aaron shot off a text letting Daniel know he'd be staying with Silas.

Daniel responded with *Yeah, you are!* which Silas thought was hilarious.

They went to bed shortly after packing items for Silas' new drawer.

Aaron stretched against the sheets then rolled onto his side to pull Silas closer. They lay face to face in the dark sanctuary of the bedroom, and Aaron remembered the first time he'd finally felt safe.

"I'm really sorry," said Aaron.

"Stop apologizing," said Silas. "You came back. That's all I care about."

He was warm and solid and real in Aaron's arms. Even in the darkness, he was beautiful. "I want to give you more," said Aaron quietly. "You deserve more."

"Baby steps."

"I want to eventually—um"—Aaron cleared his throat—"to—you know. I want to do more, too."

"Do more what? Dates? I assumed those would continue."

"No, not just dates. The other stuff. Sex stuff." Aaron stumbled over the last word and kicked himself for being such a teenager about it.

"Oh," said Silas. "That can wait, of course."

Aaron tracked the glimmer of Silas' eyes in the darkness. He licked his lips and brushed a lock of hair from the other man's forehead. He'd tried to contain his desire until it simmered down to something less overwhelming, but the longer he tried to control it, the hotter it burned. He wanted Silas and the need to have him was terrifyingly close to the surface.

"I want to try," said Aaron. A shiver ran through him the moment the words left his mouth. He licked his lips again.

"Um, when?" he asked.

At least Aaron wasn't the only one consumed by nerves. They were pressed against each other, sharing heat through thin pajamas. The more Aaron thought about their closeness, the more his stomach fluttered.

Silas took Aaron's hand and brought it to his lips. He placed a gentle kiss against his fingers. "You're trembling," he said.

"Yeah," breathed Aaron.

"You must know I don't expect anything," said Silas. "If you never want to do more than this, I would still be very happy."

Heat trickled into Aaron's stomach and he burned. "I want more," he said. "Is that okay with you?"

Silas nodded. "But we should take it slow."

"Yeah," agreed Aaron, his eyes locked on Silas. "Slow is good." He didn't have to move far to make their lips meet. He pushed a little closer. Emboldened, he placed a hand on Silas' hip and slowly slid his fingers beneath his T-shirt.

Silas inhaled sharply and wrapped an arm around Aaron's waist. They were chest to chest, together in bed. Aaron tried not to think and instead trust what he wanted.

He kissed the edge of Silas' lips then made his way down to his neck. He sucked at the soft skin and Silas moaned. Aaron went with his instincts. He pushed Silas onto his back and straddled his hips. He let his hand slide all the way up Silas' shirt, touching as much skin as he could. With his other hand he cradled Silas' cheek, holding him in place as he continued to lick his neck.

Silas moaned again. His hand found Aaron's thighs and he gripped him hard.

Still pushing the boundaries, Aaron rocked his hips downward. Silas shivered beneath him. He did it again, thrusting with a little more force. The sensation was everything he needed. He pressed his forehead against Silas' and breathed heavily as he lowered his body. Silas dug his fingers into Aaron's back and they slowly began rocking together.

Silas brushed the hair from Aaron's face. "Are you all right?"

"Yeah," breathed Aaron. He kissed him and thrust down again.

Silas craned his neck and trailed a line of kisses down Aaron's neck. Silas held him close as they pumped their hips against each other. The angle wasn't quite right and their clothes didn't provide the same kind of friction as skin-to-skin contact, but when Aaron felt Silas' erection rub against his own, his breath hitched and heat pooled low in his stomach.

He buried his face into the crook of Silas' neck, biting back the sound desperately trying to escape him.

Silas kissed his cheek and breathed against his ear. "I've got you," he whispered. "You're safe."

Aaron took a sharp breath and thrust against him harder. Silas held him tighter to his chest. Aaron's hips stuttered as he came. Silas arched off of the bed and gasped as his orgasm followed.

Aaron kept his face pressed into Silas, panting, delirious. They dry-humped like virgins. It was sweaty, messy and undignified, but it was what he wanted.

Desire chased away his perpetual thoughts of shame, but as the pleasure faded, the thoughts crept back.

Silas didn't push him away. He turned his face to nuzzle against Aaron's neck and began stroking his back. "That was," panted Silas, "my God, that was hot."

Aaron snapped out of his dismal spiral and laughed. "I can't believe we dry-humped," he said, mumbling into Silas' skin. He raised his head. "For the record, I can do better. Next time will be better."

Silas took Aaron's face into his hands and looked up at him, suddenly very serious. "That was the best—I don't know…" He scowled. "I enjoyed that very much. It was a big step for you—for us—and it was good. Accept the fact that it was good."

"Okay," he muttered. "I guess it was pretty good."

Silas kissed him again. "Let's get cleaned up," he said. "Then we can come back here and never leave this bed ever again."

They took turns in the bathroom. Aaron was tempted to suggest they strip down and rinse off together, but the proposal was anchored somewhere in his gut and he couldn't make himself say the words. The thought of *more, more, more* pounded in his head, keeping rhythm with his heart.

When he got back into bed, Silas quickly curled up behind him and pressed his lips to the back of Aaron's neck. He wrapped Aaron in his arms and made a contented little sigh.

"This might be the best I've ever felt," said Silas.

Aaron laughed. "Then you're pretty easy to please."

Silas squeezed him against his chest. "Maybe you're just exceptionally pleasing."

Aaron huffed.

"Why are you so tense?" asked Silas.

"I'm not," answered Aaron. He tried to relax and realized Silas was right—he was tense.

"You're relaxed now, but you were tense a moment ago."

"Sorry. Knee-jerk reaction."

"To?"

Aaron thought for a moment. It was most likely because he wasn't in the dominant position. Silas had hold of him and Aaron couldn't see him. However, despite his instinct, it felt nice to be held, to surrender and know the other person wasn't going to inflict damage.

"Are you all right?" asked Silas.

Aaron felt him pull away. He looked over his shoulder and saw Silas propped up on his elbow, waiting for an answer. "I'm not used to, um, cuddling like this I guess."

"I can move," offered Silas.

"No," said Aaron. "I like it. Do you like it?"

Silas nodded. "Very much," he said. "I like knowing you're safe."

Aaron snorted and rolled his eyes. "I keep forgetting you're my white knight."

Silas settled back down and nuzzled against him. "I just want to make sure you're protected—and I like having someone to hold on to."

Aaron rolled over in Silas' arms. "You need to be protected, too," he said. "I'll watch your back and you can watch mine."

"One might say we're a little paranoid," said Silas.

"One can kiss my ass," said Aaron. He kissed Silas for the millionth time that night. They fell asleep wrapped in each other's arms.

Chapter Twenty-Eight

Goodbye Party

A week went by. Daniel was leaving soon and Aaron was trying to figure out how to prepare to say goodbye. Jack swore up and down nothing would change, but that couldn't be true. Daniel was leaving. He was going to live hours away, a *plane ticket* away.

Daniel promised he'd call and he'd showed Aaron how to video chat on his phone, but it wasn't the same. Everything was going to change. He wouldn't see Daniel again until Thanksgiving. Months. It would be *months* until they saw each other again.

Aaron sat on the floor in the living room waiting for Jack to return. They were throwing a surprise party for Daniel and Aaron had accidentally volunteered to take over planning and decorating. Jack was in charge of distracting Daniel for the afternoon. Guests would arrive in a few hours.

Aaron blew up another balloon and sent it wafting into the pile with the others.

"Is this even?" asked Silas. He was standing on a chair trying to hang up a 'Congratulations Daniel' sign.

"Looks good," answered Aaron.

Silas hopped off the chair and sat beside him. He leaned in and planted a loud kiss on Aaron's neck. Aaron shoved him away.

Silas leaned in again slowly. He aimed for Aaron's ear this time. He was close enough that Aaron could feel this breath against his skin. "You have," whispered Silas, "entirely too many balloons."

Aaron pursed his lips to keep from grinning. Silas was getting bolder with intimacy, more confident in testing Aaron's boundaries. Aaron was surprised to find that so far, he didn't have any boundaries.

Silas inched closer so they were sitting hip to hip. His breath was soft against Aaron's neck.

"Make yourself useful," said Aaron. "Start hanging these." He blew up another balloon. "Put them over the door or something."

Silas' lips pressed just below Aaron's jaw and he licked at the skin. "Can you be more specific?" he asked.

"You are useless," muttered Aaron.

Silas hummed and began sucking gently at Aaron's collarbone. They never got further than eager make-out sessions. Silas kept a seemingly calculated amount of space between them and Aaron wasn't sure how to get them back to awkward grinding and groping.

He suspected Silas was being overly respectful. Then again, maybe Silas didn't want more. Aaron didn't know how to broach the subject. Thinking about it made it difficult to enjoy what they were doing, and he couldn't figure out how to talk about it without killing the mood.

He wrapped his hand around Silas' waist. After a moment of internal debate, he slipped his hand carefully beneath the hem of Silas' shirt. A chill ran through him as his fingers made contact with bare skin. They had plenty of time before anyone arrived.

"Hey," muttered Aaron. He jerked his head back toward his bedroom.

Silas blinked at him.

"You want to — um…" He gulped down the rest of his words. He clenched his jaw and stood, pulling Silas up with him. Neither of them said a word as Aaron led them back to the bedroom.

Aaron shut the door, then pushed Silas onto the bed. He licked his lips and sat straddling his lap. Silas was transfixed, taking in his every move, and Aaron got a little brave. He pulled his shirt over his head. Silas swallowed hard and looked back and forth between Aaron's chest and his eyes.

Aaron wasn't sure if the expression he was seeing was one of lust or terror. Silas finally seemed to snap back to himself and he whipped his shirt over his head.

"What are we doing?" asked Silas. His eyes were still scanning Aaron's body. He cautiously moved his arms to encircle Aaron's waist.

Aaron leaned forward and licked at Silas' lips then kissed him slowly. Silas was already hard and his fingers twitched against Aaron's back.

"I want to try something new," whispered Aaron. He eased Silas down onto the mattress and moved his hips in a slow circle.

"You don't," began Silas. He licked his lips and tried again. "You don't have to do anything." Aaron nipped at his neck.

He placed a hand on Silas' chest.

Silas' eyes fluttered. He ran his fingertips gently over Aaron's back.

Aaron kissed his way down Silas' neck to his collarbone, then to his chest. Silas' hips bucked slightly, so Aaron let his teeth graze over the sensitive skin. Aaron turned his attention to the other side of his chest, nipping and sucking as he went. He moved his hand carefully down Silas' body and paused between his thighs. Silas bucked again and Aaron decided that was a signal. He palmed Silas' erection, rubbing it slowly through his jeans.

"Aaron," breathed Silas.

He looked up, but Silas didn't appear to be talking to him. His head was thrown back as he arched against the mattress.

Aaron grinned. At least teasing and foreplay were more or less the same between genders. He'd always been good at this part. It was the next part that scared him. He tried to go by what he enjoyed and what women had done to him in the past.

He breathed against Silas' skin as he kissed down his chest to the top of his jeans. He slid from the bed and knelt between Silas' legs. Aaron nibbled again at his hips and began undoing the top button.

Silas shot up, mouth hanging open.

Aaron looked up at him through his lashes and grinned again as he undid the zipper. He pressed his mouth to Silas' boxers and tongued at his cock. He undid his own jeans and let them slide down his thighs. He pulled his shorts down and began stroking himself. He didn't expect the sensation to be quite so intense. He closed his eyes and brought his free hand up to Silas' pelvis.

He caressed Silas through his boxers, groaning slightly when his own euphoria grew in intensity. He finally took pity on Silas and tugged his boxers down.

Silas propped himself up on his elbows as Aaron freed him. Silas gasped and Aaron felt the muscles in his stomach clench. He bobbed his head slowly, trying to gauge how far he could go.

Something hit the mattress with a thud. Aaron looked up and saw Silas was flat on his back with an almost white-knuckle grip on the sheets. His skin was covered in a thin layer of sweat, and when Aaron licked the underside of his cock, Silas arched against the bed.

Aaron gripped himself a little tighter and stroked a little faster. He timed his mouth and hand so he and Silas were sharing the same rhythm.

"Aaron," whimpered Silas. "I'm close."

With his free hand, he dug his nails into Silas' thigh and sucked harder. Silas came in his mouth with a muffled cry and Aaron followed right behind him.

"Oh my God," panted Silas.

Aaron kissed his hips and the light red marks he'd left on Silas' thigh.

Silas propped himself up again. "I want," he said between breaths, "to blow you."

Aaron laughed.

"I'm serious," said Silas. "It's all I can think about right now."

"Sorry," said Aaron, still snickering. "I've got to recharge." He stood up and Silas held out a hand. When Aaron took it, Silas tugged him onto the bed.

"You are amazing," said Silas.

Aaron laughed again and rolled onto his back. Silas took the opportunity to kiss him and curl against his chest.

"Was that — that was because you wanted to, right?" asked Silas.

"Yeah," answered Aaron. "I've been wanting to for a while."

"Teach me how to do it. I want to do that to you."

Aaron just laughed harder.

"I have no idea why you find that so amusing."

"I don't know," said Aaron. "You're so blunt about it."

"I prefer to be direct."

"Yeah, I picked up on that."

Silas hummed against his skin. "That was incredible. I've never felt anything like that before."

"How is that possible?" asked Aaron. "What about porn? Didn't you get off?"

"Yes, but not like that." Silas sighed. "I was exceptionally terrible at that job. I didn't get along with my troglodyte co-workers and, according to Farley, I asked too many questions. Apparently, 'do we have a business license?' was an inappropriate inquiry."

Aaron snorted. "I still can't wrap my head around the fact that you worked with those people."

"I was stupid. I thought it was easy money. I didn't account for moral quandaries or obsessive STD testing."

Aaron blushed. STDs hadn't even occurred to him. He was clean, but he hadn't thought to ask Silas. He'd just assumed.

"I'm disease-free, by the way," said Silas.

Aaron felt a knot in his throat as more questions bubbled up within him. What had Silas done while he worked with Farley? Had he slept with Ralph or Regina? Why was he a Dom? Did he tie people up? Was Aaron the first person he'd saved? Why hadn't they talked about this before?

"Uh-oh," said Silas. He propped himself up and hovered over Aaron. "Where'd you go?"

"Um, what?" asked Aaron.

"You disengaged. What happened?"

"I don't know."

"Yes, you do," said Silas. "Talk to me. What happened? Did I say something?"

"No," answered Aaron. "I guess I spaced out for a second."

Silas sighed again and his head dropped to Aaron's shoulder.

Aaron clenched his jaw. They'd had a good day. He didn't want to ruin it. "I guess I was thinking about how we—I—don't talk about sex that much. I was thinking maybe we should talk about it more."

"I agree," said Silas, lifting his head. He looked down at Aaron, clearly waiting for more.

"I'm clean, too," said Aaron. "STD-wise, I mean."

"I assumed you were," said Silas. "Thank you for telling me."

Aaron chewed on his lip. "Silas, I want to talk about this, I swear I do, but I've got to take it slow."

Silas lowered himself back onto Aaron's chest. He threaded his fingers in Aaron's hair and kissed his neck. "I understand," he said.

"You deserve to know what I'm thinking, though," said Aaron. "And I'm not thinking anything bad, I swear. It's hard to put into words." He sighed and ran a hand over his face. "Fuck me."

"Take your time," said Silas. "I know you'll tell me when you're ready. It doesn't have to be today."

It didn't *have* to happen right then, but Aaron *wanted* it to happen. He needed to nut the fuck up and talk. His face felt like it was burning. "I want to talk about porn," he said quickly.

Silas sat up again.

"You and porn," said Aaron. "Like, what happened? What did you do? Did anybody else get hurt and stuff? Did you get hurt? Did you fuck anybody? Did they fuck you? How did you get into Dom/sub stuff? Was I the first one? Did you save other people? I've got to know. Maybe it's not really important. I didn't know I wanted to know, but I guess I do. Surprise." He stopped rambling and caught his breath.

"I'm sorry," said Silas. "I should have addressed this much earlier." He kissed Aaron's forehead. "Farley wanted someone with experience in dominating others. I lied and said I could do it. I was on the receiving end of oral sex on two occasions and I gave one man a hand job. I started a scene with a woman and another with a man, but Farley didn't like what I was doing."

Silas brushed his thumb over Aaron's cheek. "I didn't engage with Ralph, Regina or Farley. No one hurt me and I didn't see them assault anyone else. That doesn't mean it didn't happen. I doubt you were the first. All the more reason to lock them away."

Aaron searched Silas' eyes. "That's it?" he asked.

"That's it."

Aaron reminded himself to breathe.

Silas frowned and suddenly looked worried. "Does that information change anything?"

"No," answered Aaron quickly. He didn't know what to do with the answers, but he knew felt better. "Thank you, I— Fuck. I don't know what I'm doing." He closed his eyes. He was going to cry if he let himself go any further. He struggled to regain control. He knew better. He knew not to let himself disconnect. He wasn't all right and this was only the tip of the iceberg of his current problems. If he kept going, the whole damn thing would come to the surface and rip him apart.

He couldn't think about sex because it made him think about porn, which made him think about Ralph, then Robert, then losing Daniel — and he was going to lose Daniel again, but this time Daniel wanted to go. Aaron clenched his jaw again.

"Breathe with me," murmured Silas. He gently pulled Aaron into a sitting position. Instead of sitting across from him as he usually did, Silas crawled behind him and sat with his chest pressed to Aaron's back. He placed one hand over Aaron's heart and his other hand on Aaron's shoulder.

Aaron automatically started counting. He felt Silas smile against his shoulder, felt his body relax and the panic subside.

"You're safe," whispered Silas. "We're throwing a party today and it's going to be so much fun." A party to celebrate the fact that Daniel was leaving. Aaron pushed the thought away and exhaled.

"Fun," he echoed.

Silas kissed his neck. "We're going to stay up too late, maybe drink too much, then fall asleep beside each other."

"I can get behind that plan," said Aaron.

"We're going to wake up together and hope Jack has enough coffee to cure our hangovers."

Aaron grinned. "He does."

Silas kissed him again.

Aaron gave himself another minute to come back to normal. "We should finish decorating," he said.

"I'll try not to distract you," said Silas.

"I don't think you can help yourself," said Aaron.

They put their clothes back on and cleaned up before returning to the living room. Silas was only marginally less distracting. Aaron was grateful. It kept him from thinking about saying goodbye.

* * * *

Liam brought enough pizza to feed an army. Aaron pulled the cake from the fridge and set it in the middle of the table. Balloons were everywhere. He'd overestimated and they ended up leaving a pile of inflated balloons on the floor to kick around.

Aaron did a quick head count to make sure everyone was present. Friends and co-workers parked around the back of the house so Daniel would be surprised. He tried not to think about the fact that most of the people there had also been at Robert's memorial. He tried not to compare saying goodbye to his brother to saying goodbye to his father.

When he heard Jack's truck pull into the yard, he signaled for everyone to hide. They crowded into the hall to wait. Silas took his hand. Aaron couldn't remember if they'd held hands in front of everyone at Robert's service. He couldn't remember if everyone knew.

Silas squeezed his hand and Aaron squeezed back.

Jack was the first one through the door. As soon as Daniel was inside, Aaron flipped the lights on and leaped out.

About thirty people yelled "Surprise!" at once and Daniel jumped back.

Aaron clapped his brother on the back and congratulated him, then let friends move in to talk to Daniel.

As the evening went on, Aaron found excuses to keep himself busy. He picked up trash, set out more drinks, checked on Daniel. By the end of the night, he'd run out of tasks. He snuck out of the house and told himself he wasn't hiding. Daniel was the only person in the world with the power to trigger every emotion Aaron tried to bury. The outburst with Silas hadn't been coincidence—it was just the first thing to surface.

He'd begun to sulk when Daniel found him.

"You know," said Daniel, "at first I thought you were actually busy, but now I kind of think you're avoiding me on purpose."

"I'm not avoiding you," said Aaron.

Daniel leaned against the railing across from him. "It's insulting when you think you can lie to me."

"I'm not lying," said Aaron.

"Can we skip the part where you're in denial? I want to get straight to the point."

Aaron crossed his arms over his chest. "Go for it," he said.

"Don't be a dick," said Daniel. "I got you a present, but I need to say something first."

"What'd you get me?"

"I need to say something first," repeated Daniel. "Can you listen?"

"Fine," said Aaron, fighting the urge to roll his eyes.

"I'm going to Stanford," he said slowly. "I'm going to be all the way across the country. We've never been that far apart for that long and it's going to suck."

Aaron stared at the ground. He wasn't ready for this. Daniel was pulling everything up at once, everything he'd worked so hard to bury.

"This year has sucked hard. I think this has been our shittiest year since Mom died. I don't remember her dying, so this my shittiest year ever."

"It's been my shittiest year, too," said Aaron quietly.

"I talked to Jack about it and he agrees," continued Daniel. "I can't deal with more shit right now, so I made a decision. And before you ask, yes, I'm sure. I've talked to Jack and my advisor and my new advisor and I'm absolutely sure I want to do this."

Aaron looked up.

"I've been accepted to the university here," said Daniel. "I can get my undergrad degree, then go to Stanford Law after I graduate. I'm going to take online courses from Stanford just to make sure I stay on their radar, but I'm going to school here. I'm staying with Jack. Campus is about twenty minutes away."

Aaron couldn't find the words. He wasn't sure what he wanted to say.

"That's your present," he said. "Me. Surprise, I guess. I hope you like it."

"Danny," said Aaron slowly. "You can't do that. What about your future? You can't do that just because of me."

"I'm not," said Daniel quickly. "I don't want to leave. I already thought I'd lost you once this year. Then Dad died. I still don't know how to feel about that and I know you probably don't either. I can't—I'm not ready. I can't leave." Daniel's voice cracked. "I know this wasn't the plan. I don't want you to think I'm slacking off or that I don't care about school. I do care. I just know that if I leave now, I won't be able to think about anything other than getting back home. I won't be able to do my best and I want to do my best. I hope you're not disappointed."

Aaron stood and pulled his little brother into a hug. "You've never disappointed me," he said. "I just want to make sure you're doing what makes you happy."

"I want to stay home," said Daniel. "Home makes me happy."

"Then fuck Stanford," said Aaron. "Stay the hell home."

"I was going to tell you earlier," said Daniel. "But Jack said I should surprise you."

"Best fucking surprise ever," said Aaron. "Do your friends know?"

Daniel shook his head. "I'm going to tell them tonight, but I wanted you to know first. You can go ahead and tell Silas, though."

It still hurt, because Daniel was still going to leave one day, but Aaron wasn't alone anymore. Daniel was hurt, too. They were together in everything, even pain.

"On a scale from one to someone totaled your car, how mad are you that I didn't tell you sooner?" asked Daniel.

"I am way too fucking relieved to be mad," said Aaron. "But holy shit, next time don't keep me in suspense."

"So," said Daniel, "to clarify, next time I know something big I should tell you ASAP."

"Yes," said Aaron.

"Even if Jack says we should surprise you?"

"Yeah. Screw surprises. I'll be surprised anyway. Just tell me."

Daniel grinned. "Good, then Jack owes me twenty bucks."

"Did you assholes bet on how pissed I'd be?"

"Yeah," answered Daniel. "Technically we tied. Jack bet you'd like the surprise and you wouldn't be mad. I bet you wouldn't like being left out of the loop and you'd be furious."

"We'll tell him I threw a fit and you talked me down. If keeping me in the dark was his dumbass idea, then he deserves to lose twenty bucks."

"I agree," said Daniel. He nodded to the front door. "You ready to actually join the party? Your boyfriend's been worried about you all night."

"He's always worried about me," said Aaron.

"We're all kind of worried about you," said Daniel. "Like I said, it's been a shitty year and you got the worst of it. I vote we go in and talk Jack into letting me have another beer."

"Lush," said Aaron.

They laughed and returned to the party together.

Chapter Twenty-Nine

Treading Water

Daniel and Aaron had learned to swim, fish, and paddle a boat in a lake about an hour north of town. It was quiet, comfortable, clean and the perfect place to spend the day.

Aaron took his shirt off and was rewarded with a dazed look from Silas. They had a blanket spread out near the shore and Aaron had packed lunch and drinks. The lake was quiet during this part of the day and they had the beach to themselves. Aaron left his shoes by the blanket and headed for the water.

"Come on," he called over his shoulder. He was knee-deep in the lake and he turned to see Silas still had his shirt on and had only made it to the edge of the water. "You can't swim in the dirt," said Aaron.

"Is it cold?" asked Silas.

"A little, but that's kind of the point, isn't it?" Aaron waded back to the shore and held his hand out. "Come on. I'll be gentle."

"I am a truly terrible swimmer," said Silas. "And I probably should have mentioned I have a slight tendency to panic when I'm in deep water."

"We're not going into deep water," said Aaron. He tugged on Silas' shirt.

Silas rolled his eyes, but allowed Aaron to pull the T-shirt over his head and toss it back to the blanket.

"Much better," said Aaron. He took Silas' hand and guided him into the lake. He stopped when the water was up to their waists.

"It's deep."

"It's not deep. We're halfway out of the water."

"It's cold."

Aaron sighed. He stepped back then submerged himself. He swam underwater and came up behind Silas. He made a bigger splash than was necessary and wrapped his arms around him.

Silas shivered. "You are a monster," he said.

Aaron planted a kiss behind his ear. "Get in the damn water. We'll splash around a little bit. I'll at least teach you how to tread water so you don't drown. Then we'll go back to your place and get nice and warm."

"How warm?"

"Super warm," said Aaron, kissing him again. "You'll be all hot and bothered by the time I'm done with you." He grazed his teeth over Silas' neck. Aaron took his arm and circled back to stand in front of him.

Silas' face was bright red. "It's very difficult to argue with you," he said.

Aaron tugged on his hand and crouched so that most of his body was submerged. After another gentle tug, Silas surrendered and sank into the water. "Look at that," said Aaron. "You're halfway there."

"That seems like an overstatement," said Silas.

"You're pretty cute when you're grumpy," said Aaron.

Silas blushed again and rolled his eyes.

"We'll work on your top half first," said Aaron. "Cup your hands and move your arms like this." He made a sort of sweeping gesture with his arm in the water.

Silas mimicked him. "Like this?"

"Yeah, but with a little less splashing. The goal is to keep yourself upright." He watched as Silas altered his movements. "That's better," he said. "You feel the resistance? Feel how you're pushing the water?"

"Kind of," answered Silas.

"Let's go out a little deeper. You'll feel more of a difference if we're standing."

"Yes," grumbled Silas, "let's go out deeper where it's more likely I'll die flailing around."

"You won't die," said Aaron, standing. He pulled Silas into his arms and swept him off his feet and out of the water. "If you start flailing, I'll carry you back to shore."

Silas wrapped his arms around Aaron's neck. "Are you sure you didn't bring me out here just to show off?"

"Not just to show off," said Aaron. "I also wanted an excuse to get you out of your clothes." He waded out a little deeper with Silas still in his arms.

Silas cleared his throat. "I should probably tell you that this is fulfilling many lifeguard fantasies I had when I was younger."

"Lifeguards," echoed Aaron. "That's good to know." Aaron couldn't remember many of his own fantasies. There had been a period of time when he'd been afraid Robert would know what he was thinking and be punished for it. Even if there weren't any fantasies to fulfill, Silas soothed an ache that had plagued him for as long as he could remember. Being around him just made sense. Silas had settled into his life so smoothly it was difficult to imagine the rest of his life without him.

"This is far enough," said Silas. "If we go any farther, I'll probably panic, and that would be terribly undignified."

Aaron lowered him back into the lake. The water was just up to his shoulders. "You feel all right here? You can touch the bottom and everything?"

Silas splashed him. "I'm not that much shorter than you."

Aaron glanced back at the shore to make sure they were still alone. "Okay," he said. "Come here." He spun Silas around and pressed against his back. He took Silas' hands in his again and slowly moved their arms through the water. "You feel that? Feel how you're pushing against the water?"

"Yes," answered Silas quietly. "I think so."

Aaron pressed a kiss to his shoulder and grinned. He was allowed to have fantasies now. He could imagine anything he wanted, and better still, all of his fantasies would probably be about Silas.

"At some point I'm supposed to move my legs, too, right?" asked Silas.

Aaron sighed against his neck. "Yeah."

Silas hummed and laced their fingers together, arms still moving slowly through the water.

"I am one lucky son of a bitch," said Aaron. He nuzzled into the other man's hair, lips pressed against his ear. "You're beautiful, Silas." Aaron felt him tense and he squeezed Aaron's fingers. Aaron wasn't sure what to make of that, but he didn't like the idea of Silas flinching at a compliment. "You're the kindest, smartest, strongest, most hard-headed person I've ever met."

That earned him a small snicker from the man slowly curling in on himself in Aaron's arms.

"You fought for me," said Aaron. "And I'll fight for you for the rest of my life."

Silas released Aaron's hands. "You don't owe me that," he said.

Aaron circled to stand in front of him. He chewed on his lower lip, bit down a little too hard and let himself feel the pain. He felt the sand under his feet, the water touching his skin, the sun beating down on his neck and shoulders. He felt Silas, shrinking in his arms, made sure to notice the way his tan skin felt beneath his fingers.

He breathed deeply and grounded himself in the moment. He wanted to remember this. "Silas," he said, voice shaking. "I love you. I am stupidly in love with you."

Silas looked at him wide-eyed, with his lips slightly parted, staring like he'd never seen another human before.

For a split second, Aaron felt panic creeping through him, but he quickly dismissed it. He didn't care if Silas didn't answer. He needed to say it and Silas needed to hear it. He curled his toes against the rough, sandy floor of the lake. *No regrets.*

Silas suddenly seemed to remember how to move again. He cupped Aaron's face in his hands and kissed him fiercely. Aaron lost himself the sensations—Silas' tongue licking against his lips then exploring his mouth, Silas' hands moving to tangle in his hair, his teeth scraping against Aaron's lower lip, their bare chests pressed together, the way Silas smelled like sex and home and freedom. Aaron breathed it in and surrendered.

Falling wasn't something to fear—it was exhilarating. Landing didn't hurt—it strengthened him. He tightened his hold around Silas' body, suddenly hungry for a way to be closer.

They broke apart just enough to catch their breath.

"I love you, too," whispered Silas. "I'm sorry. I should have led with that."

Aaron laughed. "Don't worry. I got the message."

Silas kissed him again.

They spent the next hour splashing and stealing touches and kisses. It was a miserable excuse for a swimming lesson. Aaron called it a day after Silas 'accidentally' groped his thigh for the fifth time. They packed the car and made it back to Silas' house in record time.

They made it as far as the living room before Aaron pinned Silas against the wall and began rolling his hips against him.

Silas panted into his skin. The journey to the bedroom was urgent and clumsy and Silas kept making noises that short-circuited Aaron's brain.

Moments later, their swimming trunks were on the floor. Aaron didn't have a plan and he wasn't letting himself think ahead. He made sure to feel everything, every inch of skin pressing and grinding against his body. He was on his back with Silas writhing on top of him.

"I love you," panted Silas.

"I love you, too," breathed Aaron.

Suddenly Silas pulled away from him, and just as suddenly something warm and wet wrapped around his aching erection. Aaron looked down just long enough to watch Silas swallow him. He fell back against the bed, unable to stop the sound that escaped him.

Silas made an obscene noise and dug his blunt nails into his thighs. Aaron wanted to watch, to take in and appreciate everything that was happening, but his muscles weren't responding to his mind. He was completely at the mercy of Silas and his tongue. His mind was slow to catch up with his libido and his thoughts trickled in one at a time. He wanted Silas to fuck him. He wanted, needed, to feel Silas inside him, needed to hear Silas gasp and feel their bodies twist and curve together. Aaron shivered and grabbed him by the arm, yanking him up so they were face to face.

Silas didn't miss a beat. He latched on to Aaron's neck.

Aaron whimpered and gasped again. He fumbled around, searching, trying to return the pleasure, but his arm was suddenly entirely too heavy. He closed his eyes. He wanted this. God help him, he wanted everything that was happening to him right now. He loved feeling Silas' weight pinning him to the bed. He loved the way Silas' long, slender fingers stroked his erection and tugged at his hair. He loved Silas' tongue and loved tasting himself in Silas' mouth. He loved that Silas was dragging this out.

He's creating a memory.

The realization hit Aaron slowly. Silas was savoring the moment, making it last. He was carving out a memory in their collective history and making sure this day would live with them forever.

Aaron grabbed Silas' face and kissed him hard and rough. He flipped them over and pinned both of Silas' arms over his head. Mouths still sealed, Aaron lowered his hips and began to thrust, deliberately taking his time.

Aaron needed this memory and he needed to be an active part of it. He needed to remember control as much as he needed to relish pleasure. He closed his eyes, working up the courage to vocalize what he was actually craving.

He needed to feel Silas inside of him, needed to erase the last memory he had of someone thrusting in and out of him. He couldn't let Ralph hold him hostage forever, couldn't continue to ignore the fear he felt whenever he lay face down on a bed, couldn't keep hiding from the shame of letting it happen.

"Aaron," panted Silas. "Open your eyes."

He hadn't realized he'd closed them.

"Look at me."

He stared down at Silas. He'd stopped rocking his hips and they were both very still. Silas carefully slipped his wrists from Aaron's grasp and began running his fingers up and down his back.

"Sorry," said Aaron.

"Are you sure you want—"

"Yes," growled Aaron, thrusting his hips again to underline his enthusiasm.

"Then I need you to stay with me," said Silas. "Keep your eyes on me. Stop thinking and just let your body feel. Most importantly, you need to talk to me and tell me what you want."

"I want you," said Aaron.

"I want you, too," answered Silas.

Aaron kissed him again. "I want you to fuck me."

Chapter Thirty

Fuck Me

Silas was lying on top of him with one hand cupping his cheek. He pressed his lips to every bit of skin within reach. Aaron was doing his best to clear his mind and keep his eyes on the man trying to help him relax. His feet were flat on the bed and his knees were bent. It wasn't the most practical position, but it made both of them more comfortable. It was easier to see each other this way.

Silas' free hand was slick with lube. He teased Aaron's entrance with the pad of his index finger. It took everything Aaron had to keep his breathing slow and steady, and when he felt himself tensing, he'd take a second to remember this was his idea and something he desperately wanted.

The pressure against his hole increased and he clung to Silas a little tighter. "Are you all right?"

"Yeah," answered Aaron. "Keep going."

Silas kissed him and slowly inserted his finger. He pressed deeper until Aaron was almost positive the entire finger was inside him.

"Tell me if something doesn't feel right," said Silas. "My knowledge is more theoretical than practical."

Aaron nodded, distracting himself with the way Silas' lips were still kiss-swollen and pink.

It burned a little at first and Aaron felt himself adjusting and stretching to accommodate the intrusion, but it was nothing like what he'd felt before. Silas wasn't going to ram another finger inside him before he was ready. He wasn't going to force Aaron to get hard then tease and beat him.

"Still all right?" asked Silas.

Aaron realized his eyes were closed. "Yeah," he croaked.

Silas tilted Aaron's head down so their faces were closer together. "Would it help to talk through it?" murmured Silas.

"No," answered Aaron. "Just keep doing what you're doing." He felt Silas' finger shift and bend slightly, then it pressed against a bundle of nerves and Aaron gasped.

"Good or bad?" asked Silas.

"Good," stammered Aaron. "Do it again."

Silas obliged.

Aaron could feel eyes on him. Silas moved his finger in and out, hitting Aaron's prostate on every other thrust. He wasn't sure when one finger became two, then three, but it didn't take long for him to start begging.

"I'm ready," he panted. "Please."

Silas kissed his way up Aaron's jaw to his lips. "You're sure?"

"Yes," moaned Aaron. "For the love of God, just fuck me already."

Aaron brought his knees toward his chest as Silas lined himself up with Aaron's entrance. It began with a slow, steady stretch. Silas placed a hand on Aaron's chest and Aaron grabbed it, squeezing as tight as he could. It wasn't going to hurt. He wasn't afraid. He wanted this. The more he told himself those, things the truer they seemed to become.

Silas pushed himself deeper. He started with long, slow thrusts. Aaron opened his legs so the other man could lean down closer to him. His pelvis began rocking on its own, an instinctual reaction to match Silas' pace. The burn from the intrusion quickly subsided and Silas pumped his hips faster. He dug his fingers into Aaron's skin and plunged deeper.

Aaron cried out, clawing at the bed. Silas was panting above him, rocking the entire bed as they moved together.

He was drunk. His body was behaving as pleasure dictated. He couldn't think, couldn't move, could barely process the different sensations hitting him at once. He felt lips press against his. He heard Silas whisper, "I love you," and heard himself reply. He felt Silas thrusting faster and faster until pleasure stopped coming in waves and became one long, overpowering flood.

Silas made a sinful, obscene sound. Aaron felt Silas' hips stutter. Suddenly, he was empty and Silas disappeared. He quickly replaced his cock with two fingers and began a merciless assault on Aaron's prostate. He pushed Aaron's hands away and swallowed his cock, sucking and licking until Aaron was a helpless, writhing mess.

He gasped and his vision went black. He came hard in Silas' mouth and the next few moments blurred together.

When he came back to himself, he was lying exhausted and weak in Silas' arms. Aaron tilted his head up and kissed him with all the energy he had left.

"Oh my God," panted Aaron.

"Did I do it right?" asked Silas. He was drenched in sweat and his hair stuck to his forehead.

Aaron stared at him, speechless.

"It felt good to me," he continued, blush rising in his cheeks. "Did it feel good for you?"

"Silas, that was suspiciously good," answered Aaron. "Like, I don't believe you've only fucked somebody once. That was — fuck — there aren't words. How did you — fuck — where did you learn that?"

Silas seemed to relax. "I've been doing a lot of research lately. There are some very useful instructional videos. Plus, I happen to have a slight advantage in that I'm very good with human anatomy."

Aaron kissed him again. "I can't feel my legs," he said. "Next time, I'm going to fuck you. You've got to know what that felt like."

Silas grinned. "I'm pretty sure I had an equally leg-numbing experience." He was absent-mindedly stroking Aaron's hair.

Aaron laughed and nuzzled against him. "I'm starving," he said. "Let's get cleaned up and I'll make us something to eat."

"No," groaned Silas. "I'm too comfortable."

Aaron wriggled free and tugged at Silas' arm. "Come on," he said. "We can get comfortable on the couch and watch another Jurassic-something movie."

"You still haven't seen the new one."

"There you go," said Aaron. "We'll get clean, get food, get comfortable and watch the new one."

Silas groaned again. "Fine, but only because you insist."

Apparently a post-sex, committed-relationship Silas had no concept of personal space. They cleaned up together, made food together, found the DVD together and got comfortable on the couch together. Through it all, Silas was either playing with Aaron's hand, kissing his neck, fussing with his hair or wrapping Aaron in his arms.

He stretched out on the couch to watch the movie. Aaron curled up on top of him with his head resting just under Silas' chin. He felt disgustingly domestic and completely satisfied. Silas fell asleep halfway through the movie and Aaron spent more time listening to his heartbeat than watching the screen.

* * * *

They went to the lake again after breakfast the next day and again they had the beach to themselves. This time Silas didn't hesitate. He went straight for the deeper water. He grinned and splashed around waiting for Aaron to join him.

"You are a giddy moron," said Aaron.

Silas splashed him. "So are you," he said. "You've been blushing since yesterday and I'm not sure I've ever seen you smile so much."

Aaron splashed him back. "I have not been blushing since yesterday."

"Yes, you have, and it's only endeared me to you more."

Aaron rubbed his cheeks, wondering if that could possibly be true. "Well, you've been blushing too," he said.

"I don't doubt it," said Silas. "The last time I felt this good, I passed out and had to have my stomach pumped."

Aaron's face fell. "Jesus Christ, Silas. What happened?"

"I've told you that story, haven't I?" asked Silas. "It was when I was living with David."

"You haven't told me anything about David," said Aaron. He couldn't remember what Silas had actually said to him versus what he'd overheard the night Sara had gone to the house.

Silas rubbed the back of his neck. "Ah, well, to be fair, it was one of the most embarrassing periods in my life and I'm not exactly proud of it."

"You've already witnessed a lot of my most embarrassing moments," said Aaron.

"There isn't much to tell, and honestly I don't remember most of it."

"But you remember overdosing?"

Silas sank lower in the water. "I wasn't at my healthiest."

"Who's David, what did he do to you, and do I need to kill him?"

"He didn't do anything. He wasn't well and I thought I could fix him—save him." Silas sighed. "It's an unremarkable story. I sold him some stuff. He kept coming back. I started supplying him for free because he lost his job. Then he moved in with me. It wasn't romantic, but I cared for him deeply."

Aaron couldn't help but log the similarities between this story and his own.

Silas shrugged. "In retrospect, we brought out the worst in each other. I came home one night, and he had acquired some new drug I'd never heard of and offered to share. I wanted to impress him, so I accepted without question. His tolerance was obviously much higher than mine. I remember thinking air tasted blue and that I could fly." He glanced up at Aaron. "I'd like to say I wholeheartedly regret it, but in all honesty, I was blissfully happy."

Aaron raised an eyebrow. "But?"

"But I blacked out and woke up in the hospital alone."

"Where was David?"

Silas scrunched his nose. "I'm not entirely sure what happened. From what I pieced together, I must have been unresponsive long enough that he panicked. I think he called 911, gave them my address then ran. In his defen—"

"What the fuck do you mean he ran? He *left* you?"

"I think so. I talked to the EMTs who found me. They said I was alone, but I really don't remember much."

"That little bitch. You could have died!"

"He was a very broken person."

"No, fuck that guy. He almost killed you."

"Aaron."

"Did he try to see you again? Does he know if you're all right? You helped him out and he fucked you over. Where does he live? Does he live here?"

"It was years ago. I lived on the coast. I didn't hear from him again and, to be fair, I never tried to contact him either."

"Good fucking riddance. I hope that fucker is rotting in a crack house."

"I knew what I was getting myself into. I told myself I'd treat him like a patient, but I didn't."

Aaron took Silas' face in his hands. "Fuck. That. Guy. You could have died. He betrayed you."

Silas sighed. "I was mad at him at first," he said. "Being angry was exhausting. It took me a long time, but now I recognize the relationship for what it was and I'm really not upset about it anymore. It was a good lesson to learn, both about myself and other people."

Aaron shook his head. "No fucking wonder your family thinks I'm a sketchy asshole."

Silas laughed. "My family hasn't exactly trusted my judgment since that incident. They've *never* really trusted my judgment."

"I can't believe you almost died," said Aaron.

"I would have died very happy," said Silas. "Whatever he gave me was extremely effective."

Aaron kissed him, if only because he wasn't sure what to say. Wishing David dead didn't feel good enough. Holding Silas wasn't good enough. Silas was a beautiful bright spark in an ugly world. He was good like Daniel and Jack, and their goodness made them vulnerable to needy bastards like David and Robert. Aaron wasn't good like they were, but he wasn't needy either. He didn't fit.

"Come back," said Silas.

Aaron scowled. "What?"

"You were off in your head."

"Sorry," muttered Aaron.

Silas huffed and pressed his forehead against Aaron's. The world was small and quiet for a moment. Aaron focused on the way it felt to lean against Silas, to capture his fingers, to breathe into him.

"I love you very much," said Silas quietly.

"I love you, too," said Aaron.

Chapter Thirty-One

Bang

Good things didn't last for Aaron. Peace was a concept, not a reality. Danger was never far away and the people he loved were never safe. He knew that. He knew better than to let his guard down. He knew not to get too comfortable, no matter how deceptively calm his life had become.

Daniel started school. Aaron finally returned to his job. Silas stopped selling drugs and started looking for real work. Jack remained the same. At the end of his shift, Aaron stopped by Jack's office to let him know he was leaving.

"I'm heading out," he said. "I'm making dinner for Silas tonight."

"It's a wonder that boy ate anything before he met you," muttered Jack. "Take this with you." He handed Aaron a sheet of paper.

Aaron took it and frowned at what looked like a real-estate listing. "Whose house is this?" he asked.

"It was a rental," he answered. "It butts against the north end of my property."

"Are you going to buy it or something?"

Jack scribbled something on the slip of paper in front of him, then handed that to him as well. It was a check for six grand made out Aaron.

Aaron looked at the check, then back at Jack.

"Sold those cars you worked on," said Jack. "Figured you might want to start a savings account."

Aaron opened his mouth, then closed it again.

"It's not much," said Jack. "I know how much work you put in and a few of them were worth a lot more than what I could get, but it's a start and you deserve it."

Aaron started to shake his head and hand the check back.

"Don't put up a fuss," he said. "Just take it. You earned it." He jabbed a finger at Aaron. "Don't turn around and give it to Daniel. I'm taking care of him."

"But," began Aaron, unsure of where the rest of that sentence was going to go, "I don't—I can't— They were *your* cars."

"They were going to rust and die with the rest of my crap. You saved them, you get the reward."

"How much is Daniel's tuition?" As if he didn't already know. He really wanted to ask how much Daniel got in loans and scholarships and how much Jack was paying.

Jack held up another check. "This is two grand," he said. "Got that for another one of your cars. If you want to help Daniel, you can buy him books for the next four years. Tuition is covered mostly with scholarships. We'll worry about student loans later."

Aaron nodded quickly.

Jack smirked. "I know you're proud of him and I figured you'd want to contribute to his education."

"Hell yeah, I do," said Aaron.

Jack gave him the other check. "This will be your share of the cost of college."

"What about law school?"

"We'll cross that bridge when we come to it," answered Jack. "I'm not worried and you shouldn't be either."

Aaron glanced back at the flyer in his hand. "And this?" he asked.

Jack sighed. "I'm not stupid," he said. "You're a grown man. You won't be happy living with me forever and neither will Daniel." He sighed again. "But I thought you might be happy living near me."

He pursed his lips, and for the first time since Aaron had met him, he looked nervous.

"It's small," continued Jack, "and it needs some work, but the bones are good. It's a good price and if you need to expand it, I could give you a couple acres to stretch out."

"I can't—"

"You can," said Jack. He pointed to the check. "I looked into it and that will cover the down payment. I'll make sure you stay covered."

"No," said Aaron. "I mean, this is too much."

"Don't be stupid," said Jack. "I don't have any kids. I'm not married. I hate everyone. You and Daniel are all I've got. You two have been in my will for years. Everything I own will eventually go to you anyway."

"I don't know what to say," said Aaron. 'Stunned' didn't accurately cover how he was feeling.

"Say thank you and that you'll think about it." He cleared his throat. "I've scheduled a walk-through of the property for tomorrow. It hasn't been rented for a few months. I wanted to check it out. You're welcome to come with me."

"Thank you," murmured Aaron.

"You're welcome," said Jack. "Now go make dinner for your boyfriend."

Aaron tried to say more, but Jack waved him away. He wondered if Daniel knew. He stared down at the flyer as he walked out to his car. He took a picture of it and sent it to his brother with the caption *want to buy a house?*

As soon as he got behind the wheel, his phone rang. "Hey, Danny," he said.

"Are you going to buy it?"

"I don't know," answered Aaron. "Jack just handed me some info for a house and a check for six grand and said I should think about buying the house."

"Oh, cool," said Daniel. "He gave you the car money?"

"You knew?"

"Duh," answered Daniel. "He was going to tell you what he was doing and make sure you were all right with the prices. I told him to just do it because you'd never agree to take the money unless it was already in cash or check form."

"I'd agree," said Aaron.

"No you wouldn't," said Daniel. "I bet he had to talk you into taking a check. Did he tell you about his will? I told him he'd have to go ahead and tell you that before you'd take anything."

"So you're just in on all of it."

"Yeah. It's a pretty cool house, too. You should think about buying it. That plus the two acres would be sweet. You'd have room for your own garage. I could build a house next to yours or we could just make the original one really big."

"God dammit," muttered Aaron.

"I had a long talk with Jack about it," said Daniel. "I promised him if he talked it over with me, he wouldn't have to repeat himself with you. You don't have to buy the house, but the land is already ours. I gave him a dollar for it. I think you still need to sign some paperwork."

Aaron huffed.

"He almost cried while we were talking," said Daniel. "He said he wanted to do something nice for us because we're like sons to him. We have to take it. And we have to let him help. I think he feels guilty. If this makes him feel better, we have to let him do it."

"He doesn't need to feel guilty," said Aaron.

"I also think he loves us a lot," said Daniel. "This is like a hug or something. You know Jack, he's not really a touchy-feely kind of person. This is his way of saying he cares."

"I don't know what to say," said Aaron.

"I said thank you."

Aaron rolled his eyes. "Yeah, so did I."

"Then that's all you need to do. I have to go to class. Are you staying with Silas tonight?"

"Yeah, planning on it."

"Okay. I'll see you tomorrow for the walk-through."

"Know-it-all," muttered Aaron. "See you tomorrow." He hung up and headed to Silas'.

He parked in the driveway and, after a moment of debate, tucked the checks and the flyer into the glove compartment. Something in his chest stung when he thought about the house and Silas.

What if he doesn't stay here forever?

The sting grew, radiating up into his neck and down into the rest of his body. He took a deep breath and looked at where his hands were gripping the steering wheel. They suddenly seemed closer, connected. He recognized them as an extension of himself. He felt the wheel in his grip, noticed how cool the air was around him. He felt whole. He came back.

He blinked in surprise, then got out of the car. Everything seemed normal. He looked at his hands again. They were still his and he felt everything down to the tips of his toes. He rushed into the house.

"Silas," he called. "I've got something awesome and weird to tell you."

"Are those two separate things or the same thing?" asked Silas.

Aaron followed the voice into the kitchen. Candlelight made the room glow and something smelled delicious.

Silas stood by the table looking thoroughly pleased with himself.

"You cooked," said Aaron.

"I cooked," confirmed Silas. "And I didn't burn anything. I even made dessert."

Aaron sniffed. "Oh my God, is that cake? Did you bake a cake?"

"I did," answered Silas.

Aaron crossed the kitchen and pulled the other man into a kiss. "I don't deserve you," he said. "What's for dinner?"

"Braised beef ribs and mashed potatoes."

Aaron examined the table as Silas pulled the lid off the Dutch oven Aaron had left at the house. "That was ambitious," he said. "And no fires?"

"No fires, no smoke and I didn't burn myself either," answered Silas. "But you have something to tell me. What is it?"

Aaron squeezed Silas a little tighter and buried his face against his shoulder. It was too much. He'd left his shitty life behind, and when he'd finally come back to himself, things were suddenly better. Robert was still dead and Ralph was still loose, but everything else had improved so much he barely recognized this life as his own.

Maybe Silas knew that. He always seemed to be in Aaron's head, know what Aaron was thinking without needing an explanation. He sighed against Silas' skin as he realized he could feel him again. Silas was real and solid and Aaron was actually standing in the kitchen holding him in his arms. They were together and free and Aaron loved him.

He couldn't name everything he was feeling, but it didn't matter because it was all so vibrant. It took him a moment to realize Silas was rocking them slowly side to side.

"I've felt so hollow for so long," muttered Aaron. "I don't know how it happened, but I started feeling things again today."

Silas squeezed him and pressed his lips to Aaron's ear. "You came back," he whispered.

"Yeah," answered Aaron. "I guess I did."

* * * *

Aaron was happy. The emotion was bright and present and he knew without question he was the happiest he'd ever been. Silas was snuggled on top of him on the couch. 'Snuggled' was the only way to describe it. His head was tucked beneath Aaron's chin, and he had one arm under his cheek and the other curved around Aaron's chest. Their legs were tangled together under a light blanket.

They both ate too much, but it was too early for bed so Aaron put on some music and they ended up snuggling on the couch. Aaron was absentmindedly tracing patterns up and down Silas' back. It didn't feel dirty or wrong—it felt perfectly normal, as if they'd always done this, as if there was never a time when one of them had existed without the other.

Silas' phone buzzed on the coffee table. "Go away," muttered Silas, reaching blindly. Aaron handed him the phone.

"Whoever you are, I'll have you know you're interrupting a very pleasant evening," said Silas as he answered the call.

Aaron could hear the voice on the other end. When they spoke, his blood ran cold.

"I know what you did," said the caller. "I know it was you and I know you think you'll get away with it."

Silas sat up and quickly pushed away from Aaron. "Where are you?" he asked.

"Closer than I was before."

Aaron snatched the phone away. "You son of a bitch," he growled. The line was quiet. The voice on the other end was gone. "That was Ralph. Why is he calling you?"

"I don't know," answered Silas. He suddenly looked very pale.

"What was he talking about? What does he think you did?"

"I assume he's mad about Farley and Regina," answered Silas.

"He said he was closer than he was before," said Aaron. "What the hell does that mean?"

"I don't know," answered Silas. "He's mad. He's probably just trying to scare me."

"I need to warn Jack. He might try to go after him or Daniel."

Silas nodded. "Call Jack," he said. "I'll make sure the doors and windows are locked."

Aaron grabbed his phone and pressed the button for Jack. Silas headed to the back of the house, so Aaron made sure the windows and door at the front were locked.

"Hey, Aaron," answered Jack.

"Hey, uh, so don't panic or anything, but Ralph just called Silas. He said he knew what Silas did. Silas asked where he was and he said 'closer than I was before', whatever that means."

"That bastard," muttered Jack. "I want both of you over here pronto."

"I don't want to lead him to you and Daniel."

"I dare him to set foot on my land," growled Jack. "It'll be the last thing he ever does." Aaron heard something click in the background. "I've got to call Liam. Get what you need and head over here. I'll call you again in five minutes. You better be in the car and on the road."

"All right," said Aaron. "See you soon." He hung up.

Satisfied with the security of the kitchen and living room, he went to collect his bag and his boyfriend. "Silas," he called. "We've got to go." Before he'd managed to set foot in the hall, he heard a gun go off. Without thinking, he ran toward the sound.

Chapter Thirty-Two

Beyond This Point

"Aaron, run!" Silas' voice rang out from the bedroom.

The gun went off again as Aaron rushed into the room. He saw everything in a blur and didn't stop to process any of it. He knew Silas was on the floor. He knew the man shooting at him was Ralph. He knew throwing himself at a man with a loaded gun was a bad idea. He knew Ralph's last shot had missed.

They crashed to the ground, each of them gripping the weapon. Aaron slammed his forehead into Ralph's nose. Ralph's finger was still on the trigger and all of his strength seemed to be going toward reclaiming control of the gun. His eyes were wide, madness and rage pounding just below the surface.

"Aaron," he hissed. "I remember you."

Aaron hesitated for one second too many. Ralph managed to roll them over and straddle Aaron's waist, pinning him to the floor.

"Maybe you and I can have some fun tonight," said Ralph. "I don't know about you, but I had a hell of a time during our last encounter."

Something moved behind Ralph. Aaron looked up and saw Silas was on his feet.

Ralph ripped the gun from Aaron's hands, but instead of shooting him, he whipped around and aimed the gun at Silas.

"No," shouted Aaron.

Ralph pulled the trigger and Silas collapsed. He hit the floor with a guttural, choking sound. Ralph turned his attention to Aaron again. "Be good, or I'll kill him." He pressed his hips down against Aaron's body.

Aaron wasn't sure what he said next. His vision turned red. He reached for the gun and snatched it from Ralph's grip. It flew across the room. He planted? his feet, grabbed Ralph by the shoulders and flipped them over. Next thing he knew, his hands were around Ralph's throat and he was watching his eyes bulge out of his face. Ralph clawed at Aaron's hands and gasped for air. Aaron shifted his weight forward, putting all of the pressure on Ralph's neck.

Kill him.

It wasn't fast or clean or easy. A blood vessel burst in one of Ralph's eyes. He tore skin away from the back of Aaron's hands as he fought for his life. His tongue stuck out of his mouth, swollen and discolored, and saliva trickled down his cheek. His muscles constricted and recoiled. He kicked and squirmed beneath Aaron.

He wasn't sure how long it took Ralph to die, but he knew his hands were getting tired. He could still hear Silas' labored breathing behind him. Finally, the man beneath him stopped struggling. Aaron got off him and retrieved the gun. He shot Ralph once in the face for good measure, then hurried to Silas' side.

He'd been hit in his stomach and chest and he was still bleeding. Aaron grabbed a blanket and tried to press down to stop the blood flow. "Can you hear me?"

Silas' eyes were glossy and half closed. His breath hitched as he inhaled.

"Don't leave me," said Aaron. "Don't you dare leave me."

Blood trickled from the corner of his mouth. He took another breath and his eyes seemed to find Aaron. He lifted a hand and laid it over Aaron's.

"You're not going to die tonight," said Aaron. "I'm going to call for help. I'll be right back." He didn't look to see if that registered. He hurried to the living room, grabbed his phone and rushed to Silas' side. He put his phone on speaker and resumed putting pressure on the wounds.

"911, what is your emergency?"

"Multiple gunshot wounds to the torso," shouted Aaron. "He's dying." He had to repeat the information and Silas' address several times before the operator understood him. He couldn't calm his voice, couldn't make himself stop shouting.

"An ambulance is on the way."

Aaron didn't hear the next question. He focused on Silas, watched the way he slowly blinked, then finally closed his eyes. He kept his hands firmly pressed against Silas' chest and stomach, keeping track of his breaths.

The door is locked. They can't get in.

Aaron scooped Silas up in his arms and ran to the front door. He fumbled with the lock, trying not to jostle Silas, and managed to get it open. He burst outside into the cool night air and dropped to his knees on the grass. He heard a siren in the distance, but it wasn't the first car to arrive.

Jack's truck screeched to a halt in the driveway beside the car. He tumbled out of the vehicle and rushed to Aaron's side. Aaron must have missed his check-in call.

He pulled Silas out of Aaron's arms and onto the grass. He removed the blanket and checked his wounds.

"Where's Ralph?" he asked.

"Dead," answered Aaron.

"How, and who did it?"

"I strangled him," answered Aaron. "Then I shot him."

"No you didn't," said Jack. "Don't admit to anything yet. Get in the ambulance with Silas. Don't give them information about Ralph. I'll handle the rest."

Bright lights poured into the yard. Two police cars stopped in front of the house, followed by an ambulance and a fire truck.

"You're distraught," hissed Jack. "Go with him and don't say anything unless it's to save his life."

Aaron nodded as a small team in varying uniforms swarmed the yard. Jack stood up and flashed a badge Aaron had never seen before.

"Robert Miller, CIA," he said. "I've called for backup. We'll take it from here."

* * * *

Aaron refused medical treatment. His hands shook as he tried to scrub away the blood in the hospital bathroom. Silas was still in surgery. He stared at the water as it faded to a pale pink.

The bathroom door opened. "Aaron?"

"I'm okay," he said.

Daniel showed up at the hospital not long after he and Silas arrived. He assumed Jack sent him. "I've got some stuff for your hands," said Daniel, holding up a small black bag.

"I don't need it."

"It's to hide the scratches," he said. "Jack's orders."

The door swung open again and Liam entered. He locked the door behind him.

Silas is going to die and I'm going to jail.

Aaron shook his head and presented his hands to Daniel and Liam.

"Holy shit," breathed Daniel.

"This is going to sting," said Liam. He took the bag and set it on one of the sinks.

"My skin is under his fingernails," said Aaron. "They'll know I killed him."

"You didn't kill him," said Liam. He pulled a small brown bottle from the bag and unscrewed the lid. "He broke into the house looking for Silas. He broke the lock on the back door and forced his way in. He shot Silas and you jumped him. You two struggled, lost the gun, and in a panic you tried to strangle him."

The lid of the bottle had a small brush attached to it. Liam began painting the back of Aaron's hands with something sticky and transparent.

"Silas got up, you got off Ralph to find the gun and call for help," continued Liam. "While you were watching Silas, Ralph found the gun and shot him again. You tried to get the gun away from him. You two fell and when you did, the gun went off in his face."

"Sounds legit," said Daniel.

"It's hard for you to talk about it right now," said Liam. "It happened so fast, you're not really sure what you remember." He pointed to the dryer in the corner. "Stick your hands under that so they'll dry faster."

Aaron followed his instructions. "Do you know anything about Silas?" he asked. "Have you seen him?"

"Fractured rib and a punctured lung," answered Liam. "The upper bullet missed his heart and I think the lower one missed his stomach. I've seen injuries like that before. I'm sure he'll be fine."

"Have you seen him?" asked Aaron again.

"No," answered Liam. "Just read the report."

Aaron felt a hand on his shoulder. Liam pulled him away from the dryer and back over to the sink.

"He's going to be all right," said Liam. He reached in the bag and pulled out a tube. This time the liquid he spread on Aaron's hands was white. It dried quickly and turned a pale tan color.

"Is that latex?" asked Daniel.

Liam nodded. "Liquid bandage, latex, then some concealer and his hands will be good as new." He looked up at Aaron. "Did you wash your feet already?"

He nodded. Daniel was the one who'd sent him into the bathroom to get cleaned up. Aaron had arrived barefoot, so a nurse had given him a pair of slippers.

"Almost done," said Liam. "We've got shoes and clean clothes for you. Don't leave anything here."

As soon as his hands were painted and dry, Daniel brought in a plastic bag with a new outfit. Aaron changed in the stall and shoved his other clothes into the bag along with the slippers.

Liam looked him over, then nodded. "I think you're good to go," he said. "I'll wipe down the bathroom. You boys go to the waiting room."

Daniel steered Aaron back outside. Daniel pushed him into a chair and Aaron tried not to fidget with his hands.

"So," said Daniel. "Liam is FBI or something?"

"I guess so," muttered Aaron. He fixed his eyes on the doors that led to Silas.

"CIA, FBI," said Daniel. "Or maybe neither. Maybe it's all a cover for something else. They know a lot about crime, that's for damn sure."

"I can't complain," said Aaron.

Daniel nudged him gently. "He's going to be all right."

It was hours before anything happened. Aaron kept wandering up to the desk to see if there was any news. Daniel had to put him on a schedule—he was only allowed to ask every forty-five minutes.

Around midnight, a familiar-looking woman rushed up to the desk. "Is Silas Anderson still in surgery?" she asked.

Aaron jumped up. He knew her.

"I'm his sister," she continued. "What room is he in?"

"Sara," he said. "Silas is still in surgery, but they think he's going to be all right. Did you just get here?"

"Actually," said the woman at the desk, "he just got out. They're moving him to the ICU. I can show you where he'll be."

"Thank you," said Sara.

"He's okay?" asked Daniel, suddenly appearing right behind Aaron.

"Yes," answered the woman. "Are you family?"

"No," answered Sara quickly. She didn't even look at them. "His brothers — our brothers — are on the way. One will be here later tonight."

"I'm his boyfriend," said Aaron. "I need to see him."

The woman glanced at Sara. "I'm sorry," she said slowly. "Only family is allowed beyond this point." She put her hand on Sara's shoulder to lead her away.

Aaron clenched his jaw and followed them. "Sir," said the woman, "you need to wait here." Sara didn't turn around.

"I need to see him," said Aaron. "Just let me see him."

"It's hospital policy," she said. "Only family at this time."

"That's a damn lie. You're covering for Sara."

Daniel tugged at the back of his shirt. "Let it go," he muttered. "We'll see him later."

"This is bullshit," said Aaron.

The woman winced and almost looked apologetic. "I'm sorry. It's our policy."

"Sara, tell her I can see him."

Sara turned around, tears in her eyes. "Aaron, right?"

"Yes."

"I don't know what you did to him, but as long as I'm alive you'll never see him again."

Daniel grabbed him and pulled him away.

"You don't know what happened," said Aaron. "Please, he trusts you. Just let me look at him. I need to see that he's okay."

She turned stiffly and followed the woman.

"Dammit," said Aaron. "Sara, come back here."

Daniel pulled him out of the waiting room. "Shut up," he hissed. "If you make a scene we'll never get to see him."

"This is bullshit and you know it," shouted Aaron.

"Shhh. For the love of God, stop yelling. We'll figure it out. At least we know he's all right."

"It's not fair," growled Aaron.

"I agree, but we can't do anything about it right now. When Silas wakes up I'm sure you'll be the first person he asks to see."

"That bitch called his brothers," said Aaron. "They won't let me in. I fucking know. They're going to block me."

"Silas can override them. Don't worry." Daniel dragged him into an elevator.

Aaron shoved him away. "Dammit, Danny. We live in bumfuck nowhere. No one is going to give a shit if some man doesn't get to see his boyfriend. Nobody cares. Nobody's going to listen to me or Silas. His family is loaded. They could have him airlifted out of here and I'll never see him again."

"Don't panic," said Daniel. "I know you're pissed. I'm pissed, too. But right now, Silas is still here and we don't know what anybody is going to do next. You've got to chill and stop drawing attention to us."

Aaron clamped his mouth shut and started pacing. The elevator dinged as they hit the first floor. Daniel took hold of him again and led him out into the parking lot. They stopped at Daniel's car.

"I'm not leaving," said Aaron.

"Fine," said Daniel. "Just get in the car."

"No."

"Yes," said Daniel.

"I'm not leaving him."

"I told you, you don't have to. Just sit here until Jack shows up."

"I'm going to the ICU waiting room," he said. "They can't keep me from sitting there."

Daniel dropped his voice to just below a whisper. "Get in the car. I need to say something that I can't say out here." He opened the passenger door.

"Fine," muttered Aaron.

Daniel walked briskly around the car and got in. He locked the doors. "I know you're upset," he said, still whispering, "but please, for the love of fuck, think about yourself for just a second."

Aaron crossed his arms over his chest.

"You killed somebody," whispered Daniel. "All jokes aside, I don't how much Jack can help. Maybe this will go away, maybe it won't. But if you get arrested and charged with murder, it's not going to help your case if you were seen lashing out at hospital staff."

He didn't answer. Daniel was right, but that was way too much to think about.

"We'll wait for Jack," he said. "He'll know what to do."

"I should be in the waiting room," muttered Aaron.

"We can go inside if you promise me you'll stay calm."

He ran his hands over his face. "I'll be calm," he said.

Chapter Thirty-Three

Silver Lining

Aaron sat between Jack and Daniel in a row of small gray chairs outside the ICU. They'd been in the waiting room for too damn long, but Aaron was doing his best to stay calm. He channeled his rage into a glare, which he focused on the front desk. His knee was bouncing, but there was nothing he could do to stop that. He had to do something, and Daniel had made him stop pacing an hour ago.

Jack had showed up shortly after they'd gone inside. Daniel had asked about the attack and Jack had said they were in the clear.

The official story was that Jack had arrived just in time to see Aaron struggling with Ralph and witness the fall and accidental shot. Accident. It wasn't murder. It was self-defense that led to a fatality. No one knew why Ralph was after Silas. That part was actually true. Aaron knew it was revenge, but he wasn't sure if Ralph had intended to kill Silas or wreak havoc in some other way.

Aaron might need to give a statement and they might need information from Silas as well. He wasn't sure who 'they' were. Jack kept telling him not to worry.

A blonde woman in scrubs peered into the waiting room. Her eyes brightened when she saw Aaron. She jerked her head toward the hall then vanished around the corner.

"I'll be back," said Aaron.

"Do you know her?" asked Daniel. Apparently he'd seen her too.

"Know who?" asked Jack.

Daniel started explaining as Aaron left. He ducked around the corner and came face to face with the woman.

She had a chart in one hand and a cup of coffee in the other. She handed the drink to Aaron.

"My name's Jenny," she said. "I think you know my mom."

He took the cup and tried to figure out if he'd seen her somewhere before. "You're Aaron," she said. "My mom's Ava Davis."

"Oh," he said. "Yeah, I'm her patient."

"I've seen you at her office," she said quickly. "I mean, that's how I recognize you. I don't want you to worry about a breach of trust or anything. I don't know you. I've just seen you around."

"Okay," said Aaron, raising an eyebrow.

"I'm a medical student," she said. "I've got friends in different parts of the hospital. I heard through the grapevine that you've got somebody in ICU."

Aaron didn't realize he'd been holding his breath until he exhaled. "Yes," he said. "Silas Anderson."

"I also heard his family isn't letting you see him."

"Can you get me in?"

She shook her head. "No, but—" She snapped her mouth shut as a few nurses walked by. She waited until they were around the corner. "Laugh," she hissed.

"Why?"

"Just do it. We're just two friends catching up."

Aaron gave his best fake laugh and took a quick sip of coffee.

"He's going to be all right," she whispered. "Don't tell anyone I told you." Aaron's knees almost buckled. He leaned against the wall.

"His sister won't let me in."

"I know," she said. "I'm sorry, but this is the best I can do."

Aaron rubbed his forehead. He had a massive headache and he wasn't sure when it had started. "But he's okay?" he asked.

"I'm pretty confident he's going to come out of this good as new."

He let out a deep breath. "Thank you," he said. "I owe you big time."

"Just drink your coffee and try to relax. I'll keep an eye on him." She smiled and squeezed his arm. "I thought you deserved to know, but you didn't hear it from me. Got it?"

"Got it," he said. He watched her walk away, feeling a thousand pounds lighter. He found his way back to the others and collapsed in his chair.

"What was that about?" asked Daniel.

"Silas is all right," said Aaron. He sighed and relaxed in his seat.

"Did you know her?" asked Jack.

"She's my therapist's daughter," answered Aaron. "She said she's seen me at her mom's office. I've never talked to her before."

"I feel like there're more than a few HIPAA violations in there somewhere," muttered Daniel.

"Has she seen Silas?" asked Jack.

"I don't know. She said she's got friends who have or something." He shook his head. "I don't care how she knows. I'm just glad he's all right."

"Can she get you in?" asked Daniel.

"No," answered Aaron. "But they can't keep me away forever."

Jack looked down at his phone. "Liam is on the way up. Daniel, he's going to ride home with you and stay the night at the house."

"I'm not going home," said Daniel.

"I'm sending you home," said Jack. "It's late, and unless I'm mistaken, you have classes to go to tomorrow."

"I can miss a few classes," said Daniel. "I haven't skipped any yet. I've only got lectures tomorrow. No one will notice if I'm there or not."

"It's not up for debate," said Jack. "We'll keep you updated. I'm going to stay with your brother and make sure he doesn't do anything stupid. Liam is going to keep an eye on you and make sure *you* don't do anything stupid."

Daniel muttered something under his breath, but he didn't argue when Liam showed up to take him home. They said goodnight to Jack and Aaron, and Daniel promised to return as soon as he could.

"I'm glad you made him go home," said Aaron. "He doesn't need to fall behind in school."

"I'd make you go home too, if I thought you'd listen," said Jack. "You need to get some sleep."

"I need more coffee," he said.

"I second that," said Jack. "Need to stretch my legs."

* * * *

Aaron still wasn't allowed to see Silas the next morning. Sometime around nine a.m., two men approached the front desk. They didn't bother looking at anyone else in the waiting room. Aaron recognized one of them, which meant the other one had to be Zach.

"Max," muttered Aaron. "I can't believe she called them."

"His brothers?" asked Jack.

"Yeah. The gang's all here."

"Silas' doctor will probably keep him in the ICU for the rest of the day," said Jack, suppressing a yawn. "I'm sure they will want to keep him under observation for twenty-four hours. He probably needed a blood transfusion."

Aaron leaned forward and put his head in his hands.

"I'm kind of surprised we haven't been kicked out yet," said Jack. "Your friend must have put in a good word."

"Where will he go after the ICU?" asked Aaron.

"Probably to a regular room. They'll want to keep an eye on him for another day or two."

"This is bullshit," said Aaron. "I should be with him."

"We'll figure it out," said Jack. "Don't worry."

Aaron yawned for the third time in less than ten minutes.

"Let me take you home," said Jack. "It's good for the staff to know we're not going to lurk around here for days on end. Besides, you're going to want to be alert when you see Silas. We'll go home, catch a few hours of sleep, then head right back up here."

Aaron shook his head. "I can't go."

"You're not doing any good just sitting here stressing yourself out. Silas wouldn't want you to sit here without taking a break." He paused. "And, no offense, but you look like hell. You're starting to get crazy eyes. You need to recharge."

Aaron blinked heavily. Sleep was tempting, but he couldn't bring himself to leave.

"We need to regroup," said Jack. "I might know somebody who can help. If we go home, I'll check my contacts and see if I can cash in any favors to get you in to see him."

"Are you trying to bribe me with more of your 'contacts'?"

"Yes," answered Jack.

"Fine," he muttered. "We can go home, but only for a little while. I don't want to miss anything."

Jack promised to let Aaron return in the evening. They went home and Aaron collapsed on the couch. The car was in the driveway where it belonged. Aaron's keys, wallet and phone were in his room. He didn't know what Jack and Liam had had to do to cover his ass, and wondering about it wasn't the distraction he'd hoped it would be.

He couldn't eat or sleep, so he made a pot of coffee. A shower and three cups later, he was pacing outside on the porch with his phone in his hand. He didn't expect anyone to call him, but holding it made him feel closer to Silas.

An hour later, Jack was still asleep. Aaron made an executive decision. He'd been very patient and had waited long enough. He grabbed his keys, cranked up the car and headed into town.

At the hospital, he returned to his post and resumed staring at the doors to the ICU. If he knew Silas' room number, he could just walk back there and wait for the other Andersons to take a break. He'd seen enough people go in and out of the doors to know he didn't need a code to get through. Technically, there wasn't anything stopping him from wandering back there. He could pretend to be lost if anyone questioned him.

He eyed the woman sitting at the desk. She'd been there since eight a.m. and hadn't seemed to take note of him earlier. She didn't seem particularly aware of him now. Still, it was better to play it safe.

A few minutes later, she stood up and wandered away from her post. Aaron got up quickly and, as casually as he could, strolled through the doors to the ICU.

The area was not as big as he'd expected, but everyone seemed busy. A few doors were closed and Aaron wasn't sure if they were closets or patient rooms or something else. He wasn't desperate enough to check just yet. Most occupied rooms had a sheet of paper with a name written on it hanging outside them. He turned a corner and was about to restart his search when he finally saw the name he was looking for.

The door was closed. It was too risky to barge in and he didn't want to get kicked out. He took note of the room number and walked back down the hall. Just knowing how many steps away he was from Silas was an improvement.

He walked through the doors and immediately locked eyes with a very disgruntled-looking Jack.

He ran a hand over his beard and patted the seat next to him.

"I'm not sorry," whispered Aaron, sitting down. "I waited as long as I could."

"You should have told me you were heading out," said Jack. "Thank God your car is so damn loud, otherwise I wouldn't have known you were gone."

"I found his room."

"Good for you."

"That counts for something, doesn't it?"

Jack raised an eyebrow. "Did anyone see you?"

"No," answered Aaron.

"Did you remember to cover the scratches on your hands?"

His hands were exposed and it was obvious he'd forgotten about the marks.

"That's what I thought." Jack handed a small black bag to Aaron. "Go into the bathroom. Do the best you can to cover them up. I'm going to get you some water and a God damn granola bar."

Begrudgingly, he did as he was told. His cover-up skills weren't as good as Liam's, but his hands looked convincing enough. True to his word, Jack was waiting for him with a bottle of water and a snack. He made Aaron eat and drink, all while maintaining an expression very close to pouting.

They sat together in silence. Aaron was sure there was a way around the bullshit, but he hadn't figured it out yet.

Suddenly the doors leading from the ICU to the waiting room swung open. Sara marched across the floor with her eyes on Aaron and Jack.

"Walk with me," she said. She didn't bother stopping to see if they followed. She led them down a long hallway and two flights of stairs to the main level of the hospital. She finally stopped just outside the gift shop.

"Is he okay?" asked Aaron.

"No," she answered. "He won't talk to anyone. Max and Zach, I understand, but me?" She glared at him.

"Let me guess," said Aaron. "You told him I wasn't allowed to see him and he's pissed because you're being an asshole."

"No," she spat. "I told him I didn't know where you were and he sent me to look for you."

"What?"

"He doesn't even know Aaron's here?" asked Jack.

"I told him I couldn't find you and he didn't believe me," she answered, arms crossed over her chest.

"You fucker," growled Aaron.

"Save it," she said. "I already figured out I screwed up, that's why I'm here confessing."

"This better end with you taking me to see him," said Aaron.

"I can get you in tonight."

"Why not now?" asked Jack.

"Our brothers are against you going anywhere near him. Max is still in the room. He and Silas are trying to out silence-treatment each other. Max will wear himself out by tonight and go back to the hotel."

"How long do I have to wait?" asked Aaron.

"Come back at nine. Zach is gone for the day. He and Max won't return until after lunch tomorrow."

Aaron looked at his watch. Nine o'clock was an eternity away.

"Look," said Sara. "I'm sorry. I fucked up. I get it. I'll fix this, I swear, but this is the best I can do for now."

"Fine," said Aaron. "I'll take what I can get."

Chapter Thirty-Four

Silas

Waiting was akin to torture, but Aaron reminded himself that Silas was waiting at the other end. Sara told them to stay away from the waiting room. She'd meet him and Jack on the first floor again. Daniel showed up just after seven p.m. and that took the edge off just enough to keep Aaron sane.

He'd packed an overnight bag, just in case. If he got the opportunity to stay, he wasn't going to miss it. He adjusted the backpack slung over his shoulder.

When nine p.m. finally came around, Aaron was bouncing on the balls of his feet just to keep his adrenaline at bay. Sara was one minute late. He saw her walking swiftly down the hall and almost sprinted to meet her.

"I don't need to take all three of you, do I?" she asked.

"We're all going upstairs, but I'm the only one who needs to see him," answered Aaron.

She eyed the group. "You guys really care about him."

"We do," said Aaron. "I'm not another David."

They followed her to the waiting room. It was after visiting hours and the doors were locked. Sara didn't have any trouble getting in. She nodded to the woman at the front desk and the woman hit a button to open the doors. Aaron wondered if Sara had already lifted her ban on him. Maybe he'd be able to see Silas again without needing her permission.

He wasn't supposed to know which room was Silas', but Sara was walking too slowly. Aaron didn't remember passing her, but suddenly he was opening Silas' door and Sara was behind him.

Silas was propped up with pillows in his bed. His eyes were closed. He was on his back scowling at the ceiling. He had an oxygen tube in his nose and an IV in his arm.

Aaron set his backpack on the floor and approached quietly. His hands were shaking, but for once fear wasn't the cause. Silas was too pale and too small. Aaron brushed a lock of hair from his forehead.

His eyes snapped open and he was suddenly moving too quickly. "Aaron," he said, pushing himself up.

"Don't get up," said Aaron. "You're going to hurt yourself." He sat on the edge of the bed.

As soon as he was within grabbing distance, Silas took hold of him and pulled him into his arms.

"I'm so sorry," said Silas. "He came in through the back of the house. Are you hurt? What happened?"

"It's okay," murmured Aaron. "I'm okay. He's dead. You're alive. I couldn't be happier."

Silas pushed him up. Still gripping his shirt, he looked over Aaron's body.

"I'm fine," said Aaron. "Just a few bumps and bruises." He cupped his hand against Silas' cheek. "He's gone."

"Zach and Max are trying to move me to a hospital closer to home," said Silas. "I thought I might not —" His voice cracked and tears leaked from the corners of his eyes. "I knew you were here. You have a very helpful friend."

"Who?" asked Aaron.

"A medical student," answered Silas. "She was watching you and telling me what you were doing. She said she spoke to you."

"She did," answered Aaron. "She was the only reason I knew you were all right."

Silas pulled him down again. Aaron kissed every inch of skin he could find until he got to Silas' lips. They sealed themselves together and Aaron consumed every detail. Silas was still strong. His lips were a little chapped, but soft. He smelled the same, tasted the same. He was all right. Two gunshot wounds were not enough to break him.

When they parted, Silas tangled his fingers in Aaron's hair and kept their foreheads pressed together. "I'm never speaking to my family again," he muttered. "I'm just lucky my mother didn't show up. Her health is failing. I suppose I should be grateful."

"You can hate the rest of them," said Aaron, "but you might have to forgive Sara. She's the one who got me in here." He glanced out of the corner of his eye and realized she wasn't in the room. The door was closed and they were alone.

"She's also the reason you weren't allowed to see me in the first place."

"That's true," said Aaron, "and I'd love to keep hating her, but she was just looking out for you. She thought she was doing the right thing."

"She was very wrong," said Silas. "I'm sure I'll eventually forgive her, but it's not going to happen anytime soon."

Aaron leaned in for another kiss. It seemed like they'd been apart for weeks. He sighed. "I killed him," he whispered.

"Good," said Silas. "I hope he suffered."

"Does your family know what happened?"

"No," answered Silas. "It's driving them crazy and that is no less than they deserve." There was a knock at the door. Aaron looked up and Silas glared at the interruption.

Sara entered with her head slightly hung. "I won't be spending the night tonight," she said. "The chair in the corner is open, if Aaron wants to use it. They can also bring in a cot."

"I'll take the chair," said Aaron. He turned to Silas. "I can take the chair, right? You're okay with me staying?"

"Of course, but aren't you exhausted? I heard you didn't get much sleep."

"I won't sleep if I go home. Honestly, I probably won't go home."

"Then stay," said Silas. "But you have to promise to rest."

Sara cleared her throat.

Silas finally looked at her. "You're dismissed," he said.

"Thank you," said Aaron.

Silas huffed.

Sara nodded and left the room. She closed the door behind her.

"You have to forgive her eventually," said Aaron. "I'd be just as overprotective if Daniel were in the hospital."

"She knows how I feel about you," said Silas. "She's called me every other day since that fight we had to see how things were going. She knows how much I love you." He frowned. "I should probably tell you, I called her that night you left. She came over and commiserated with me, but we've seen each other since then and I've told her I love you. She's even said I seem happier than I've ever been."

Aaron must have made a face, because Silas' eyes locked on him and began scanning.

"What?" asked Silas. "Something I should know?"

"Kind of," answered Aaron. Silas had been honest, he should probably fess up too. "I, uh, I kind of snuck back to your house that night. After the drawer-war, I went back and saw someone else was there."

Silas put a hand over his face and groaned.

"I might have spied on you guys a little bit."

"How much did you hear?" he asked.

"You said you loved me," answered Aaron. "Sara was trying to explain that I was broken. She was right, by the way. I'm still pretty broken."

"Aaron, no."

"It's okay," he said. "I told Ava about it. She set me straight. I talked to her the day I went back to see you."

"You're not broken."

"Everybody's a little broken."

"So you already knew a little bit about David?"

"Yeah," answered Aaron. "Sorry, I probably should have told you sooner."

"It's all right. She wanted to meet you before this happened."

"Well, she's met me now."

"This really isn't how I imagined it going." Silas ran his thumb over Aaron's cheek. "You must be exhausted."

"Relieved is more like it," he said.

"You know you don't have to stay," said Silas.

Aaron snorted. "Yeah, I'll just head on home and drive Jack and Daniel crazy. I'm sure they'd love that."

"Do you want to go home and pack some things to stay?"

"I came prepared," said Aaron. "This ain't my first rodeo."

Silas examined the bed. "You don't have to sleep in the chair. There's room for both of us. I can move over. I don't need to sleep in the middle."

"No. You need to be comfortable and there's no way in hell I'm going to risk rolling over on you or something."

Silas snorted. "I'm fine," he said. "I could probably go home tonight. They're just coddling me at this point to make sure the hospital doesn't get sued."

"You've been shot, you moron. Nobody is coddling you. I'll move the chair right beside you and you can get comfortable and relax."

Silas rolled his eyes. "Fine," he said. "But I really am all right. I can stand and walk around. I'm not even in pain."

"That's because you're all doped up." Aaron kissed his forehead and went to reposition the chair. He sat sideways in it with his chin propped on the bed, looking up. Silas wiggled around until they were closer to eye level. Aaron had one arm stretched out with his hand holding Silas'.

Silas frowned and looked down at where his thumb was rubbing against Aaron's skin. "What happened to you?" he asked. He brought Aaron's hand up closer to his face and began wiping away the tan makeup.

Aaron knew pride was not the right emotion to feel when thinking about murder, but that didn't stop the emotion from swelling in his chest. Grinning, he pulled his hand away and picked at the latex, then did the same to his other hand. He held them both up for Silas to inspect.

"What is this?" he asked.

"I strangled the shit out of that bastard," whispered Aaron. "Watched his eyes roll back in his head and everything."

"Oh my God," breathed Silas.

"He shouldn't have shot you," said Aaron. "I mean, I really wanted to kill him anyway, but he fucked up big time when he messed with you."

Silas wasn't nearly as amused as Aaron. "What about the police?" he hissed. "Have you been questioned? Did they find his body?"

He shrugged. "Jack said he took care of it. I'm not so sure he's actually retired. And it turns out Liam is FBI, or CIA. Well, at least, he claims to be."

He looked at Aaron's hands. He frowned, then took hold of them again. "I'm so sorry. I thought I could hold him off."

"What happened?" asked Aaron. "I called Jack then heard the gun go off."

"He was already in the house when I went to lock up," said Silas. "The door was open. When I went to check the bedroom, he was waiting for me. We could hear you talking. I think he wanted to wait to fire the gun until you got off the phone. He didn't want anyone else to hear it." He sighed and tugged on Aaron's hands. "Just come up here for a little while. It will be another hour before someone comes in to check on me."

"I don't think your doct—"

"I'm my doctor," said Silas. "I approve. Come up here."

Aaron kicked off his shoes and Silas moved over to make room. It was a tight fit with Silas on his back and Aaron curled around him on his side, but for whatever reason, as soon as they were pressed together, Aaron felt them both relax.

"I thought I could take him," said Silas. "I hit him a few times, but as it turns out my hand-to-hand combat skills are outmatched by ranged weaponry." He sighed again. "He kept telling me he was going to kill you."

"Yeah, well, lucky for us I have a shit ton of pent-up aggression."

"How did you get the gun away from him?"

"I honestly don't remember," answered Aaron. "He shot you that second time and I kind of blacked out. Next thing I knew he was clawing the shit out of me trying to breathe. I shot him in the face after he passed out. You know, just in case."

"No one can say you weren't thorough," said Silas.

"Jack showed up just before the police. He had his badge ready and everything," said Aaron. "I'm lucky."

"I'm so glad you're all right. It was driving me crazy not knowing what happened." Silas closed his eyes. "The last thing I saw was him on top of you."

Aaron carefully draped his arm over Silas' chest. "He didn't hurt me," he said. "I hulked-out big time. I hope that fucker rots in hell."

Silas wriggled closer. He moved his arm so that Aaron's head was partially resting on his chest.

"We're safe now," said Aaron. "Nothing in the world can keep us apart—not even your rich-bitch family."

Silas laughed softly and hummed in agreement. His breathing slowly evened out. Aaron stayed silent and let him drift off to sleep. Aaron waited for a while to make sure he was comfortable, then he slipped out of bed and curled up in the chair.

He snapped a picture of Silas and sent it to Jack and Daniel to let them know he was staying and everything was right in the world again. He fell asleep listening to Silas' steady breathing.

Chapter Thirty-Five

Shooter

Aaron woke up first and spent the first part of the morning watching Silas sleep until the nurse came in to check on him. Silas muttered to himself as he blinked his eyes open.

The nurse buzzed around the room, taking notes on her chart and updating any changes. "Your vitals are much better today," she said. "I think we can move you out of the ICU this afternoon."

"Can I go home?" asked Silas.

The nurse seemed startled. She stared at him for a moment or two and glanced at Aaron. "Oh," she said. "You're talking. That's great!"

"I am," confirmed Silas.

She cleared her throat. "You shouldn't leave yet. We'd like to keep you for twenty-four to forty-eight hours."

Silas sighed. "I suppose that's fair."

"Could I persuade you to eat something?" she asked.

"Yes," he answered.

She beamed. "Wonderful. You really are doing so much better. I can't believe how much you've improved."

Aaron raised an eyebrow at his boyfriend.

The nurse handed Silas a small menu. "I can bring breakfast up for both of you," she said. "Do you see anything you'd like?"

Aaron's stomach growled.

"What do you want?" asked Silas, showing him the menu.

"I'll get whatever you get," he answered. "All food sounds good right now."

Silas requested some mixed berry oatmeal something or other and orange juice. The nurse left and Aaron moved from his chair to perch on the side of Silas' bed.

"So," he said. "You took a vow of silence and went on a hunger strike. In your professional medical opinion, was that such a good idea?"

"I was angry," answered Silas. "But you heard her. I'm doing much better."

"You made yourself sicker."

"My family made me sicker. They're determined to take me home."

"Sara won't let them," said Aaron. "Don't get me wrong, at first I thought she sucked, but now I'm pretty sure she was just worried about you."

"I can't believe she called for backup," muttered Silas. "And I can't believe they actually came. Both of them. It's been years since we were all in a room together." He huffed and threw the covers off.

"Going somewhere?"

"The bathroom," answered Silas. "Don't get up. I don't need help."

Aaron had never seen Silas so grouchy. He was prickly and indignant and adorable. Aaron crossed to the other side of the bed and lowered the railing.

"I can do this on my own," said Silas. "Really, you don't need to help."

"You're a terrible patient," said Aaron. "I'm surprised they're willing to keep you here."

Silas swung his legs over the side of the bed and Aaron untangled his IV tube. He helped Silas stand so he wouldn't put pressure on his wounds. Once he was in Aaron's arms, he leaned forward and took a deep breath.

"I should probably wash up before I get distracted," said Silas.

"Do you need help?"

"No. I'm perfectly capable." He paused. "But thank you for offering."

Despite his protests, Aaron helped him walk to the bathroom and stood guard by the door just in case. They spent the rest of the morning basking in the relief of each other's presence until Sara returned.

"The guys are on their way over," she said. "They probably won't stay long."

Aaron nodded. "I'll head out for a while and come back when they're gone. Daniel and Jack might want to see you," he said to Silas. "If you're up for it."

"I am," he said. "I am not 'up' for seeing my brothers." He pressed the call button by his bed.

"Don't do it," warned Sara. "If you do what I think you're about to do, they're going to be pissed."

His nurse entered. "Everything all right?" she asked.

"I have unwelcome family members attempting to visit me today," answered Silas. "I'd like to block them."

The nurse glanced at Aaron and Sara.

"These two can stay," clarified Silas. "My brothers are the people I want to block. There are two other men coming to visit, but they are allowed. I can write the names down for you."

"All right," said the nurse. She produced a pen and a slip of paper.

"They're not going to like that," said Sara.

"Frankly," said Silas, "I don't give a shit." He wrote his brothers' names and a woman's name on the sheet then circled them and added '*These are my older brothers and my mother. Please block. Do not allow visitation under any circumstances including, but not limited to, my death. Everyone else is allowed to visit.*'

"Dude," said Aaron. "That's a little extreme."

He handed the pad to the nurse.

"You can always change your mind," she said.

"I won't," said Silas. "But thank you."

The nurse glanced at them again. "Everything else okay? Are you feeling all right?"

"Honestly," answered Silas, "I feel fantastic."

She smiled and nodded, then left the room.

"I can't believe you did that," said Sara. "They're going to cut you off. Mom's going to write you out of her will. Dad left the trust to her. You won't get anything."

"I don't want it," said Silas.

"You're uninsured, you idiot," said Sara. "How are you going to pay your medical bills? What about rent and utilities and food? You're unemployed. What about trying to get your license back? I thought you wanted to be a doctor again."

"Well, fuck it," said Silas. "I've got enough money for now. I knew I'd cut ties with them one day. I took precautions. I have money saved. Today just happens to be the day I'm brave enough to actually do it."

"I hope this isn't because of me," said Aaron.

"Don't be ridiculous," said Silas. "Not every stupid thing I do is because of you." He took a deep breath and a slow, toothy grin spread across his face. "I feel strangely liberated." He laughed. "Had I known it would feel this good, I would have written them off years ago."

"I guess I should be glad I'm not on that list," said Sara.

"I'm still mad at you," said Silas.

"What about your rich-guy perks?" asked Aaron.

"Again," he said, "fuck it." He nodded to himself. "It's what Joshua would have done."

Aaron squeezed his hand and kissed his cheek. "I wonder where you're going to live now," he mused. "It's a shame you don't have a charming boyfriend to move in with."

"It is a shame," said Silas. "But I have a regular boyfriend. I suppose he'll have to do."

"Man," said Sara. "I was so sure I was going to hate you."

"Gee, thanks," said Aaron.

She rolled her eyes. A phone range somewhere in the room. Sara retrieved it from her pocket. "Guess who," she muttered. "I'll take this outside." She answered the phone and headed out of the door.

"I should apologize in advance," said Silas. "They're going to blame you."

"I don't care if you don't care," said Aaron. "I'm not a fan of Max and it doesn't sound like Zach is any better. I'm kind of surprised your mom hasn't come to see you."

"Mother doesn't travel unless it's an emergency."

"You were shot. Twice."

"But I recovered. Besides, she'd have to take her jet and she doesn't like paying for fuel and a pilot unless she absolutely has to."

"She has a *jet*?"

"She *leases* a jet. My father always said leasing was a better investment, especially with planes."

"You gave up private-jet money?"

Silas nodded. "I guess I did."

Aaron relaxed in the chair. "Damn. You sure you don't want to reconsider?"

"Positive."

Sara came back into the room. "I'm supposed to be in here 'talking some sense' into you," she said. "Don't worry. I'm just going to pretend I tried." She nodded to Aaron. "They're really not happy about you being here."

"The feeling is mutual," said Aaron.

"Silas," she said, "I think they were trying to get you to come back to work for the family. I guess they saw this as their opportunity."

"Obviously," said Silas. "You didn't think they came to see me because they cared, did you?"

"I guess I hoped that was the reason," she said.

Aaron's phone buzzed and he checked it. "Daniel and Jack are heading over," he said, reading the message.

"Your family?" asked Sara.

"My brother and my uncle," answered Aaron.

"I'm sorry I made such a big deal about you guys visiting," said Sara. "I didn't realize how much my brother meant to you."

"In spite of the fact that I've specifically told you how kind and welcoming they are," said Silas. "You know we love each other. You know how much his family cares and you know how much I care about them."

"How many times can I say I'm sorry?" she asked.

Aaron leaned into Silas. "Hey, baby," he said, "maybe cut her some slack. I'm not mad at her. Daniel and Jack probably aren't mad. She thought you were dying and that it was my fault."

"Don't use pet names to mitigate my anger," said Silas.

"I would have been just as crazy if it was Daniel in the hospital and some chick I'd never met was the reason he got shot."

"You are not the reason that bastard shot me."

"You know the shooter?" asked Sara.

Silas snapped his mouth shut and Aaron realized he had no idea how much Sara knew.

She crossed her arms over her chest. "What exactly happened to you?"

Aaron looked to Silas, who seemed just as unsure as he was.

"You said it wasn't drug-related," said Sara, eyeing her brother.

Aaron needed to talk to Silas alone so they could get their story straight, but Sara clearly wasn't going to let that happen. Aaron decided to sacrifice subtlety for the sake of coordination. He leaned in and whispered to Silas.

"Does she know about the porn thing?" he asked. "You can just say yes or no."

"No," muttered Silas.

"Does she know anything about Ralph?"

Silas tugged on his shirt collar and whispered. "I told her I sold you some weed and there was someone else with us who became aggressive. I admitted to pulling out my gun to scare him away, but I told her I didn't fire it. I also told her your father was homophobic and abandoned you, but that's it. She doesn't know the shooter was really Ralph from the fake drug deal."

Aaron let his head slump to rest on Silas' shoulder. He wasn't ready to explain his stupid life to someone again, though part of him was relieved Sara didn't know how deeply fractured he was.

"Clearly," said Sara, "there's a story here. Why can't I know?"

"We should wait until Jack gets here," muttered Aaron. "He's got the official story."

"What official story?" asked Sara. "Why is there an official story?"

"My uncle works for the CIA, or at least I think he does. He says he's retired, but at this point I'm not sure what he actually does and doesn't do."

"Are you two in legal trouble?" asked Sara.

Aaron looked up at Silas, whose eyes were wide. Silas shook his head ever so slightly.

"Will Jack tell me what happened?" asked Sara.

Aaron lowered his voice again. "We should at least tell her how we really met. I'll do it if you want me to. You had to tell my family, so I'll tell yours."

Silas ran a hand over his face. "Oh my God," he muttered.

"Somebody has to tell me something," said Sara.

"I wasn't actually selling to Aaron when we met," said Silas. "We were, um—how can I put this delicately?"

313

"Just say it," said Aaron. "Daniel handled it well."

"I was sort of an actor," said Silas.

"In porn," finished Aaron.

"Good lord," muttered Sara. "Silas, porn? Really?"

"Don't judge," said Aaron. "I did it, too. We were supposed to do a scene together but Silas got replaced for being too nice."

Sara opened her mouth, but Aaron held up a finger.

"Let me finish," he said. "I need to say it while I'm on a roll. The guy who replaced him was a major asshole. He, uh, he had an assistant, I guess. They kind of tied me up and things got out of hand."

Silas put his arm around Aaron and leaned into him.

"I'll spare you the details," he continued. "Long story short, Silas kicked down the door, fired off a few warning shots and scared them. He, uh, he saved me." Aaron swallowed hard.

Sara had her hand over her mouth.

"He saved me a couple of times," said Aaron. "My dad had a pretty strict 'women only' rule. He found out I'd done stuff with guys, kicked me out, I was homeless. I'd also stolen some of the porn guys' money—"

"I took it," interrupted Silas. "It was rightfully yours."

"Fine, *we* stole it. Porn guys showed up at Silas' house to find it, but I'd gone and taken the money with me. To give back," he added quickly. "There was this whole ultimatum thing. Man, this story sucks." He sighed.

Sara looked horrified.

Aaron took a deep breath. He did his best to summarize the rest of the story up to Robert's death. He wasn't sure if it made sense. He wasn't sure it had made sense the first time they'd tried to tell it. "It's a lot," he finished. "A lot of shit happened."

"I'm so sorry," murmured Sara. "I didn't know."

Aaron pushed his hair away from his forehead and realized he was sweating. Silas squeezed him.

"The man who shot you," began Sara, "was he — was he the same one?"

"I'm not sure," answered Silas quickly.

Aaron didn't correct him. They both knew better than to say something that might contradict Jack's story, and Aaron was having trouble remembering what he could and couldn't say. Though it was fair for her to assume, by now, that Ralph was the shooter.

"It all happened so fast," said Aaron. "My uncle knows what happened. He can tell you."

"All right," she said. "I guess I'll just wait here for Uncle Jack." She grabbed a folding chair from a hanger behind the door and settled at the foot of the bed.

Silas didn't seem to trust himself to say anything without saying too much, so he stayed quiet. Aaron decided that was the safest tactic, so the three of them sat in silence until company arrived.

Chapter Thirty-Six

Getting Better

"You killed him?" asked Sara.

"He didn't kill him," said Jack. "The gun went off when they fell."

"But he's dead?" asked Sara.

"Yeah," answered Aaron. "He's way dead."

"Good," she said. "And you're sure it's the same guy that attacked you before?"

"Positive," answered Aaron.

Jack and Daniel had arrived just in time to stop Sara from continuing to pressure Silas and Aaron for details. Aaron told Jack that Sara knew most of the story and everyone kept quiet while Jack, once again, gave the official explanation.

"Was he trying to rob you guys?" asked Sara. "Did he know Aaron was there?"

"We don't know what he was doing," answered Aaron.

"We think he was after Silas," answered Jack. "But there's no real way to tell for sure at this point. You all don't need to worry about anything though. It's been taken care of, and Silas and Aaron are safe."

Sara stared ahead at her brother. She sighed heavily, apparently still processing the story. "What about the others?" she asked after a moment. "Weren't there other people from the porn shoot?"

Aaron cringed at the word 'porn' and realized he hadn't watched anything erotic since the incident. Silas, seemingly always tuned in to Aaron's emotions, leaned his head on Aaron's shoulder.

"I checked on them," answered Jack. "Their group was busted on other charges. Ralph was the only one missing. Everybody's accounted for now."

"How long will the others be in jail?" asked Sara.

"A long-ass time," answered Jack. He cleared his throat. "I guarantee you they're not going to bother anybody ever again."

"If you don't mind," said Silas, "I'd like to take a walk with Aaron. I've been in bed too long."

"Do you want us to stay here?" asked Daniel. "We can leave if you want. We know you're tired."

"No," answered Silas. "I'd like you all to stay. We'll be back in a few minutes. I just need to stretch."

Aaron went to help Silas out of bed and this time Silas actually let him. He leaned heavily on Aaron as they made their way out into the hall.

"You all right?" asked Aaron, keeping his voice down.

"Yes," he answered. "I thought you might like a break." He straightened up, supporting most of his own weight once they were several feet away from his room.

Aaron kissed his cheek. It didn't occur to him to be insecure until afterward. He realized he didn't care.

"I'm okay," said Aaron, smiling. "If you're okay, I'm okay."

* * * *

Silas went home after spending four days in the hospital. He didn't go back to his house and, once again, at Jack's insistence, Aaron's family was under one roof. He started making meals for Silas, then quickly fell into the habit of cooking for the household. The routine became something comfortable. Aaron looked forward to waking up early to make breakfast. Silas usually got up with him to make coffee and Daniel usually took care of dishes before leaving to go to class. Aaron would make lunches for everyone, make sure Silas was comfortable, then kiss him goodbye and head off to work with Jack. In the evening, he'd make dinner and maybe have time to work on his next project car, then fall asleep beside Silas.

Sara visited about once a week. During her first visit, she said their brothers had blocked Silas' access to the family fortune. Her second visit, she said their mother was writing him out of her will. During her third visit, she informed Silas that her piece of the fortune was still secure and handed him a check for fifty thousand dollars. She promised him, no matter what, he would get half of anything she received from their family and no one would know about it.

Aaron took Silas on a walk-through of Jack's property one evening. He stopped at an open spot near the edge and pointed to the neighboring yard. "What do you think of that house?" he asked.

"It's nice," answered Silas. He furrowed his brow and looked up at Aaron. "Why?"

"If I bought it, would you live there with me?"

"Is this a hypothetical question or are we actually talking about moving in together?"

Aaron pulled a set of keys from his pocket. "These open the front door," he answered. "Jack worked out a plan for me and Daniel to have some land and a place of our own. The land we're standing on now is mine and that" — he pointed across the field to a small tree — "is where Daniel's land begins."

Silas looked to the tree, then down at the grass, then back to Aaron.

"The house is mine if I want it," said Aaron. "Daniel wants me to buy it — says we should put down roots somewhere. This place is pretty much our home and I think I'd like to keep it that way."

Silas had that deep crease between his eyebrows that meant he was still thinking.

"If the town has too many bad memories for you, I get it. We can figure something else out. We can rent for a while or something, but I want to stay close to Daniel and Jack and I want to live with you."

"Yes," said Silas.

"Yes to moving in?" asked Aaron. "You can say no, it's okay. I get that it's a lot of pressure, but I had to say something or else Daniel was going to blab. I mean, he's going to Stanford for his law degree, but he keeps saying this is home and this is where he expects us all to end up."

Silas silenced him with a kiss. "Yes," he said again. "Buy it. How much do you need? I can pay half."

Aaron bit his lip, but Silas didn't give him a chance to even process his hesitation.

"If you want to own it outright, I understand," he said. "This is a place for you and Daniel, not you and me. Moving in together is one thing, but buying a house together is another. This is something married people do and we haven't even discussed that idea. I want to give you money though. I can pay rent, cover half the mortgage—something."

Aaron nodded.

"You want to take it slow," said Silas. "That's all right. I understand. We have to be practical. If something happens and we're not together anymore, co-owning a home would just complicate things."

Aaron was thinking all of those things—worst-case scenario preparation was in his DNA. His worst-case scenario was always somehow, for whatever reason, ending up alone without his family. It wasn't because he couldn't stand the thought of being alone. He loved them. He couldn't stand the thought of not loving them, of not loving Silas.

There would always be another leap to take with him. Aaron would never stop falling for Silas. Marriage, children, retirement, death—and those were just the leaps he knew about. He was sure there'd be others.

He took Silas' hand. "My mom used to say she loved my dad through every season," he said quietly. "She said to know someone, you have to know them through all kinds of weather, and she'd seen Dad through every storm she could imagine."

"Death changes people," said Silas. "I'm sure she never thought he'd hurt you."

"What if," said Aaron, "you love me through all the seasons, and I change?"

"You will change," said Silas. "I'm sure you'll change. I'll change too. It's a risk, but it's one we took when we fell in love."

Aaron nodded, biting back the question on the tip of his tongue. He couldn't imagine a world where he wouldn't love Silas. June couldn't have imagined a world where Robert would hurt their children.

He toyed with the keys in his hand. "I want to live with you," he said. "I don't know what comes next, but I know I want to go through it with you."

Silas' lip twitched with the little half-smile that meant he was pleased with himself. "Can I see inside?"

"Yeah, I'll show you our room."

"You've already picked it out?"

"Yeah," answered Aaron. "I picked the one with the best view. You'll see." He took Silas' hand and led him to the house. As they crossed the threshold, he imagined what it would be like to carry Silas in his arms and into their home.

Aaron would carry him because Silas wouldn't care, but Aaron liked tradition. They'd be exhausted from the wedding and ready for the honeymoon, but they'd go home first. They'd crack open the good scotch and laugh because one of them still had cake on his face.

Aaron was going to marry him. They were going to be together forever.

Silas wandered through the empty home, checking light switches and opening and closing closets and cabinets. "I like it," he said. "The kitchen is massive."

Aaron watched him walk from room to room inspecting the home. He couldn't stop the grin blooming across his face. Of course he was going to marry Silas. They made sense together.

He crept up behind him and wrapped his arms around Silas' waist. He took a deep breath and buried his face in Silas' neck. He pressed his lips against soft skin and marveled for a moment at how much his life had changed.

Silas leaned against him. "Are you going to show me our room?" he asked.

"Yeah," answered Aaron. "It's upstairs."

Aaron led the way, tugging Silas along behind him. Since the attack, they were always connected in one form or another. They sat next to each other, stood shoulder to shoulder, held hands — they did whatever it took to remember they were together.

He pushed the bedroom door open. There were no curtains on the windows and the white walls seemed blue in the moonlight. It came pretty damn close to matching the vision in Aaron's head. He'd bought a new bed and had the mattress on the floor with fresh sheets and a new bedspread. Beside it, he'd placed a dozen red roses. Aaron bit his lip and watched Silas for a reaction.

Silas tilted his head. "What's the occasion?"

"Ralph's dead. You're alive. We're moving in together," answered Aaron. "Figured we should celebrate."

Silas grinned and pulled Aaron to the mattress. Without warning, he let himself fall and brought Aaron tumbling down on top of him. They landed in a heap on top of the comforter. Silas rolled them over and sat straddling his lap. His eyes glittered like stars as he smiled down at Aaron.

He grabbed Silas by the front of his shirt and pulled him into a deep kiss. It didn't matter how long they stayed together. He was lucky to share any portion of his life with this man. He wrapped his arms around Silas' neck and slowed the kiss. This was the best his life had ever been, and if it was the best his life would ever be, he was more than willing to accept it.

"You're beautiful, Silas," he whispered. Even in the darkness, he knew Silas was blushing.

"You're beautiful, too," he said.

Aaron bit his lip. "So," he began. "Hypothetically, how do you feel about getting hitched?"

"You mean 'getting hitched' to you, right?"

"Yeah," answered Aaron. "Hypothetically."

"Hypothetically, I'm very much in favor of the idea."

"Good," said Aaron. "Me too. I never want to be stuck in a waiting room again just because I'm not 'family'."

"With any luck, I won't get shot again and that won't be an issue."

"You know what I mean." He pulled Silas to his chest. "I almost lost you. Jesus, what if you'd died? What if I didn't get to say goodbye?"

"But I didn't die and we're together. Don't dwell on what could have happened." He placed his hand over Aaron's heart. "We're in your house, on our bed and we're both fine."

"I'm lucky," said Aaron. "I like to think I'm pretty well prepared for what life throws at me, but I swear I never saw you coming."

Silas started to speak but instead he hid his face against Aaron. "I'm lucky, too," he said.

Aaron kissed his cheek. His lips drifted down to Silas' jaw and he sucked lightly at his skin. That was all the encouragement Silas needed. It was all he ever needed. He rolled his hips against Aaron and tangled his fingers in his hair. Their lips locked in a deep and hungry kiss.

Silas wedged his leg between Aaron's thighs and began rubbing his palm over his cock. Aaron did his best to stay focused as he wrestled Silas free from his shirt. The next moments were a blur of zippers, shoes and fabric. Something about being with Silas, in their room, in their house created a frenzy in Aaron.

As soon as they were both naked, Aaron rolled Silas onto his back and slipped beneath the covers. He took Silas in his mouth all at once and Silas moaned. Aaron had one hand wrapped around the base of Silas' cock and the other resting on Silas' chest. Silas took Aaron's free hand in both of his and clung to it.

Suddenly caught up in the rush, Aaron released his cock and grabbed Silas' wrist. He led Silas' hand to the back of his head and left it there. He returned his attention to pumping and sucking and teasing. He hollowed his cheeks and dragged his lips over the pulsing member. Silas shivered and his nails scraped against Aaron's scalp. Aaron moaned and sucked harder.

Silas seemed to get the message. He clutched Aaron's hair, almost holding him in place. Aaron relaxed his jaw but kept his lips tight. He gripped Silas' hip and encouraged him to thrust. Silas was hesitant at first, clearly testing the boundaries, so Aaron brought Silas' other hand down to tangle in his hair.

He gave a shallow thrust, pushing himself into Aaron's mouth. Aaron moaned again and began rubbing his thumbs into Silas' thighs.

Silas thrust again, deeper this time. Aaron closed his eyes and relaxed completely, overwhelmed by the heat and the sounds coming from Silas. His legs trembled beneath Aaron's grip. His breathing was erratic. Then it suddenly stopped.

He pulled Aaron from beneath the comforter and latched on to his mouth. It was like kissing fire. Silas' cock was still wet with saliva and it slid perfectly against Aaron's. Silas grabbed his ass, blunt nails digging into the muscles.

Aaron groped in the darkness for a box he'd tucked at the head of the mattress. He found it and brought it closer. Silas fumbled with him until one of them found the lube.

Silas took it from there. Still panting beneath Aaron, he slipped a finger between Aaron's cheeks and massaged his entrance. "Tell me," said Silas, "if I do something you don't like."

Too dazed to quip back, Aaron just nodded. He wondered if sex with Silas would always take his breath away.

Silas slipped out from under him and encouraged Aaron to prop up on all fours. Silas' finger slipped inside him and immediately went for his prostate. Aaron's elbows buckled and he found himself face down with his ass in the air.

Silas used that to his advantage. He wrapped an arm around Aaron's waist and took his cock in his hand. Another finger slipped into him. Aaron arched his back and clutched the pillow beneath him.

Soon Silas' fingers were gone and something thick and hot pressed against his hole. Silas took hold of his hips. Aaron braced himself as Silas pushed inside him. He bit his lip hard and rocked back until his ass met Silas' pelvis.

Together they set a merciless pace. Aaron ended up flat on the bed. Delirious, he began rutting against the mattress. His senses were overwhelmed by a blissful assault on his nerves.

One last broken cry followed by rapid-fire thrusts and Aaron was done. He came hard, spilling against his stomach and the bed. The intensity of his orgasm doubled as Silas pounded against his prostate, then finally shook and collapsed against him.

It was almost a full minute before either of them could speak. Silas rolled off him and onto his back. The comforter lay in a forgotten heap on the floor. They were too hot to need it right now, anyway.

"Was that all right?" panted Silas.

Aaron had enough energy to turn his head and give him a grin and a thumbs up.

Silas nodded. "That was — different."

"Did you like it?"

Silas nodded again quickly. "At this point it's safe to assume I enjoy everything we do," he said. "Especially when we're both nude."

"Good," breathed Aaron. "Want to clean up and rinse off?"

Silas groaned. "No," he said.

"What if I told you we have a Jacuzzi tub?"

"That would change my mind."

Aaron rolled his eyes. "I've got bubbles and other bath crap in there." He pointed to the master bath. "I'll clean up in here, you're in charge of the tub."

Silas sighed, but didn't argue. He kissed Aaron and left for the bathroom.

Ten minutes later, they were both submerged in bubbles and warm water. They sat back to chest, Aaron leaning against the tub and Silas leaning against Aaron.

"You were right," said Silas. "This was a very good idea."

"After this we can go to bed and stay there until noon tomorrow."

"Or we could go for round two," said Silas.

"Seriously?" asked Aaron. "Aren't you exhausted? You're still supposed to be taking it easy."

"I assure you," he said, "I'm fine."

"We'll play it by ear," said Aaron. He hugged Silas against his chest and kissed his shoulder. He'd do anything Silas wanted. He was defenseless against those blue eyes and soft, dark lashes. Silas could ask him for the Andromeda Galaxy in a snow globe and not only would Aaron pilot the first intergalactic mission, he'd take up glass blowing to make sure the globe turned out just right. He belonged to Silas and he was going to marry him.

Chapter Thirty-Seven

Say Yes

Aaron was getting ready to leave the shop when an angry-looking man stormed out of Jack's office and slammed the door behind him. The man cursed under his breath and walked away fuming. Aaron hurried to investigate. He found Jack sitting calmly at his desk, looking a little smug.

"What was that about?" asked Aaron.

"What was what about?" asked Jack.

"That guy. What happened?"

"Nothing much. He's with the local police — or state. I can't remember. It doesn't matter."

"Are we in trouble?" asked Aaron.

"Nah," answered Jack. "They've just got their shorts in a twist."

"Why?"

Jack sighed. "Seems they're having trouble tracking down some evidence from a home invasion resulting in a death from a few months ago." He cocked his eyebrow and looked up at Aaron. "I guess there was some kind of clerical error. The intruder was never identified and police are still investigating, or trying to."

Aaron frowned. "Is that good or bad?"

"It's bad for them," answered Jack. "Someone must have misfiled something. The John Doe was accidentally cremated and the carpet samples were accidentally destroyed. They can't find the gun he used and they've only got partial prints from the crime scene."

"Did you —"

"I wouldn't worry about it," said Jack. "They lost the original coroner's report. The only copy they've got is a mess of redactions. They don't have the clearance to look at anything else. Shame their office is so unorganized."

Aaron opened his mouth then closed it again.

"If they *are* able to dig a little deeper," said Jack, "they'll find out he was part of group that produced child pornography. The other people in the group are already in prison."

"Wait, is that true?" asked Aaron. "Are we still talking about the same thing?"

Jack scratched his beard. "The evidence found with Farley and Regina suggested they were into some nasty stuff. After further investigation, officers found a lot of disturbing images on their computers. Seems true to me."

"Yeah," said Aaron, "but did you frame th —"

"Seems true," repeated Jack. "Don't worry about it. Listen, you need to know two things. One, as long as I'm alive no one, I mean no one, is going to mess with my boys. You're safe and I have the power to keep you safe."

"What's the second thing?"

"I plan to live forever."

Aaron huffed a laugh. "Guess that sums it up."

"Go home," said Jack. "Relax, enjoy the house. Daniel's staying on campus tonight and I've got plans. You and Silas are on your own."

"Thanks, Jack," he said.

"Don't mention it."

Aaron left the shop and tried to forget about the policeman at the garage. He stopped by the pharmacy closest to home. Ava had recommended medication to help with his anxiety and post-traumatic stress disorder. She said he had both, or maybe the PTSD was a byproduct of his anxiety, or maybe it was the other way around. He didn't know and he didn't particularly care. Ava had sent him to a doctor for his prescriptions. He was on a schedule now. He took a pill every night before bed, and one milligram of Xanax as needed. Both drugs came from the pharmacy instead of from Silas.

He retrieved his prescriptions and set the bag beside him in the car. This was his first refill. He'd taken them for a month and, according to his doctor, he should feel small improvements. He knew he wasn't taking miracle drugs. He knew this wasn't a cure. That didn't stop him from hoping.

Generally speaking, things were better. His life was much better. Silas was better, Daniel was better, even Jack was better. When Aaron and Silas had finally finished moving into the house, everyone seemed to relax—probably because, for once, their lives were settled. Aaron at least felt grounded, but pills didn't do that. He wasn't sure what did that. Ava said it was probably a result of him feeling safe again, of him dropping his shield.

He still couldn't think about his father. Sometimes his dreams would replay the night he'd found him. Sometimes they'd replay Silas getting shot. Sometimes he'd wander through his old house and find Silas in the bathtub instead of Robert. Sometimes Robert would be waiting for him beside the car. Sometimes Daniel was with him. Anytime Robert and Daniel were in the same dream, Robert would shoot him. Daniel would fall and Aaron wouldn't be able to stop the bleeding.

He told Ava about his dreams, but no one else. In his opinion, his biggest improvement was that he didn't let his problems spill out anymore. He was able to keep his trauma between him and Ava. He was able to keep it in perspective, where it belonged. Sometimes — though it was happening less and less — he'd wake up at night, after a vivid nightmare, and find himself wrapped in Silas' arms.

Silas never asked him what he saw. He probably didn't need to. He'd hold Aaron close, kiss his cheek and remind him he was safe. At first, Aaron felt guilty. He had everything else under control. Then he'd realized Silas had nightmares too.

One night, he'd awoken to find Silas curled into himself on the opposite side of the bed. He'd thrown the covers off and sweat covered his face. Their room was cool and Silas' skin was cool. He'd pulled Silas to the middle of the bed and held him until he stopped shaking. Silas didn't wake up. He never woke up. His breathing would eventually slow and his muscles would relax, but he never spoke or indicated he knew what was happening. They never talked about it, but Aaron decided the next nightmare would be different. Since they'd moved into the new house, Silas' dreams had become more frequent.

He entered the house and found Silas glaring at his laptop on the couch. He was typing something and didn't seem to notice he was being watched.

Aaron cleared his throat and Silas jumped. "Oh," he said. "Hello, Aaron."

"What are you working on?" he asked. He crossed the room and dropped next to his partner on the couch.

"Job applications," answered Silas.

Aaron looked over at the screen and raised an eyebrow. "You're applying to a gas station?"

"I could be a clerk."

"No." Aaron grabbed the laptop and began clicking through the tabs Silas had open.

"It's just a job," he said. "It doesn't really matter where I work."

"You have a medical degree," said Aaron.

"And a bad reputation."

"That doesn't mean you don't have options." He started closing out of the tabs Silas had open. "This is an application to be a line cook. You don't even like cooking."

"But thanks to you, I'm much better at it than I used to be."

"No." Aaron shut the laptop. "There's no rush and you don't need to do something you'll end up hating. We'll be all right for a while. I'm making money. You can afford to wait for something that makes you happy."

"I don't think anyone else will hire me."

"Then you can just be my trophy husband," said Aaron. The word *husband* slipped out automatically. "What do you want for dinner?"

Silas grinned at him, but didn't say anything.

Aaron blushed and hid his smile behind his hand.

"How about pizza?" asked Silas.

"I could go for pizza," he answered.

"Pizza and wine?"

"Good enough."

"Good," said Silas, still grinning. "I vote we relax tonight and drink a little too much."

"You trying to seduce me, Mr. Anderson?"

Silas tilted his head and frowned. "Not at the moment."

"I meant like in the movie. *The Graduate*? Dustin Hoffman?"

"I haven't seen it."

"Then I guess we know what we're going to watch tonight."

Silas rolled his eyes and grabbed his cell phone. "Do you want the usual?"

"Yeah," answered Aaron. He leaned against Silas while he placed their order. He was in his own home with his soon-to-be fiancé and they had a 'usual' takeout order.

Silas hung up and Aaron kissed him. He moved his hand to Silas' lap and began undoing the button on his jeans. "Thirty minutes or less, right?" asked Aaron.

Silas nodded.

"I bet I can deliver in ten minutes or less."

"I don't know, I think—" His sentence was lost as Aaron lowered his head.

* * * *

Silas was the first to fall asleep that night. Aaron stayed awake. He wasn't sure if Silas would dream. He had still been buzzed when they went to bed. He might sleep more soundly tonight. Aaron waited. Silas was pillowed against his chest and, so far, seemed calm. He had a pitch, a plan and a few suggestions he hoped would help Silas relax.

A little after two in the morning, Aaron realized he'd fallen asleep. He also realized Silas wasn't resting against him anymore. Silas was across the bed, out of the covers with his back turned, and curled in the fetal position. Aaron sat up carefully and reached across the bed. He encouraged Silas to roll over and pulled him toward the center of the mattress. As usual, he didn't wake up.

Aaron settled down next to him and held him. He kissed his cheek and pushed Silas' hair away from his forehead. "It's okay," he whispered. "You're safe."

Still asleep, Silas pressed himself closer.

"It's all right," whispered Aaron. "It's just a dream."

Silas let out a muffled cry against him.

"It's okay, baby. You're safe." He took Silas' hand and held it against his chest over his heart. "I need you to wake up." He kissed his cheek again. "You're having a bad dream, but it's just a dream. Everything's okay."

Silas jerked against him and blinked. He looked at Aaron and took a few unsteady breaths.

"It's okay," said Aaron.

Silas frowned and tears leaked from the corners of his eyes. "I'm sorry," he said. "That's never happened before."

"Do you want to tell me about it?"

Silas shook his head. "It must have been the wine. It's not a big deal. I just haven't had a dream like that in a very long time."

Aaron bit his lip, unsure of how to proceed. "Are you sure?" he asked. "Lately you've been a little, um, weird, I guess, when you sleep."

Silas groaned. He pulled away from Aaron and rolled onto his back. "I'm sorry," he said.

"It's okay," said Aaron quickly. "It doesn't bother me. I normally wouldn't wake you up, but it's happened almost every night this week. I'm kind of worried about you."

"I'm fine," muttered Silas. "Just embarrassed."

Aaron wiggled closer to him and propped himself up on his elbow. "Tell me about it. You know I have nightmares. You know I understand."

"I am normally a very light sleeper," said Silas, sighing. "Most nights I don't dream at all. Actually, I should amend that. Before I started spending my nights with you, I didn't dream much."

Aaron winced. "Am I a trigger or something?"

"No, not at all," answered Silas. "I sleep more soundly with you and stay asleep longer, so I dream more often."

"But?"

"There isn't really a but," he said. "Usually I have good dreams. Sometimes very good dreams." He glanced at Aaron. "But I used to dream about Joshua when I was younger. I stopped sleeping for a while. Mother sent me in for a test and I got a prescription for something to help me fall asleep. I never used it. I threw the pills away and switched them with Tic Tacs." He sighed again. "I dreamed about him again after you and I met."

Aaron tugged him closer and Silas let him. They lay on their sides facing each other. "Sometimes I dream about Dad," he said. "But usually the bad dream's about losing people I love."

"I dream about Ralph," said Silas. "He doesn't always have a face, but I know it's him. He doesn't shoot me, but it doesn't matter. I never get to you in time."

"Roll over," said Aaron.

"Why?"

"You're going to be the little spoon and I'm going to tell you some things."

Silas eyed him, seeming a little skeptical. "All right." He did as instructed.

Aaron made sure they were tightly pressed together. He wrapped his arms around Silas and tilted his head so that he could speak quietly and directly into Silas' ear. "First of all, Ralph is very, very dead. I murdered the shit out of that bastard and Jack had his body burned."

"You're not supposed to say you murdered him."

"Well, I did, and I'm kind of proud of it. I should probably feel a little guilty for taking a life or something, but I don't. Heads up, if I ever become a serial killer, this is probably the first red flag."

"Obviously I'd be your accomplice."

Aaron laughed and squeezed him. "Second of all, you've been through a lot of traumatic shit."

"So have you."

"I know, and I'm on medication. I've talked to Ava about you and she thinks you could benefit from talking to someone, too."

"Aaron, your sessions are not supposed to be about my problems."

"I can't help it. You're my favorite subject," he said. "You don't smoke as much and I haven't seen you take as many pills. I check your secret stash pretty regularly. Seems like you use something once or twice a week."

"You're spying on me?"

"Yeah. That's not the point. Also, I'm sorry for spying, but only a little sorry."

"I suppose that's fair. I spy on you as well."

"I know. Sometimes Daniel spies on you spying on me."

"Beaumonts," muttered Silas.

"Point is, you need to take care of yourself. I'm glad you're sleeping better, but I think Ava would say you've been repressing some stuff. She tells me that a lot."

Silas huffed again.

"You got shot. You almost died. People don't usually walk away from that kind of thing without problems."

"People also don't usually walk away from killing someone without problems."

Aaron ignored him. "I'm going to wake you up from your nightmares from now on," he said. "You like to be in charge of stuff and you like to know you have control of a situation. There've been two really fucked-up events where you had no control and I think that's what's haunting you."

"You actually listen to Ava when she talks, don't you?"

"Yeah. She's smart. I think you and I are similar in a lot of ways, so whatever helps me might help you."

"That's thoughtful, but you don—"

"You were completely powerless when Ralph attacked. He did that on purpose. That was his thing. He took people's power, made them feel helpless. He did that to both of us."

Silas was silent.

"You were helpless when Joshua died, too," said Aaron. "You legitimately couldn't do anything about that. Even if you'd been with him, you were too small to help or fight."

"We spend a lot of time psychoanalyzing each other, don't we?"

"No one knows us better than we do."

"True."

"I'm going to take some control away from you for a while."

Silas flinched and turned to look at him. "What does that mean?"

"That came out a little more BDSM than I meant. Unless you're into that."

"I don't understand."

"I'll steer the ship for a while, you just relax."

"I need specifics. The ship metaphor isn't helping."

Aaron sighed. "You're a doctor, Silas. I know, firsthand, how good you are at helping people. I want you to do whatever it takes to get your license again. I've got our future as a couple under control. You need to focus on yourself."

"It's a long process. I don't—"

"Whatever it takes," said Aaron. "If we need to pay somebody off, just tell me where to send the check. If we need to forge some documents, Jack probably owns a printing press."

"I'm sure there's a legal option," said Silas.

"Either way. And I don't care how long it takes. Your job is to figure out how to get it done. No more gas station applications. I've got you covered, baby. You need to get your dream job back. The world needs people like you."

"I can't do it," he said quietly. "We have money now, but we're going to need more eventually."

"I'll cross that bridge when I come to it," said Aaron. "Besides, Jack's got me covered."

"Your family has already done so much."

"I'll worry about that."

"It's not fair to you."

"I've got my dream job," said Aaron. "It's not glamorous, but I love it. I've got a boss who is biased as hell in my favor, and a lot full of cars I fix and sell for a profit. I'm set. You need that too."

Silas scowled and pursed his lips.

"I want you to be happy."

"I am happy."

"The day we met, you told me you'd always be a doctor."

Silas sat up and placed hand over his eyes.

Aaron didn't let him get far. He sat up and quickly pulled Silas into his lap. "Why is it," he began, "that every time I get upset your first reaction is physical contact, but when you get upset you pull away?"

"I have no idea," muttered Silas.

"Do I need to take a hint and leave you alone? I don't really want to, but I will if it will help."

"No," said Silas. "It's a knee-jerk reaction. I'm sure it was something I developed when I was a child."

"So clinging to you like a barnacle is okay?"

"Yes, though I'm not sure 'barnacle' is the right analogy. Your hold is more like an anaconda's."

Aaron squeezed him. Silas laughed and uncovered his eyes.

"The first time Dad kicked my ass, he took me to the hospital," said Aaron. "I was pretty fucked up. I think the doctor was suspicious. Our story didn't really add up. But he didn't question us. If I'd had a doctor like you, I'm pretty sure my life would have been a lot different."

Silas leaned heavily against him, returning the embrace.

"You can read people like a book," said Aaron. "You're caring, smart and sincere. A guy like you needs to be front and center in the world. People like you change things."

"What if I can't get my license back?" asked Silas. "What if it's a waste of time?"

"If there's any chance at all of this working, it's not a waste of time."

He shook his head. "I don't know what to say."

"Say yes."

"I'll think about it. There might be a job I enjoy just as much."

"Say yes, Silas."

"But—"

"No buts."

Silas rubbed his eyes and let out a deep breath. "Yes," he said quietly.

Aaron kissed his cheek. "There you go."

"I suppose it could work." Silas sighed again. "I can't express how much this means to me. You don't have to give me a second chance at my life. That's not your job."

"I'm an idiot for not thinking of this a long time ago." Aaron kissed him again. "You deserve so much. I'd give you the whole damn world if I could."

Silas buried his face against Aaron's shoulder.

Aaron grinned. "You're going to be a doctor again."

Chapter Thirty-Eight

Tomorrow

Sara and Daniel stood on either side of him, both studying the ring in his hand. Aaron shook his head and returned it to the man behind the counter. "It's pretty," he said, "but it doesn't say Silas."

Sara groaned. "You have to pick something."

They'd been to eight different stores. The one they were currently investigating was full of antiques and Aaron was holding out hope for something original.

"I will," said Aaron. "When I find something I like, I'll buy it."

"Silas will like whatever you pick out," she said.

"That's probably true," said Daniel. "I don't think you can really go wrong."

"I don't even know what stone to get."

"I thought you settled on a diamond," said Daniel.

"What if it's a blood diamond?" asked Aaron. "Silas would hate that."

"You've done too much research," said Sara.

"What if the previous owner was a dick or something?" countered Aaron. "Can't diamonds be cursed? What if I get him something that's bad luck?"

"Curses aren't real," said Daniel.

"And Silas isn't terribly superstitious," said Sara.

The man behind the counter smiled and took a step back. "I'll give you another moment to discuss."

"Everything's really nice, but nothing is right," said Aaron. "Hell, I'm not even sure if I should go with gold or silver."

"You said silver originally," said Sara. "Go with your gut."

"My gut says it's hard to get jewelry information from him without being obvious," said Aaron. "Hasn't he ever said anything about what he likes? Did he have any of this crap when he was a kid?" He gestured around the store.

"No," she answered. "He didn't really like jewelry."

"But I'm sure he'll like a ring," said Daniel quickly.

"Right," said Sara. "He'll like anything you get him."

The man behind the counter returned. He cleared his throat and set a new ring display on the counter. "Have you considered something less traditional?" he asked.

Aaron eyed the new rings.

"These are all one of a kind," said the man.

Aaron stopped. He carefully picked up a ring with a gold band and an ornate, almost vine-like engraving. The center stone was a dark blue sapphire and there was a small diamond on either side. It wasn't a large ring like some of the others. The band was wide, with just enough room to accommodate the stones and designs.

"Silas would want an emerald," said Sara. "Since your eyes are green." She pointed to a similar ring, but Aaron didn't pay it much attention.

He shook his head. "This one is perfect."

Sara started to protest. Out of the corner of his eye, he saw Daniel quickly shake his head.

"It looks like him," said Aaron.

Daniel cleared his throat. "It's missing something," he said. "I think you should consider the emerald."

"The sapphire is the part I really like."

"Maybe emeralds instead of diamonds?" said Daniel. He pointed to the sides of the ring. "Then it would match your eyes and his eyes instead of just his."

Aaron felt heat rise in his cheeks. He never meant to be as obvious as he was. Of course he liked it because it matched Silas' eyes. He lowered the ring. "That's really sappy, isn't it?" he asked.

"Honestly, you guys are already pretty sappy," said Daniel.

Aaron elbowed him. "I want to get him something nice but not corny."

"He loves your eyes," said Sara. "I vote emeralds." She looked to the salesman. "Can we get a quote on what it would cost to replace the stones?"

He nodded and retrieved a book from behind the counter.

"Is it too small?" asked Aaron. "Maybe I should go back to diamonds."

"No," said Sara and Daniel together.

Aaron glanced at them.

"That's the ring," said Daniel.

"Just replace the diamonds," said Sara.

"Emeralds would be pretty," said Aaron. "Right? That's pretty, isn't it? Do I have bad taste?"

"No," answered Daniel. "Emeralds are pretty."

"I agree," said Sara.

"You're sure?"

"Yes," they said, again answering together.

The man returned with a quote. He explained how much the ring would cost with changes, without changes, and showed him the resizing fee. "If you would like to change the stones and have the ring sized, I can have the order ready in roughly two weeks," he said.

Even with the alterations, the ring came in under budget. Then again, Daniel and Sara had agreed his budget was too high.

"Do it," said Sara.

"It's perfect," said Daniel. "One of a kind and you went straight for it. You haven't liked any of them as much as you like this one."

"And you're positive about the emeralds?" he asked.

"Yes." This time the salesman answered with them as well.

"Then I guess we're doing this," said Aaron.

* * * *

Two weeks came and went. The ring was finished. Everything was ready. He wasn't on a schedule, but he wanted to be mindful of the day he picked to pop the question. He'd already decided on a location. He considered asking on the anniversary of the day they'd met, but that day was an anniversary on its own. And that day belonged to more than just the two of them. Too many lives changed that day.

Their anniversary came and went. To honor the day, Silas shut them inside the bathroom and lit what he called "a commemorative joint". They were a little overzealous and Aaron ended up not going to work the next day.

The ring stayed hidden away in Daniel's room. When didn't really matter. He knew where he wanted to ask. They'd been together for over a year. All of Aaron's criteria had been met. Daniel kept telling him to *'just pick a fucking day already'*.

"What if I pick a shitty date?" asked Aaron. He was pacing in Daniel's room, fidgeting with the ring box. Daniel was sitting on his bed watching him. "Wait, do people celebrate engagement anniversaries or just weddings?"

"Oh my God," muttered Daniel. "Just ask him."

"I'm working on it," snapped Aaron.

"Do it tomorrow," said Daniel. "It's Friday. I'll be home for the weekend. Sara's not busy. Jack's free after five. You can take him down to the lake, propose, then come back here to celebrate with us."

"I can't just do it tomorrow," said Aaron.

"Why?"

"It's not right."

"Why not?"

"I don't know."

"Just do it," said Daniel. "What are you waiting for?"

"I don't know," muttered Aaron. "I want it to be perfect."

Daniel rolled his eyes. "It's going to be perfect whenever it happens. Just ask him already."

Aaron opened the box. The ring glittered in the light. He'd only taken it out once. His hands had shaken so much he was too afraid to take it out again.

"If you don't ask him, he'll probably ask you," said Daniel.

"He's too busy to plan anything," said Aaron. Silas was closing in on getting his license. He needed colleagues to vouch for his ability. He needed two more people to speak on his behalf and those people were proving difficult to find. Silas said he'd burned too many bridges. Aaron had told him to keep trying.

"He's pretty sneaky though," said Daniel. "And he'd love to surprise you."

"That's true," muttered Aaron. "Has he said anything?"

"Not yet," answered Daniel. "But I feel like it's going to come up."

Aaron shut the box.

"Just do it tomorrow," said Daniel.

"Tomorrow is too random. Isn't the day supposed to mean something?"

"It'll mean something after you nut up and ask him to marry you, you moron," said Daniel.

Aaron clutched the box in his hand. "That's true," he muttered. "What time tomorrow? Sunset? That's romantic, right?"

Daniel nodded.

"Okay," said Aaron slowly. "Tomorrow." He looked toward his little brother. "Holy shit. I'm getting engaged tomorrow."

"*Finally.*"

* * * *

Aaron didn't have a good excuse to go to the lake. He didn't have an excuse to dress for the occasion either. Luckily, Silas suggested a date night. Aaron tried not to seem too eager to take advantage of the coincidence. He dug through his closet and found clothes that were nice, but not too nice, then got dressed and went downstairs.

Silas had a head start. Aaron had to scrub off oil and grease before he could change clothes. Silas was already dressed and waiting for him. A piece of blue fabric was sticking out of his pocket.

"What's that?" asked Aaron.

Silas flinched. "Wha—nothing—what's what?" He quickly crammed his hands into his pockets.

"Wow," said Aaron. "That wasn't suspicious at all."

Silas' face flushed bright pink.

"You had something blue hanging out of your pocket," said Aaron.

"Oh," mumbled Silas. He removed his hand and held up the fabric. It turned out to be a tie. "I couldn't get it right. It seemed excessive."

Aaron felt a chill run down his spine. Silas knew. Of course he knew. Aaron wasn't sure what he'd done to give himself away, but clearly the surprise wasn't a surprise anymore. He stepped forward and took the tie from Silas' hand. He looped the fabric around Silas' neck and took his time finishing the knot.

"You know I love you in this color," said Aaron.

"Yeah," said Silas quietly. His eyes were fixed on Aaron's face and his heart was pounding beneath Aaron's fingers. He was doing his best to maintain his poker face. Unfortunately for Silas, maintaining his poker face was usually his biggest tell.

"I think it looks good," said Aaron. "It's not excessive." He gave Silas a quick peck on the lips then took his hand and led him out to the car. He knew better than to tease, but sometimes Silas was a very tempting target. If the secret was already out, he might as well have some fun.

He stopped beside the passenger side door. Instead of opening it, he knelt. He looked down for a second then looked up.

Silas was watching him, wide-eyed, with his hands by his side as if he were preparing for a quick draw.

"Thought the tire was flat," said Aaron, biting back a grin. He stood and brushed the dirt from his knee. "We're good. Are you all right? You look a little pale."

Silas nodded slowly. "I'm fine," he answered. His lips twitched ever so slightly.

Payback was coming. Aaron probably deserved it. They got into the car and Aaron pulled out of the driveway. "You know," he said. "It's a clear night. It might be nice to watch the sunset."

"Instead of a movie?" asked Silas.

"Yeah," answered Aaron. He knew Silas was going to be suspicious as soon as he suggested the lake, but Silas already seemed to know. He had nothing to lose.

"I'd like that," said Silas. "Maybe we could watch it from the lake."

Aaron glanced over at him. "Yeah, I was going to say the same thing."

"How convenient." Silas wasn't even trying to mask his grin anymore.

It took Aaron a moment to put the pieces together. He remembered what Daniel said last night about Silas popping the question first. "Do you have something planned for the lake too?" he asked.

"Do you want to know or do you want to be surprised?" asked Silas.

"That's a yes," said Aaron. "By any chance, were Daniel and Sara 'helping' you, too?"

"They were," confirmed Silas.

"Bet they're waiting for us at the lake."

"I'm almost certain."

Aaron sighed. "And here I was thinking I was being clever."

"They played us."

"No shit." He glanced at Silas, his voice suddenly stuck in his throat. "Do you still want to go through with it?"

"Of course," answered Silas. "Do you?"

"Yeah," he answered quickly.

"Even if it means dealing with my nosy sister?"

Aaron laughed. "I see your nosy sister and raise you an annoying brother." He pulled the car to the side of the road and put it in park. Aaron pulled the ring box from his pocket. The day didn't need to be perfect — the moment just needed to be theirs. "Will you marry me, Silas?"

"Of course," he answered, pulling a box from his pocket as well. "Will you marry me, Aaron?"

"You bet your ass I will." He grabbed Silas by his tie and kissed him.

They exchanged boxes and laughed when they opened them. Their respective rings were almost identical. Silas' ring was the sapphire with the emeralds on the sides. Aaron's ring had a large center emerald with sapphires on the sides.

Aaron frowned when he tried to slip the ring on his finger. "It's a little snug."

"Funny," said Silas, "mine is a little large." He frowned at the ring for a moment. "Oh," he said. "We should trade."

"Why?"

Silas took the emerald ring from Aaron's hand and slipped it onto his own finger. He slid the sapphire ring onto Aaron's finger. "I believe our siblings meddled with the rings as well."

"God dammit," muttered Aaron. "I should have paid more attention at the store."

"I thought it was a bit suspicious when they led me to this ring," said Silas. "Sara doesn't go jewelry shopping. I should have known she didn't 'just happen to notice' it."

"Those fuckers."

"They know us too well."

"Maybe the jeweler made a mistake."

Silas raised an eyebrow. "Somehow I feel like this was deliberate. I'm sure Daniel and Sara will confirm as much once we get to the lake." He took the rings and returned them to their boxes. "We need to remember to act surprised."

"I suddenly regret buying a house so close to family," muttered Aaron. "I wonder if Jack's at the lake, too."

"I bet he is," said Silas. He kissed Aaron's cheek. "I want to see you through many more seasons." Aaron pulled Silas across the seat and wrapped an arm around his shoulders. "Here's to our secret roadside engagement—unless you think we should tell them."

"No," said Silas. "They worked so hard. This can be our secret."

"Then here's to secrets," said Aaron. He laughed. "Our first secret."

"Of all the things that could have been secret, I'm glad it's this," said Silas.

"Me too." Aaron eyed him and frowned. "We're about ten minutes away from the lake. You think you can become a better liar in ten minutes?"

"Potentially."

"Let me see your poker face again."

Silas scowled and pressed his lips into a tight line.

"It's like you're getting worse," said Aaron. "You're not mad at the secret, you're just hiding it."

If anything, Silas scowled harder.

"Annnd that's why we don't have secrets," said Aaron. "Maybe just be quiet and look pretty."

"They might be too excited to notice anything is amiss," said Silas. "Then again, it wouldn't be us if we didn't show up with some explaining to do."

Aaron kissed his cheek. "I guess that's true. You ready?"

Silas grinned. "I'm all in."

Southern Charm: Rules of the Chef
Nicole Dennis

Excerpt

"I can't believe you went ahead and sold the Charm without alerting me of your final decision. I thought we were considering our options, not going ahead with a contract," Dakota Mitchell said. He couldn't keep the irritation out of his voice. The familiar work he was engaged in helped him from losing complete control over his anger. Running his sharp chef's knife through a pile of onions, bell peppers, celery, and several cloves of garlic with skill and ease was one way of not using the blade on something or someone else. Lifting the knife, he waved it at his best friend and now apparently former partner in their business, Edward Schaffer. "What were you thinking? One more year I told you. One more season and we would have been fine and back in the black. The entire region is recovering from the damn oil spill, but everyone is starting to come back to the Gulf."

"Lisa and I don't have any more money to put into the Charm. Either we sold or the bank was going to foreclose on the mortgage," Edward said, shoving a hand in his pocket. "Things were at the point of no return. We're too deep in the red and I saw no other way to save the Charm. I had no other choice. We couldn't wait for another season, not with the pre-season bookings."

"Shit, Ed. I would have given you what I could—"

"No, it'll be too much on my financials and personal fortitude to lift the Charm out of the mortgage debts and keep her running. I have nothing left to invest and I'm close to losing my home. I know as well as you do what you have in the bank. You don't have that kind of capital. The one thing holding the Charm is your restaurant and I don't want you to lose it to foreclosure."

"You didn't give me the chance to help. I could have signed a new loan or some kind of modification." Dakota couldn't stop the disappointment coloring his voice.

"It's too late to argue now. I did what was best for my family, for my health, and for the Charm. It was a difficult decision, but one I had to make. I'm sorry but papers are signed passing my share over to the buyers."

"I didn't sign over my share nor do I plan on signing over anything. This restaurant is still my piece." Dakota tugged over a bowl of washed, fresh Gulf shrimp to finish preparing it for his trademark gumbo. Needing a few moments to deal with the bombshell dropped on him he turned back and checked the colour of the roux, giving it a few good stirs. In another large pot, he checked the simmering stock and his timer. He picked up the strainer and skimmed off the fat and scum from the top.

What was going to happen without Edward being the other half of the hotel? Where did the decision leave Dakota and the staff? Who had bought the restaurant? Listing the questions in his head he turned to face his friend. Edward had suffered a mild stroke last year and it had aged him.

"I told them you were keeping your share of ownership. No one is going to ask you to sign over anything. I made sure it was in the contract. They're sending one of their fellas from management to look things over."

Dakota snorted his disbelief, he couldn't help himself. "You mean they're coming here to change things," he said harshly, "It's what they're going to do, you know. No matter what they promise, they'll take all the beauty and magic out of the Charm and make her ordinary, boring and another bland place no one will remember."

"Dakota, I'm sorry. It wasn't easy to find a buyer. Please. I wish there could be another way."

"I understand. I'll deal with things." Dakota took his flash of temper out on the large grey shrimps sitting on his bamboo covered work surface. He snapped a head, fins and legs off one crustacean. A quick slice with a small knife and he peeled off the thin shell. Another slice and he yanked out the black vein and guts from the back. He tossed all the scraps into a container to make stock from the tasty shells and guts.

Dakota saw Edward shudder out of the corner of his eye.

"Must you do that in front of me?" Edward muttered with another shiver. A grimace curled his lips and emphasised the lines in his face.

When Dakota looked closely at Edward, someone he thought of like a father, he noticed he appeared tired, exhausted, but there was a spark of something in his eyes. Relief? Jeez, all Dakota was being here was selfish. Edward had attempted to talk about selling up on so many occasions and all Dakota had done was push his words to one side with his normal 'we'll be fine'. Guilt climbed inside him and with it came his usual sense of humor to dispel the emotion.

Glancing from the small crustacean to his friend, Dakota lifted and wiggled it in Edward's face. "What? Don't want to eat the little shrimp?" He deliberately deepened and thickened his Southern accent to annoy Edward further with the teasing.

When Edward smiled, it reached his eyes this time. The teasing was familiar and somehow dangling the shrimp in Edward's face was enough to break the unsettled anger. He batted Dakota's hand away. "Knock it off, Dakota," he said with a shudder. "It has eyes."

Dakota chuckled knowing the shrimp always got a rise out of his friend. He shook his head and focused back on the matter in hand. "Who bought it anyway?" *Was that a reasonable question to ask or will it just bring up the anger again?* When Edward paused, Dakota immediately knew he wouldn't like the answer.

Sign up for our newsletter and find out about all our romance book releases, eBook sales and promotions, sneak peeks and FREE romance books!

About the Author

Alyssa has always had a love for fiction. She read her first romance novel from her mother's collection. Her first love story was about a tiger that fell in love with a zebra.

Alyssa lives in a wild west with her cats. She loves cooking and writing.

Alyssa loves to hear from readers. You can find her contact information, website details and author profile page at https://www.pride-publishing.com